THE FLAMES BURNT DARK

THE TALE OF THE ARYASURA

THE FLAMES BURNT DARK

THE TALE OF THE ARYASURA

Sayantan Gupta

Foreword by Nirmal Kanti Bhattacharjee

LiFi Publications Pvt. Ltd.
New Delhi

Published by:
LiFi Publications Pvt. Ltd.
211, 2nd Floor, Gagandeep
12, Rajendra Place, New Delh–110 008, India
Phone : (011) 2574 1000
E-mail : info@lifipublications.com
Web : www.lifipublications.com

ISBN 13: 978-93-82536-57-4 ISBN 10: 93-82536-57-4

First published in 2014

Cataloging in Publication Data—DK
[Courtesy: D.K. Agencies (P) Ltd. <docinfo@dkagencies.com>]

Gupta, Sayantan, 1955–
The flames burnt dark : the tale of Aryasura / Sayantan Gupta ; foreword by Nirmal Kanti Bhattacharjee.
p. cm.
Novel.
ISBN 9789382536574

1. Rāma (Hindu deity)--Fiction. 2. Rāvaṇa (Hindu mythology) --Fiction. 3. Indo-Aryans--Fiction. 4. Religious fiction. 5. Indic fiction (English). I. Title.

DDC 823.92 23

Printed in India by D.K. Fine Art Press (P) Ltd., Delhi–52

This book is dedicated to the memory of my father,
Late Samarendra Nath Gupta,
the best English teacher I have ever had.
Miss you, father!

Contents

Book II The Saga of Ravana

Book III The Saga of Lost Hopes

Foreword

There is a spurt of novel based on mythology in the Indian English literature of late. Of course, we have their predecessors in Sivaji Sawant's Marathi classics *Maharathi* or Prativa Ray's Odia novel *Yagyaseni*. But in Indian English it all began with the Shiva Trilogy of Amish Tripathy, especially the phenomenal success of *The Immortals of Meluha*, resulting in a cascading effect. Nilanjan P Choudhury's *Bali and the Ocean of Milk*, published by Harper Collins creates an engaging mythological universe of arrogant gods, warring asuras and convoluted power play which resonates with contemporary politics. Samhita Arni's *The Missing Princess* depicts the search of a young female journalist to find out the whereabouts of the banished princess Sita, where the fast paced action is given resonance by echoes of current moral, political and social issues.

It is against this backdrop that Sayantan Gupta's *The Flames Burnt Dark: The Tale of the Aryasura* needs to be seen. A take-off from the Ramayana, this is an epic retold in a different vein. The novel is divided in three books--'The Saga of Rama', 'The Saga of Ravana' and 'The Saga of Lost Hopes'. Generally faithful to the epic of Valmiki, it tells the story of the two iconic heroes without bias or prejudice. Like John Milton, the author here also is ready to give the devil his due share. While the first book describes the well-known facts about the tussle between the Aryans represented by king Dasharath and the Rakshasas initially represented by Taraka, how the Brahmin wee being disturbed in their penance by the Rakshasas and how the Koshala army massacred them under the leadership of the young prince Rama, culminating into the abduction of Sita during Rama's exile. The last chapter of the Book 1 (Chapter 13) ends with the turmoil created by Hanuman at Lanka when he was deputed to meet Sita at the Ashok forest.

The Book 2 begins with the preparedness of Lanka for the invasion by the Banaras led by Rama. With Ravana in a self-satisfied mood on inspecting the training, the narrative goes back to the early days in retrospect when Ravana was called Dashanan and how the incidents unfolded to make him the mighty king that he was today. This portion of the book is full of generally unknown but authentic information which whip up the curiosity of the readers. Many characters here are not familiar names with the common reader. The coinage 'Aryasura' is interesting since the author has traced Ravana's parentage and established that his father was an Aryan Brahmin and mother an Asura princess.

'The Saga of Lost Hope', consisting of six chapters, takes the novel to its climax. It shows how the devastation of Lanka began and how one by one the mighty warriors of Ravana fell. Hearing the news of the slaying of Meghnad by

Lakshman, an enraged Ravana played havoc with Rama's army and apparently killed Lakshman, thus avenging the death of his son. But when he heard that an exotic herb from Gandhamadan hills had revived Lakshman, he realised the way of the destiny and saw the writing on the wall. He went to Ashoka forest, apologised to Sita and plunged into the battle next day without his armour. Obviously he was going in to fight his last battle. The episode of Pramila's entry into the war-torn Lanka and the confrontation between Meghnad and Lakshmana at Nikumbhila have been described with epical flair, often reminiscent of Michael Madusudan Dutt's epic poem *Meghnad-badh-kavya*.

The novel ends with the fall of Ravana marking the sun setting on the glory of the asuras. The era of the Rakshasa dominance comes to an end and the rise of the Aryans begins. This element of Aryan versus non-Aryans conflict gives *The Flames Burnt Dark* its special signification.

Nirmal Kanti Bhattacharjee

Preface

Our two great epics, the Ramayana and Mahabharata, had fascinated me ever since my childhood days. My first encounter with these epics had been pictorial, through comic strips, even before I had learnt the alphabets. Those pictures had made such an indelible impression in my young mind that they have stayed alive in me ever since. Even today, whenever I read about any specific incident from these epics, those pictures flash in my mind's eye.

With increasing years this fascination increased manifold and I read through all the adaptations for children and the abridged editions then available, moving on to the poetic versions (e.g. Krittibas Ojha's Bengali Ramayan, 14th century, and Kashiram Das's Bengali Mahabharata, 16th century). Rajsekhar Bose's Bengali versions in prose had been revelations. But of all that I had read, none impressed me more than the Bengali epic Meghnad Badh Kabya, by the renowned Bengali poet, Michael Madhusudan Dutt. This epic, first published in

1861, marked the dawn of the Bengal Renaissance. I had first read it in the original when I was a mere fifteen year old boy. I was simply awestruck. A couple of years ago, in pursuit of my long cherished dream, I had sat down to translate this great Bengali epic into English. During my in-depth studies I was enthralled with the classical language and was spellbound at the revolutionary treatment of the age-old story. This epic, with its new look at the Valmiki Ramayana, opened a new vista in front of my eyes. Here Michael had made heroes out of the traditional villains, the Rakshasa Ravana and his son, Meghnad, while Rama as the anti-hero and his Banara Sena were treated as intruders. It threw all traditional views to the winds. This got me thinking.

Ramayana is not an epic that can be wished away as a figment of the poet's imagination. An epic that has its roots in the heritage of an ancient civilisation, to be carried through the centuries and to be as popular today as it was in times immemorial, is bound to be based on the bedrock of reality. During my studies in the subject of history being hidden in the Rig-veda and the Puranas, I had chanced upon a family tree of the Ikshaku dynasty. How could then this be a pure fable? The problem with ancient Indians was that they were poor chroniclers, leaving yawning gaps in their accounts that need to be filled by conjectures and imagination. But, whatever it is, there is no denial of the fact that the epic Ramayana is as much a part of our history as those happenings in our recorded past.

Here the science trained brains and pragmatic minds raise their heads. The Ramayana, as in any other tale of yore, is beset with the supernatural teeming with events that cannot be assessed with harsh reasoning. Recently there has been a spate of writings that try to peer through this colourful haze, to search for the truth lying beyond. This present novel, trying to deconstruct the age-old myth in an effort to seek the logical and scientific truth behind all the events that had held everyone enthralled for centuries together, belongs to the same genre.

When we peel off the unreal garb of mysticism, folklore and superstition, what we find leaves us bewildered. We discover a treasure-trove of wondrous tale of valour, truth, glory, chivalry, determination and struggle, interspersed with lust, avarice and deceit. We can now believe in what we read. We can no longer renounce it as a product of fevered imagination. This novel, essentially a work of fiction, tries to show things as they could actually have happened.

The time setting of this tale is in a period of great transition. The original inhabitants of India of Dravidian origin were set upon by the invading Aryans, who left behind in their wake glorious cities reduced to rubbles and mounds of corpses. The non Aryans were systematically pushed back by the militarily superior Aryans, first from the Indus, then from the Gangetic valley, to settle far south and far east. It was at this juncture, that Ravana rose as a military leader of the subjugated non Aryans. His entire life was a struggle against the Aryans who were fanning out to deprive the non Aryans of whatever stretch of homeland they had. As the last act of this eternal struggle for supremacy, Ravana wanted a war to end all wars and he wanted this last battle to be fought in his own backyard, on the beachhead of Lanka, where the Rakshasas were the strongest. But this strategy proved to be disastrous. He lost the war and his life. The last of the non

Aryan resistance fell. The flames of non Aryan supremacy, burning proudly atop the Trikuta Mountain of Lanka, darkened with the fall of this Aryasura.

Interracial marriage was extremely uncommon those days. But it is on record that the Aryan Brahmin, Bishraba, had married the non Aryan Rakshasi princess, Kaikasi or Nikasha. Non Aryans are often referred to as the Asuras. Thus Ravana and his siblings, born of the union of Bishraba and Kaikasi, were Aryasuras. In the Book II, Kaikasi tells Ravana, or Dashanan, as he was then called:

'My son, your father and Kubera are Aryans. They are fair-skinned and tall. We are Rakshasas, being dark and therefore Anarya or non Aryan. You are half Aryan and half non Aryans. So he called you half breeds.'

'Is it a bad word?'

'No son. It is your proud heritage, for you inherit the best of two worlds. You are an Aryasura and so are your brothers and sister.'

At this Dashanan held his head high. He was proud of his new identity. He was proud of being an Aryasura.

This can be a new coinage, but the name seems appropriate. There is a term that is sometimes used to describe Ravana. It is Brahmarakshasa. It signifies the child born of a Brahmin father and a Rakshasi mother. Though this is an appropriate nomenclature, yet I have avoided it simply because, as far as I could make out, the Rakshasas were essentially casteless. So it would be an injustice to brand the Rakshasa king with a name that bore evidence of caste.

My wife, Dr. Puspita and my daughters, Parnasha and Shamayita, had been real sources of inspiration while this book was being written. They had been extremely supportive. I thank them all.

But, all said and done, my readers are the best judges regarding the quality of this book. I shall be happiest when they like this work.

Sayantan Gupta
Malda (West Bengal)
India.

Book I

The Saga of Rama

1

In the Wilderness

The night was pitch-dark. The wan moonlight had given up its losing struggle to penetrate the leafy canopy of the tall tropical trees. All was quiet, except for the monotonous hum of the cicada in the shrubbery. A narrow, scarcely discernible track, used more by animals than men, meandered through the dense vegetation. A shadowy group sped along this path without the faintest whisper of sound. They knew the path, like the back of their hands, having traversed this route over thousands of times or more. Moreover, their night vision was phenomenal. Thus they needed no torch to light up their way. They were the original denizens of this wild area. The marauding Aryans called them *Rakshasas* and spun a whole lot of chilling yarns about them.

The legends that have sprung up were not justified always. Neither were they of gigantic proportions with protruding canines and sharp poison nails, nor they had ugly, fearsome visage. Cannibalism was not their way of life. They did not have the ability to assume the shape of other beings. It was true that some of them were wonderful magicians and were past masters of the art of illusion, but this did not make them meaner than their Aryan counterparts. They, on the other hand, were valiant warriors of prodigious strength, and some of them were really learned, treading the righteous path. But their life, in general, was of immense hardship and was a struggle for existence as almost all the time they had to fight against the elements, on one hand, and the forest predators, their arch enemies, the Aryans, and hostile non Aryan tribes, on the other. The list was inexhaustible.

Yet just about a thousand years ago they had been masters of their own destiny. They had a flourishing civilization of city states along the banks of the mighty River Sindhu, and were at the pinnacle of glory. Then came the Aryans of the Deva tribe, led by Indra, with their horses and better weaponry and pushed them out into near oblivion. The Rakshasas were originally of Dravidian blood, boasting of one of the earliest civilizations of the world. But they succumbed to the migrating nomadic Aryan tribes who needed more space to live. They lost their homeland and moved east and south. Soon they were pushed beyond the lush Gangetic plains and were concentrated to the south of the Vindhyas, where, finally, they had firmly entrenched themselves, and to the farthest east where they were surrounded by other inimical non Aryan tribes who had been the original inhabitants of that region. These original settlers were non Aryans and were known by their family totem. Those who bore the totem of the snake were known as Nagas. Those with a monkey totem were called Banara etc. The Nagas, with famous leaders like Vasuki and Takshak were allied with the Aryans. In fact Takshak was a close friend of Indra. The Banara were not allied with anyone. They were a proud race, residing down south, where their valiant king Bali had carved out a sizable empire.

The Devas had called them all Asura as against their own nomenclature of Sura. The name Rakshasa was more or less self-given. When their cities were being destroyed by the hordes under Indra, groups of young Dravidians took upon themselves to be the protectors of their race and the precious waterways. They called themselves Rakshak, or 'the protector'. This name gradually spread to encompass their entire clan and became Rakshasa through regular usage. Other groups of Asuras who got scattered away earlier, were known by different names, such as Danavas, Daityas etc.

The group that was now trotting along the jungle trail was a small one, comprising about ten persons. All were dark skinned, well built, with long, unruly hair. Their black clothes rendered them almost invisible in the dark. They were lightly armed for fast travel, carrying only a spear apiece, in their right hands and a sword hanging from their waistbands. One of them carried a rather strange looking bundle in his free hand. The bundle dripped blood.

This strange group was led by their chief, a woman called Taraka. A woman as the chief of a tribe was not at all uncommon amongst the Rakshasa tribes of Aryabarta. Her husband, Sunda, the original chief, had been treacherously killed by the Aryan Brahmin Agasthya. Since then Taraka had assumed the mantle of leadership. Taraka, herself, was an exceptional woman, of insurmountable leadership abilities. For a woman, she was tall and muscular. Her strength and skill in combat were legendary. In battle she was mean, vengeful and almost appeared to be blood-thirsty. Now she ran at the head of her column with a raw feline grace, jaws set and eyes blazing. She wore nothing but a black sari, hitched high and wrapped tightly around her, accentuating her heavy breasts which bounced enticingly as she ran. Her spear, she carried in her left hand and a naked sword was clutched in her right.

The path culminated in a wide clearing in the forest. It was a small settlement of a handful of huts, housing a few intrepid Brahmin *Rishis* or sages. A huge fire burnt in the centre of the clearing. Five sages sat all around this fire chanting *mantras* and pouring ladles of *ghee* in the roaring flames. The flames, apparently elated at the addition of fuels, leapt up higher with every offering. The sages were performing a *yajna* of some sort. The forest all around was quiet as the flames sprang higher and higher throwing the huts into sharp relief from their glare. The sonorous chanting rose in volume as the yajna reached near its culmination, when, suddenly, something huge dropped out of nowhere with a resounding thud, straight into the yajna fire, with a vengeful splattering and flying sparks, all but putting it out. The Rishis gasped in horror. It was the head of a bull, recently slaughtered. The dripping blood sizzled. The Rishis jumped up from where they sat and looked around in alarm. Taraka, followed by her soldiers, sauntered arrogantly into the clearing and stood there with head thrown back and hands akimbo.

"So, it is you, *Rakshasi*, who had the audacity of disrupting our yajna?" cried the chief Rishi.

"Ah, you know me, Brahmin, do you?" asked Taraka in reply. The naked sword in her hand flashed wickedly as it caught the glare of the dying fire.

"How dare you?" The voice of the sage trembled with rage.

"Why Brahmin? Had I not repeatedly warned you earlier that you are not to perform any yajna in my territory? Had I not told you that the consequences of such Aryan encroachments in our hunting grounds will be disastrous?"

"This land is in the kingdom of Koshala and I, being a loyal subject of King Dasharatha, am entitled to perform a yajna in his territory. Who are you to stop me?"

"Don't cross me Brahmin. Pack up all your things and leave. My men will escort you to safety. I shall not tolerate such infringements. And about Koshala? The King's jurisdiction ends right there, where the deep forest begins. My forefathers have always stayed in these areas, as we do today. We are peaceable people, Brahmin, minding our own business. But we shall not be silent onlookers while you encroach to rape and plunder our home territory. Now, away you go!"

The Brahmins were thus unceremoniously evicted and a tenacious peace prevailed. But soon it was apparent that the Aryans would not leave the Rakshasas in peace. News began to filter in from different parts of Taraka's territory about newer Brahmin settlements coming up. Now the enraged Taraka was goaded into action. What followed was sheer mayhem. One after another settlement fell to her sword. Yajnas and other rites were unceremoniously disrupted. The offending Brahmins were ruthlessly slaughtered and their huts torched. Very few could escape to tell the world their tales of woe.

✦ ✦ ✦

2

The Rishi

Rishi Vishwamitra was rudely awakened from his meditation. It was early in the morning. The clime was mellow and the eastern horizon was just tinged with a touch of rosy hue. At first he could not be sure as to what had disturbed him. Then he heard the voices of anguish calling out for him over and over again. Vishwamitra rose, rubbed his hands over his face and strode out of his small hut. The sight that greeted him startled him out of his wits. A large number of Rishis were gathered in front of his hut, crying out for him.

"Save us, *Maharshi,*" cried they. "Save us from the blood thirsty Rakshasas."

The members of the delegation were all in sad states. Their clothes were torn and covered with blood and grime. Some were wounded, with blood still welling up from their wounds. Tears ran down their dirt besmeared faces and drenched their beards. Rage mingled with pity and compassion surged through Vishwamitra. He ushered the supplicants in.

Vishwamitra seethed with pent up anger. He had given patient hearing to the Brahmins and had sent them off to wash themselves before taking some refreshments. Now, he sat in his small room thinking about all he had heard.

The Brahmins' tales had been uniformly gruesome. All of them had settlements in different parts of this forest. They, with their students and disciples, had fought nature to reclaim parts of it as their own, where they were carrying out their scholastic pursuits in peace. But as soon as they started their yajnas, all hell broke loose. They were attacked by the Rakshasas, who plundered their *yajnasthals* like persons possessed and killed with wanton blood-lust, all without any apparent provocation. All campaigns were led by their leader, Taraka, the firebrand merciless female. These Brahmins had managed to escape alive from the carnages and they had rushed up to him for help. They knew that if anyone could help them, Vishwamitra would.

Vishwamitra stood up. He went over to the earthenware pitcher kept in a corner and had a long, cool, refreshing drink. Every muscle of his body was taut, crying out for action. It was sometimes difficult to forget his Kshatriya past. But now he was no longer a mere Kshatriya, or guardian of peace. He was now a Brahmin, at the peak of the social order. He paced about in the confines of his room, brows knitted in keen thoughts and deep concentration. The suffering Brahmins had rushed to him for help and salvation. They had come to the right place. Soon he made his decision devising a concrete line of action. He would go to Ayodhya, the capital city of Koshala.

Ayodhya was a sprawling, bustling city, situated on the right bank of the River Sarayu. It was an important trading centre and was the seat of the ancient Ikshvaku dynasty of the

Suryavanshi clan. The city owed its name to King Ayudh, one of the earliest of the Ikshvaku kings. The present king was King Dasharatha, the sixty third monarch of this illustrious dynasty, an able and a just ruler, well loved by his subjects.

The sentries at the main gate of the walled city knew Rishi Vishwamitra well enough and respected him too. With great veneration they allowed him entry and asked for his blessings. Militarily the city was well defended, with the River Sarayu guarding one side of it. A strong contingent of the Royal Infantry and Household Cavalry took care of the city defences. The robust walls were interspersed with towers where strategically placed teams of archers kept their vigil. The outer ramparts had four huge, well manned gates. These led to the inner wall where three gates were eccentrically placed for better defence. These gates opened into three wide, straight roads that led up to the immense Royal Palace in the heart of the city. The Palace itself was a treat to watch, being an architect's delight, resplendent with sculptures and artefacts of rare elegance. The roads were lined with houses of the Ayodhya residents, with the immediate vicinity of the Palace accommodating the chief officers of the Imperial Government. Each house was surrounded by a garden, big or small, every one of which was very well maintained.

Vishwamitra was eminently successful in his mission. King Dasharatha was extremely courteous and had come down from his throne to touch his feet. On hearing the tales of woes of ascetics and other Brahmins at the hands of the Rakshasas he had decreed that from now on, all Brahmins from Aryan descent will be protected and their Ashrams guarded by armed soldiers. So far so good! But the problem had begun when Vishwamitra had asked that the two Princes, Rama and Lakshmana accompany him the King had seemed to be less than co-operative then.

"Why, oh sage? Why them? They are so young! If you need help I'll personally lead a military operation to wipe the forest tracts of non Aryan settlers!" said he, in desperation.

"No, my king," replied Vishwamitra. "That wouldn't serve my purpose. I do not want massacre. Moreover, a full scale military operation will call the Rakshasa Emperor Ravana into the fray. I do not want war. It would be detrimental to the Aryan interest. Ours should be a defensive move, not an offensive one."

"But, oh learned Rishi, two kids against a horde of marauding Rakshasas! Will it be prudent?"

"It will, my king. Don't underestimate your sons!"

Even then the king worried. His boys were mere boys after all.

✦ ✦ ✦

3

Initiation by Blood

The clearing was large and expansive. A large contingent of sages, from all over the forest tracts had assembled for the grand yajna, organised by Vishwamitra, intent on self-determination. Right from sunset, the jungle reverberated with the chanting of hymns and mantras. Now, it was past midnight and the yajna was going on still. Ladles of ghee dropped in to fire made the flames soar skyward in glee. All birds had flown away from the surrounding trees. The animals too, had slunk away to save their skin.

The ever-watchful Rama and Lakshmana patrolled the perimeter of the clearing. Both were armed to their teeth. Complete in gold-plated armours, helmets, arm and shin guards, bows, arrows and swords, they appeared to be ready to take on the most formidable adversary. The King had not taken a chance. He had sent a contingent of Imperial Guards as their escort. These seasoned campaigners had concealed themselves in the bushes and had been keeping vigil.

Taraka had the inkling that something was wrong. After the vicious onslaughts against the Brahmins, there had been a total cessation of forays into the jungle by the Aryans. She had breathed a sigh of relief, although at heart she knew that this peace was illusory. The Aryans were not the ones to give in that easily. They had a peculiar never-say-die tenacity. This tenacity alone was gradually making them masters over this land which was not theirs originally. Taraka knew her history. She had heard it all on the knees of her grandfather.

For quite some time her son Maricha had been pestering her to move further south with their clan, into the realms of their own Emperor, Ravana, but Taraka had resisted him. She could not abandon the homes of her forefathers. Rakshasas had run enough. This time they were going to stay put and fight the marauders.

The footfalls of someone running in broke through her reverie. It was Vikata, a young Rakshasa soldier. He came up panting to her. Taraka sat up straight.

"Vikata, what is it? What makes you run in alarm?"

"Dear queen, the Brahmins have started another yajna." He was still out of breath.

"What!" exploded the queen. "After all we had them put through? Who has shown the audacity? Do these people never learn?" She was furious. Normally she did not enjoy bloodshed, especially of defenceless people, even if they were Aryans. But times have necessitated extreme steps.

"The Brahmin sage Vishwamitra is organising a huge yajna, my queen," informed the youngster. "But I do not like the way things look this time. To me it looks like a decoy to bring us out in the open. They have hidden armed guards all around the encampment with two princes of Ayodhya prowling about looking for trouble."

"Sound the alarm," Taraka ordered. "This time we go in full strength and smash all the resistance they have to offer. It is them or us now, with no holds barred. And tell them, Vikata, we take no prisoners."

A long row of Rakshasa soldiers jogged along the jungle trails. They were absolutely silent, communicating with hand-signs and calls of night-birds alone. There was no tell-tale snap of dry twigs or swishing of leaves being brushed by their clothes. They flitted like shadows, almost invisible to any look-out the Aryans might have stationed. This was a formidable force. Taraka had mustered all able-bodied men and also some women for the raid.

As they closed in to the camp-site, Taraka signalled them to stop. With both her hands she made sweeping movements and two groups of Rakshasas fanned out from the original column to form a trident. The side-arms of the trident then melted deeper into the darkness to encircle the camp-site. A call of an owl signalled that everybody was in position. A faint tinge of ochre from the distant camp-fire vaguely lighted up Taraka's sweat-drenched features. Her eyes were burning like two glowing pieces of charcoal. At her hand signal, the column moved forward. A lone wolf howled from the far side of the camp, signalling that the soldiers there, too, have started moving forward.

Rama was restless. He did not like it. His sixth sense was telling him that something was afoot. This feeling had made him an unparalleled warrior. He could almost smell trouble. He muttered to Lakshmana to take action station. At once all chanting stopped. The silence was eerie. Rama listened hard. Even the cicadas had stopped whirring. An owl called, followed soon by the howl of a lone wolf. It was strange, Rama felt. There was no wolf in this part of the jungle. Rama fitted an arrow to his bow and emitted a low whistle. The soldiers, so far waiting, concealed in the bushes, stepped into the clearing and formed a tight ring around the fire. Then all hell broke loose.

Taraka saw that the soldiers of Ayodhya had formed a tight defensive ring around the fire. She realised that further concealment was pointless now. She yelled, "Attack!" The cry was taken up by all Rakshasa soldiers who dashed into the clearing.

Rama's first arrow took its mark. He did not stop to see or think. Like a machine he began to draw and fire, making every arrow count. He was a superb marksman and so was Lakshmana. Both were famous for their rapid fire. Soon the Rakshasas were all over them and a hand-to-hand combat broke out. The clearing was strewn with the dead Ayodhya soldiers and Rakshasas. Rama dropped his bow and drew his sword. The cold iron caught the gleam of the yajna fire and flashed like a streak of flame in his hand. In his left hand he held a dagger. Lakshmana, too, had done likewise. Verbal communication was not needed between the two brothers.

Taraka saw that her forces were being decimated by the well disciplined Ayodhya soldiers. Even the valiant Rakshasa Subahu had been killed by Rama. She understood that if something was not done immediately, then all her men would be killed in no time. Although quite a few Ayodhya soldiers had been killed, yet the elite Imperial Guards had not broken their defensive formation. Like whirlwind she hacked through the four soldiers facing her and breached the defence.

The sages had sat there, petrified, as the skirmish broke out. Most of them were seeing an armed combat for the first time. But Vishwamitra, with his strong military background, was unperturbed. He picked up his ladle and poured ghee into the flames. The chanting resumed as the flames leapt higher.

Taraka let out a blood-curdling whoop and lunged at Rama. She cut a strangely erotic but menacing figure. Blood was splattered all over her. Her black sari was draped tight with her right breast exposed to allow unhindered movement of her right hand. She leapt straight towards Rama who whirled around to face her. Iron clashed and sparks flew. She was immensely strong and well trained in combat. But she was no match for the Kshatriya prince. Rama feigned tiredness and drew her onwards. Sensing victory, Taraka leapt up for the final cut. In one fluid movement, Rama fainted towards her left and made a sharp upward swing, his sword intent on decapitation. The blade cut through the neck muscles, windpipe and vertebrae as easily as a hot knife slicing through butter. The battle was over. The Imperial Guards cut the rest of the Rakshasas down with clinical precision. Taraka's clan was wiped out. Soon the soldiers would raid their settlement. The old people would be butchered, all women raped and slaughtered along with the children.

There was one Rakshasa who had survived the mayhem—Maricha, the son of Taraka. He was one of the few Rakshasas who wore an armoured breast plate, and this had saved his life. At the very outset of the battle, he had been struck full on his chest by a lance thrown by Rama. At its impact he had been thrown backwards, unconscious. As he regained consciousness, he saw his mother die in front of his eyes. Devastated, Maricha had slipped through the cordon of fighting men, and had run away into the forest, tears flowing unchecked over his dark, handsome countenance.

✦ ✦ ✦

4

Maricha

Maricha ran blindly on, his feet unerringly picking up the trail out of instinct. He did not know where he was going. He only knew that he had to run southwards, for there lay the realm of Ravana, the sole saviour of Rakshasas. He was totally lost in the forest. After running almost through the night, he emerged out of the trees into wide grassland. Now he could run unhindered. He ran on.

At the other end of the grassland, where the forests began anew, stood a lone cottage. Maricha had no idea as to who resided there. But he was beyond caring. His feet could not carry him further on. As he closed in upon the cottage, a man came out of it, an elderly man, with shoulder-length hair and flowing beard, all gone white. Maricha came up to him and fell in a dead faint.

When he opened his eyes, he found himself lying on clean sheets in the cottage. It was morning and the merry chirping of birds could be heard. He tried to sit up, but had such an attack of dizziness that he promptly fell back on bed.

"Don't get up in a hurry. You were wounded and utterly exhausted. You had lost a fair amount of blood. Who are you? Where are you coming from? Where are you going? From your appearance and clothes, I presume that you are a Rakshasa." The elderly man came over and sat beside him. Maricha said nothing. He was too tired to speak.

"Come, my son. Sit up slowly and drink this broth," said the old man. Maricha sat up and took the broth. Then he fell back and slept.

When he awoke, it was evening. Now he was feeling rested and stronger.

"Can you walk?" asked the old man. Maricha nodded. "Fine, then go outside. You shall find a stream flowing. Drink your fill and take a bath. I've laid out this fresh loincloth for you. Go on. We'll talk afterwards."

When Maricha returned freshened, he found that another bowl full of broth waiting for him. He took the bowl up in both hands and sipped. It was scalding hot, but tasted wonderful. He put the bowl down and began his tale.

The old man was thoughtful. He sat quietly for a while. No one spoke a word. A moth flitted about the flame of the lamp burning in one corner. Then he sighed.

"So, Taraka and her clan are wiped out. That is sad. I had heard about her. She was a brave woman. But such a waste!" He fell silent again, sitting there, pensive.

"Tell me your plans now, son. What do you want to do next? Where do you want to go?"

Maricha sat silently for a long, long time. Actually he did not know what he would do, or where he would go. He had no living relation in this world. A single night had robbed him of all he had.

"I would like to take refuge in the realm of Ravana. I want nothing else. That is the only reason of my running southwards all through the night. But I know not where Lanka lies or how far it is."

"You are already in his area," said the elderly man. "Ravana's empire is huge. While coming here you had to cross a grassland, remember? That is the no-man's land. The kingdom of Koshala ends right where the forests end. This side of the grassland is under Ravana's control and is ruled by his governor, Khar. But if it is Lanka that you search, then I can only tell you that it is thousands of *Kosh* away, straight due south, across the deep waters. I can draw the route up for you, if you want to go there. I know that part very well."

"No, I don't want to go to Lanka. I am content to stay wherever the Rakshasa banner flies, not Aryan."

"Then I see no reason for you to travel further. Your own people have been exterminated. Therefore you can stay here if you'd like. See, son, I am a Rakshasa too, as you might have guessed already. Like you, I too had lost my family in the hands of Aryan soldiers. I am known as Rudra. After losing everything, I had roamed about all over the land, ultimately to come and settle here, for this is my land and I belong to this place."

"Koshala had wiped out your people too?" asked Maricha.

"Yes, my son. But I don't blame Dasharatha. It is a relentless war for supremacy. It is a question of rule or be ruled. This struggle will continue forever."

"You said father, that you had once roamed all over the country. Why was that?"

"To ease my ailing heart son," said Rudra. "I was very good at magic, like many Rakshasas are. I went from state to state, from kingdom to kingdom. I attended the village fairs and wedding ceremonies. I was the hot favourite of everybody. I was in command!"

"Father, will you teach me magic?" Rudra stayed silent for a while. Then he nodded.

"Yes, I will. But tell me why do you want to learn it?"

"I have an intuition that my magic, someday, will cause intense agony to the killer of my mother."

So, Maricha stayed back with Rudra as the son he had never had. He performed the daily chores diligently and under the tutelage of the older man learnt the Vedas and other texts during daytime and the ancient art of magic at night. Soon he became a master of his art, with mind control and hypnosis as his forte.

✦ ✦ ✦

5

Ahalya

It was as if they had stepped into the Land of the Dead. What was once a clearing amongst the trees, was now being reclaimed by the forests. Young trees sprouted about here and there in a gay abandon, screening from view the Sarayu river flowing nearby. Weeds and wild bushes overran whatever clearing that remained. Dry leaves and twigs lay strewn about giving the place an unkempt appearance. A cracked and broken down stone hearth bespoke of a homestead that once was here. But nothing remained now. Right in the centre of this macabre area, was a huge, misshapen boulder. Not a flower bloomed. Not a bird sang. The silence was eerie. It seemed as if the place was cursed. Rama and Lakshmana were stunned into silence. Something was wrong with this place! Seriously wrong!

"What is this place, dear Rishi?" asked Rama of Vishwamitra. They were on their way to Mithila after last night's vigil, where King Janaka was hosting a magnum Yajna. On their way, Vishwamitra had told them that he was planning for a little detour. "Believe me, it will be worthwhile," he had said.

"This, my boys, had once been the *Ashram* of the celebrated Rishi Gautama. He used to reside here with his beautiful wife, Ahalya," Vishwamitra replied.

"But everything is so run-down now, as if this place had been abandoned in a hurry!" Lakshmana was intrigued.

"There must be some reason, otherwise you would not have brought us here," Rama said.

"Indeed there is a reason. It is a long, sad story of a woman who had never found love, but had to embrace death with ignominy. It is a tale of deprivation of the basic rights of a woman, whose love had been manipulated.

"Come, let's make ourselves comfortable beneath that tree and I'll tell you all about her and why I had brought you to this place.

"Prajapati Brahma, the foremost of the Devas, had a daughter. Such unblemished was her beauty that she was named Ahalya, for, in Sanskrit 'Hala' meant 'blemish'. As the days rolled by, she grew from a lovely girl into a comely damsel that all desired. Academically too, her knowledge was profound as her father oversaw her trainings himself. Soon enough there was a long line of suitors waiting in queue for her hand, amongst whom the foremost was Indra. The hapless girl was head-over-heels in love with this handsome King of the Devas, who, in turn, was also very much drawn towards her beauty. Brahma, however, was averse to this union, as he was well aware of the amorous overtures of this lecherous man. His attention had fallen upon a total outsider who was not amongst the suitors at all. He was an elderly sage, a man of profound knowledge, a great teacher who had relinquished all the worldly pleasures in pursuit of his academic dreams. He was Rishi Gautama. To him Brahma gave his beautiful daughter in marriage.

"Poor Ahalya did not have a say in this matter. She suffered all privations in silence. But the main thing that ate into her was that her marriage was almost not consummated at all. Night after night she lay alone in her cold bed, dying for a warm touch of love, while her elderly husband burnt midnight oil to probe into newer theories of Life and hereafter. Night after night she tossed about in her lonely bed weaving fantasies of being loved. Then Indra came into her life.

"Indra had once been a student of Gautama and was well aware of his guru's daily schedule. He knew that every morning he used to go for a bath in Sarayu. There he would perform his Surya Puja (worship of the Sun God) before returning to his cottage. This whole thing took up the better part of the morning and Indra took advantage of his absence.

"One morning, at first light, just after the Rishi had left for his morning rituals, Ahalya, who was still in bed, heard the door opening stealthily. She sat up and to her great astonishment saw the Rishi furtively entering the room. It was still quite dark and Ahalya could barely make out his features.

'You are back so early, my husband! Have you finished already?' she asked.

"The Rishi came up to her bed and put his hand on her bare shoulder.

'No my dear,' he answered in a hushed tone. 'I came back because I wanted to make love to you.'

"Ahalya was elated. Her dream was coming true. She shut her eyes and let the Rishi carry her up to the seventh heaven of bliss. But even as she felt her body merging into the Rishi's, Ahalya caught a whiff of a strange perfume. It was that of the Paarijat flower, found only in the Garden of Eden in the Deva realm of Swarga. At once she knew that it was Indra in disguise. But her pleasure was so great that she did not resist the intruder.

"This continued for days together. Indra was having his fill of the pleasures he desired and Ahalya, hers. She taught her mind to accept the impersonator as her husband. All were going on well enough till one fateful morning the real Rishi returned home much earlier than he usually did. He caught the two in bed.

"Indra leapt off and vanished into the forest. Gautama turned to his lawful wife, eyes blazing. Ahalya fell to her husband's feet.

'Pardon me, my husband, for I knew not that it was someone else in your disguise!'

'Your chastity has been sullied by your infidelity, woman, and you shall face the consequences.' With this he turned and walked away, his wooden sandals echoing in Ahalya's head. She lay disgraced on the floor.

"The sandals were heard once again. Ahalya sat up. Gautama entered the room, eyes wild, white hair and beard in disarray. He had a bowl in his hand.

'Sit up, you whore and drink this broth,' said he.

'What is it dear husband? Hemlock?'

'Asking any question now is a show of further insolence. You do as I say, woman. Drink it up.'

"Wordlessly Ahalya took the bowl in her hands and drank up the contents. Almost at once a bout of giddiness struck her and dimmed her vision. She fell back on the floor. Through a dark haze she heard her husband pronouncing his curse.

'Your memory will be lost to mankind. In your place an ugly piece of stone will adorn this home. This part will be cursed forever.'

" 'Husband,' gasped the poor woman. 'Don't be so harsh!' She could speak no further but fell unconscious. She never heard the next part of the pronouncement that said that her memory would be resurrected only after an Ikshaku prince visited the abandoned and cursed Ashram. She was not even allowed the flames of an all-purifying fire. Instead she was buried in the centre of the courtyard where, true to his word, Gautama placed a huge and ugly boulder. Then he went away. Where? No one knows."

Rama sighed and looked up, his eyes brimming over with unshed tears at the predicaments of the unfortunate girl. Lakshmana sat with teeth clenched, seething inside at the grave injustice.

"Are you a prince?" Rama started at the sudden question from a childlike voice. He turned to find a pretty, little girl draped in a small, white sari with red stripes, looking at him in awe. He smiled and drew her close.

"Yes, I am. I am called Rama."

"Are you an Ikshaku?" asked the girl.

"Yes, I am. But who might you be, my little princess?"

"No, I am no princess. I am Ahalya." All three of the visitors started and sat up as if hit by a thunderbolt. Just then a voice was heard crying, "Ahalya, where are you, my baby?" The little girl smiled. "My father," she informed the visitors.

"From her very childhood, sire, she spoke of an Ashram, a tiny, but clean cottage, of a sage called Gautama, and that she was Ahalya. No one knew who Ahalya was. But at her insistence all call her by that name." The girl's father informed them. "She also speaks of an Ikshaku prince who will deliver her from a curse."

"Please don't worry, my man," Vishwamitra reassured. "Your daughter is not abnormal at all. She appears to be the reincarnation of Ahalya. Don't be frightened at this. For through your daughter, the name of Ahalya will be resurrected."

Rama had gone up to the boulder. He laid his right palm on it and stood with bowed head as if in meditation. Then he straightened up and said,

"I shall have this boulder removed and have a beautiful image of Ahalya carved in marble placed right where this boulder is. I shall have masons build the cottage once more but this time in granite. From Ayodhya I shall have the Royal Gardener come in with his team to resurrect the garden. A man will be posted here who will keep everything ship-shape, but of course, with your help, my lady." He looked at little Ahalya as he said this with a smile.

Ahalya was resurrected at the touch of Rama.

+ + +

6

Ecstasy and Despair

The people of Ayodhya were ecstatic. All the four princes were getting married and their happiness knew no bound.

It so happened that King Janaka of Mithila had a huge bow that had once belonged to Shiva. He had declared that whosoever put the string on such a heavy bow would get the hands of Sita, his adoptive daughter. Rama, taken to Mithila by Vishwamitra, along with Lakshmana, not only could put the string on, but while bending the bow, broke it into two, winning over Sita thereby.

Sita was the beloved elder daughter of the Mithila King. Though she was not his biological daughter, yet she was never given to feel that she was a foundling, having been found by King Janaka while he was once marking a field for construction of his place for worship.

It was decided that when Rama wedded Sita, Janaka's second daughter, Urmila, was to be married with Lakshmana. As luck would have it, Janaka's younger brother, Kushadhwaj, had two daughters of marriageable age, Mandavi and Shrutakirti. They were given away in marriage to Bharata and Shatrughna, the two brothers of Rama and Lakshmana. The people of Mithila rejoiced as did those of Ayodhya.

Shortly, the people of Ayodhya began rejoicing once again. King Dasharatha had declared that he was going to retire, handing the throne over to his eldest son, Rama. Rama was the beloved of all. He was known to be brave, a valiant warrior, a just ruler and an intelligent and very sympathetic person. So people welcomed his imminent coronation.

But all singing and dancing on the street came to a sudden stop. The stunned citizens of Ayodhya looked on in silent horror when the Crown Prince Rama, together with his consort Sita and younger brother Prince Lakshmana walked out of the palace on bare feet. They were unadorned and bore only their arms with them. Even the Princess Sita wore no ornaments and was dressed in only the simplest of saris. All hell broke loose. The people came to know that at the instigation of Queen Kaikeyi, Rama had abdicated the throne in favour of his younger brother and son of Kaikeyi, Bharata, and was going away to spend fourteen years in the forests. Lakshmana, his brother's shadow, had followed him out and Sita could not be convinced at all, having firmly declared that her home was where her husband was. All rejoicing changed to wails of anguish and curses against the spineless, old king, his opportunist queen and poor Bharata, who was as yet uninformed about all this. But this was politics.

In all this commotion, no one had noticed a pair of doe-like eyes gazing at the departing figures. The eyes had brimmed up with unshed tears. No one had cared to notice. No one had bothered to inform her that her husband, Lakshmana, was leaving her and will be gone for fourteen long years. The receding figures had now disappeared from view. Urmila wiped her eyes and stood up from her seat near her window. Much work remained to be done at home. She could not waste time moping around. Fourteen years was a long, long wait.

+ + +

7

Seduction of a Violent Kind

Ten years had gone by since they had come to live in the forests. Now it seemed as if this was where they belonged to. A decade is not a matter of joke. It is enough to build up one's habit. But, of course, all was a state of mind. When they had left the palace at Ayodhya, little did people imagine that the princes and the princess, so used to the comforts the Royal Palace had to offer, could stay in the forest at ease. But the fact was that they were so very well prepared mentally that they had felt no hardship whatsoever.

Rama was sitting alone atop a hillock with his bow and arrows, waiting for a passing deer or jungle fowl to show up, for it had been quite some time since they had last tasted fresh meat. From where he sat, his cottage could be seen clearly. There was Sita, going about her daily chores. Now she was hanging up the freshly washed clothes to dry. Lakshmana prowled about the perimeter keeping his weather eye open for any predator, for in this jungle there were many, or any hostile tribes. They were in the heartland of the Rakshasa stronghold, governed by Ravana's cousin, Khar.

Rama suddenly sat up straight, alert. Something had moved in the undergrowths below. A lone stag it was, with a proud head of beautiful antlers. Rama fitted an arrow to his bow, drew, sighted and let go. The stag leapt up and fell to the ground. A single shot through the heart was enough to extinguish his daylight. Rama clambered down from his perch, slinging his bow on his shoulder. Over his free shoulder he hefted his quarry and measured his step towards his homestead.

Sita was freshly bathed. Her eyes lit up as she saw Rama coming in with the deer on his shoulder. She knew that able-bodied men needed fresh meat in their diet and was sad that over the last few days she had only served them with fruits and vegetables. But today it will be different. Lakshmana laid the whetstone aside, where he was busy whetting his arrows to a razor sharpness and came forward with a large knife to help Rama in flensing and quartering the carcass.

Soon the meat was made ready and the two brothers went for a bath in Godavari River. Generally the two of them never left the camp together. One of them usually stayed back for the protection of Sita. But over the last few weeks they had relaxed their vigil at the assurance from Jatayu.

It was late afternoon. A strange figure opened the wicker-gate of the camp. He was a man of a huge bulk, adorned with feathers of different birds of prey. He wore a head-dress of black feathers. Surely this was some non Aryan, probably a Rakshasa. The two brothers grabbed their bows. The man stopped and raised his right hand. It was strange, thought the brothers. This person was unarmed, save a long spear held loosely in his left hand.

"Greetings, oh Princes from Ayodhya! Jatayu, the king of the Birds tribe, welcomes you to his homeland. Pray, do not be alarmed. We may not be Aryans, but we are no friends of Rakshasas." Rama arose and advanced towards the intruder.

"Rama, the Prince of Ayodhya welcomes you, revered Jatayu, to his poor little home."

Rama escorted Jatayu to his seat. Lakshmana greeted him too. Sita came out with refreshment for the elderly man. He took a bite from the offered fruits and had a drink of water.

"You see, Rama, Dasharatha was more than a friend to me. He was my blood brother. Together we had spent some great times. Now, it saddens me to hear that my friend is no more. Anyway, I am very happy that you have come to live here. My village is not very far from here. This Panchavati area technically falls in Ravana's empire. But we people are independent. If there's anything you require, just call me. Moreover, if it so happens that any time both of you have to go away somewhere, don't you worry for my daughter Sita. I'll look after her." He said with a smile. It was reassuring.

By the time the brothers returned from their bath, lunch was almost ready. An appetizing aroma pervaded the environs. Soon they had a hearty meal and sat down talking about Ayodhya and their childhood. Suddenly the wicker gate creaked open. A woman entered. She was not very pretty, but had a regal bearing. Her body was voluptuous and she walked with a sensuous gait. She was Surpanakha, the sister of Ravana.

Over the last few days Surpanakha had been furtively watching this Aryan family. She had come to stay for a few days with her cousin, Governor Khar. But her wild nature precluded her staying at home for long. She took long walks in the forest, always on the lookout for fresh adventures of amorous nature, for she was a nymphomaniac. Perhaps she could find men easily enough in the royal households she habited in, but her preference ran more towards men who were valorous in nature, not the fawning types that surrounded her. Rama exactly met her requirements.

"Greetings, son of the Aryans," said Surpanakha, as she came in a seductive gait, up to where they sat. Unceremoniously she sat down unbidden in front of Rama.

"Dear Aryan, you have stolen my heart," she said without any preamble. Even as she spoke, she raised her arms, ostensibly to arrange her hair which had fallen down, but offering a grand view of her pushed-up busts, with the deep cleavage, as she wore her *stanpatta* very low. "Please be mine. Take me, my beloved." She added, almost with a feline purr.

Rama hid his discomfiture and exchanged a meaningful glance with Sita and Lakshmana.

"Dear madam," said he. "I mean no disrespect but please allow me to say that I am not in a position to fulfil your demands. You see, I am married and..." Surpanakha rudely interrupted him.

"That I can see. Yes, married to this skinny, puny woman, who can barely put up with your amorous acts!"

"You have made a small mistake, dear woman. Whatever she may be, it is a fact that I love her. Why don't you try your luck with my brother instead? He is single, as you can see, and surely he will be happy to oblige you." Lakshmana looked up at

Rama with a reassured smile and the princely trio understood the intended jape.

Surpanakha now turned to Lakshmana and batted her eyelid. Acting coy, she said in all coquettishness, "Will you have me dear Aryan, as your consort? You'll never regret it."

"I am but a servant to my elder brother, dear lady. Why should you waste your youth on being consort to a mere servant? You'd better get my brother to agree to your advances. If you try hard enough he will surely agree." Lakshmana could hardly control his laughter.

The tone of ridicule penetrated the haze of lust that Surpanakha had conjured upon herself. With a growl like a predator, she sprang up, taking out a dagger from within the folds of her dress.

"You have to die, woman," she cried. "I'll kill you and have your husband for myself." She lunged towards where Sita sat cowering behind her husband's back. Rama warded off the attack, bare-handed. Lakshmana caught her from behind and whirled her around. His eyes were blazing like a pair of glowing braziers.

"No one does that to my sister and live. But you are a woman. So I shall not kill you. I shall give you another reward for your excesses." He unsheathed his sword and in a flash, sliced off the hapless woman's nose and ears. Surpanakha screamed and ran away, her hands clutching her bleeding visage.

✦ ✦ ✦

8

Close Encounters

Janasthan was the nearest town in the vicinity of Panchavati. It was a small town, inhabited mainly by Rakshasas. As a town, it was nothing much to speak of, being smaller than many of the Rakshasa strongholds further south. But the town was clean and well planned, with a palatial edifice in the centre. This was the gubernatorial home and the place from which Khar, the cousin of Ravana, efficiently governed the province. In the Rakshasa reckoning, this was a frontier town, for no Rakshasa settlements were there further north.

Governor Khar was presiding at an important meeting on defence matters, in the Council Room of his palace. Suddenly the door crashed open. Khar looked up in annoyance as he had given the specific instruction that he was not to be disturbed. Instantly his annoyance gave way to horror. His sister Surpanakha rushed in with her hands covering her face. Blood still seeped out from between her fingers. Reaching Khar, she fell to the ground, weeping.

"What happened, dear sister? How did you hurt yourself?"

Surpanakha removed her hands from her face. All those present there sharply drew their breath in, in horror. Her nose and ears were chopped off without mercy. This was the punishment usually meted out to felons.

"Who on earth had the audacity of disfiguring you?" thundered Khar.

Surpanakha tried to speak, but she was choked with the blood still flowing from her severed nose into her mouth.

"Wait, wait," Khar cried in consternation. "Don't speak! Let's have your injuries tended to first!"

Immediately he had the guards help Surpanakha into the antechamber and had surgeons brought in to tend to the wounds. Rakshasas were genetically of a very tough breed. So, in all probabilities, she would not succumb to her wounds, but she will be disfigured for life. This was the profound observation of the chief surgeon.

After she was medicated and her injured parts dressed, she informed Khar about how she was humiliated. Khar was astounded and a mite perturbed as well. Never before had they any problem with the Aryans. But now it appeared that they had begun their forays into Rakshasa territory. Khar, himself, had no animosity towards any of the Aryans. Had the banished Ayodhya princes sought sanctuary in his area, he would have been glad to grant it to them. But, no! They had to come in without any 'by your leave', had to establish their home there and had to have the temerity of humiliating and disfiguring his cousin-sister for something which was not at all uncommon in the more permissive Rakshasa society. Khar could not allow this in his area. He called for Brihadbal, the Captain of his commando forces. Brihadbal came in and saluted.

"Brihadbal, take fourteen of your best commandoes at sunrise tomorrow, to the forest of Panchavati. There you'd find three Aryans have set up their home. Two are males and one female. Arrest those two men and bring them over to me, forthwith! I want them alive," he ordered.

"At your orders, sire," Brihadbal saluted smartly and wheeled about to leave.

"Another thing, Brihadbal, both men are armed and Kshatriyas. Expect resistance."

"Right, sire. And the woman?"

"She is not important."

Brihadbal left.

The sun was high in the sky, by the time Brihadbal and his unit reached Panchavati. They could identify the homestead from afar, from the column of smoke rising above the level of the trees. The cottage was situated at the far end of a small stretch of grassland beyond the line of trees. It was structured almost like a stockade with a wall of strong wood built all around it. Behind the cottage was a hillock, also bare of big trees. It was a good defensible position, unless one expected a full scale battle. At a signal from Brihadbal, the commandos slowed their mounts to walking pace and closed in up to hailing distance of the cottage. Then they took up a classical semi-lunar formation taking up action stations. Brihadbal cupped his hands to his mouth and hailed.

It was Sita who had first noticed the movements near the trees at a distance. She beckoned Rama over to the rampart to have a look. Rama came over, took a look and at once understood what it was all about.

"Bring me my bow and quivers of arrow. Also bring along my spear and sword," muttered Rama in Sita's ears, his eyes not leaving his adversaries for an instant.

In a sonorous voice bred in the parade ground, Brihadbal hailed.

"Aryans, we know that you are there. I come on Imperial Orders of Governor Khar, under the seal of His Imperial Majesty, Emperor Dashanan Ravana. You have committed heinous crimes that include assaulting a defenceless woman. You are requested to accompany my forces to Janasthan. I order you to surrender forthwith. I come in peace and I want no unnecessary bloodshed."

With silent speed Rama armed himself for battle. He did not utter a word in reply but stood behind the rampart with an arrow fitted to his eager bow. He had made Sita go inside and lock the door. By the time the captain had finished his speech, he had already drawn and had held him in his sights, waiting for the commandoes to attack.

Lakshmana had gone out hunting and was on his way back with a number of jungle fowls hanging from his belt. He broke his stride and came to a halt, as he heard the loud hailing outside the cottage. Instantaneously, out of long hours of hard training, he dropped behind a huge boulder and unslung his bow.

After waiting for a few breath-holding moments, the commandos moved in to attack. Rama waited for a couple of heartbeats and let loose the first arrow. Brihadbal never knew what hit him. Soundlessly he toppled over from his saddle,

Rama's arrow sticking out of his throat. At the same instant the man next to him threw up his hands and was dead before he hit the ground. Lakshmana had struck. The men scattered about in alarm at this new source of danger. Both brothers, very fast with the bow, drew and shot rapidly. Soon the entire platoon lay strewn about, dead, without a shot having been fired from their end.

A number of bird-men led by Jatayu, came running from the tree-line. They had heard the commotion and had rushed in to help, although no help was actually needed.

"I had heard of the valour of Rama and Lakshmana, but this is the first time I am witnessing it myself," marvelled Jatayu, as they sat in the comfort of the balcony of the cottage. The bird-men were busy removing the Rakshasa dead and retrieving their arms. "Feels good that you are perfectly capable of taking care of yourselves. But bear it in mind, now Khar will send a full division to vanquish you two."

"Let him," growled Lakshmana. "We are not afraid."

"But my son, we must be pragmatic," said Jatayu. "Let us sit together and draw up a battle plan." Rama nodded. He was much more level-headed than his brother.

From afar it appeared as if breakers of an enraged sea were breaking off the cliffs—such was the din of the approaching Rakshasa army. Khar had almost blown his top on learning about the massacre of his platoon sent to apprehend Rama and Lakshmana. As there had been no survivors, the Rakshasas could only guess what had happened. The rider less horses returning to their stables at Janasthan, en masse, told the story. Khar was in the throes of a blind rage already, but Surpanakha's caustic comments had added insult to injury.

"Aren't you supposed to be the governor of this province, my brother?" she had asked. "Don't you proudly proclaim that that the great Emperor Ravana is your own blood, your cousin? Yet you let two puny, mamma's darlings draw your exalted name through mud?" Her wound had improved somewhat and she was more or less legible, and painfully so. Khar could bear it no longer. He ordered his army to march. He decided to lead the assault himself, with his commanders Dushan and Trishira acting as his deputies. There shall be no prisoners, the soldiers were told.

It was dark, already. The wan moon only served to accentuate the darkness. The soldiers streamed out of the trees and halted. Foot-soldiers were there and there were chariots and the cavalry too. Only the elephants had been left behind as movement of the pachyderms in the forest stretch would have proved to be difficult.

Khar raised his right hand and the soldiers stopped. An eerie silence prevailed. There was no movement in the dark cottage too. Khar's eyes roved over the entire scene. With the amount of fire power and man power that he had brought in the Kshatriyas stood no chance at all. He had a rising doubt that perhaps the Aryans had fled the scene. Whatever it was he resolved to squash their homestead under the marching feet of his soldiers. He unsheathed his sword and pointing it straight to the cottage shouted 'Attack' and the attack began. Only Khar and his second in command, Trishira, held back, while the rest of his forces pushed forward under the leadership of Dushan.

When the advancing forces had crossed well over half the way across the plain grass land in front of the cottage, three consecutive volleys of fire arrows, two in each volley, rose from the top of the hillock just behind the cottage. The advancing troops stopped in confusion. The arrows shot right up, then curved to fall, not towards them, but away! This added to the confusion. But as the falling arrows hit the ground, there was instant conflagration wherever they fell. A gentle breeze encouraged the flames to leap higher. The fire spread rapidly at a pace that was mind-boggling. Soon a ring of fire surrounded the entire troop. Men shouted in alarm! Horses neighed and threw their riders from their saddles! Total chaos prevailed. Only Khar and Trishira were stranded outside the ring of fire. Then the arrows fell. The trapped soldiers were assailed by a veritable deluge of arrows. They had no idea where they were coming from. They just died where they stood. The leaping flames cut off their escape and made them sitting ducks by the intense illumination, while rendering them blind to what was happening outside. Khar and Trishira ran this way, then that, yelling encouragements, blindly firing arrows towards the hillock, but all to no avail. Most of his men were soon dead, either from the barrage of arrows, or trampled underfoot by their own mounts, or roasted to cinders in a bid to escape. Gradually the flames died down, and so did the soldiers, till not a soul stirred in the field of death. Khar drove his chariot forward, desperate. This was a type of battle he had never been in before.

"Where are you, you coward, show yourself!" Khar yelled at the top of his voice. Almost as if on cue, two tall figures stepped forward on the hillock and strode down its slope. Trishira yelled hoarsely and raised his long bow. Lakshmana disdainfully fired two arrows by the time Trishira had fitted the first arrow on his bow. One arrow passed through his throat and the other through his right eye. He was dead before he fell. In frustration Khar whirled his huge iron mace above his head. In the glimmer of the slowly dying flames, he cut a fearsome figure indeed. Then he threw it straight towards the head of Rama. As Rama ducked, Khar picked up a javelin and swung back for a lethal throw, but he did not have the time to complete it. Rama's iron tipped arrow stuck out from the back of his neck and he toppled in slow motion from his chariot. The charioteer was quaking all over thinking that his end had come. Rama strode up to him and stroked the frightened horses.

"Fear not, dear man," said Rama. "I do not fight non-combatants. You go back to Janasthan and tell whoever is in charge there that the army exists no more. I shall be coming soon to fly the Koshala flag from the palace staff. Now go!"

The charioteer wheeled the horses with a flick of the reins and thundered away in the darkness. At once an unearthly ululating rent the night air. From the trees all around jumped down the bird-men. They ran over to where Rama and Lakshmana stood. They had been hiding in the trees. Their hundred odd archers had added to the assault that put paid to the Governor's army. A smiling Jatayu led Sita down from the hillock. It was his plan and expertise that had won the field. He had the bird-men come in their hundreds to dig a circular trench in the clearing. This he had them fill in with twigs, brush, hay, dry branches and brambles, which were soaked in oil. He had also helped the Kshatriya brothers with the fire lit behind a boulder on top of the hillock and helped with the fire arrows, then stood guard over Sita with a vicious, naked sword in his hand. One by one Rama and Lakshmana embraced, first Jatayu, then his men. Not a word was needed at this hour.

The streets of Janasthan were deserted. All shops were closed. Most of the houses in the richer section of the town lay vacant. Only the houses of the poorer people showed signs of habitation. But even in these houses all doors and windows were hermitically shut. A street dog was sniffing around in the dust of the main street in search of some edibles and finding none. It cowered and sought shelter in a shade at the crunch of marching feet. Rama had entered town with his entourage of bird-men. The mothers in the poorer section clutched their daughters close to their breasts and waited in abject terror with bated breath. They belonged to the vanquished race and they knew that the womenfolk generally bore the burden of humiliation and suffering when a victorious army marches into an occupied town. But the bird-men were not concerned with them at all.

Rama marched straight on to the gubernatorial palace. At his orders, one of the bird-men went up to the terrace and shinnied up the flag-staff. The colours of the Empire of Lanka were struck and the orange Koshala standard, bearing the motif of the rising sun, flew in its place from the palace top. Rama walked into the palace and strode over to the court-room. He issued some orders to his officers who disappeared instantly. Then he went over to the ornate seat placed at the end of the room on a raised platform and settled down to wait.

He did not have to wait for long. His men soon escorted in five citizens of Janasthan, amongst whom was a priest. Rama came down from his seat to meet them. The citizens were sulky and looked scared. The priest spoke first.

"Why have you got us arrested? What have we done? We are peace loving people."

"Brahmin..." Rama began, but he was interrupted by the elderly man.

"Pray, do not call me by a falsely bestowed Aryan caste. Call me a priest, if you wish, but do not call me Brahmin, for that I am not."

"But you are a priest, are you not? Then that implies that you are a Brahmin!" Rama was incredulous.

"No, sire. Not in our society. Unlike you Aryans, we Rakshasas are casteless. Yes, classes we have, the priests, the warriors, the traders, the workers, etc. but we are not bound by any hereditary caste system."

"Right. Tell me, priest, which god do you worship?"

"Shiva has been our god since times immemorial, since long before you, Aryans, invaded our land. You had usurped our god and now claim that he is your very own."

"Thank you, dear priest, I stand educated," said Rama. He then walked away with his hands behind his back, musing. Then he turned and said:

"From now on you are no longer under the Lanka crown. You are a protectorate of the Koshala kingdom. Fear not, for unlike in many states, Koshala rules are just. You are the senior citizens of Janasthan. You shall rule the town in the name of the Ikshaku dynasty of Ayodhya. You decide who is to take which responsibility. I leave behind a contingent of my soldiers to maintain law and order. Is it all understood? Now you can go."

Lakshmana was a man of action. He could not sit idle. Since morning, after Rama had left with some bird-men to formally take charge of the town of Janasthan, leaving him behind for the protection of Sita, he had been working hard digging trenches. By midday, he was done. The circular trench now ran all around in a ring, to enclose the cottage. After that he began filling this trench with inflammable articles and soaking them with oil. Jatayu had taught him a good lesson in defensive tactics. After he was done, he called upon to Sita to see his handiwork.

"This, dear sister, is the Lakshmana Line. When you stay alone at home, always keep a burning torch handy. Never step outside this ring. Do not allow anyone to come inside. If any intruder tries to barge in, just throw the lighted torch in and the unwelcome guest will be toasted alive."

Sita was amused at the concern these two brothers always showed regarding her safety.

✦ ✦ ✦

9

Ravana

People say that Lanka is the City of Gold and they are not far too wrong. All houses were lined with golden trappings and the steeples and towers were plated with gold. The city dazzled in the morning sun. For the Rakshasas this was the last city. True, there were other big cities in the Rakshasa realm, but none could compare with Lanka, in its splendour. From his palace balcony, Ravana watched over his city with a sense of immense satisfaction.

A knock at the door broke through his reverie. At his summons, a guard entered and saluted smartly.

"Sire, Princess Surpanakha requests the pleasure of presenting herself to His Majesty, immediately."

Ravana let out a low, mental groan. This sister was the bane of his life. Now, what new misadventure had she found herself in, once again? She was reckless and beyond control. Even her husband, the Danava prince Bidyutjwiva was hard put to manage her.

"Usher her in, will you?" Ravana moved back to the balcony, his vacant eyes studying the horizon. The natural defensive barrier of the Island of Lanka, the deep blue sea, stretched as far as eye could reach, up to the horizon. The sparkling waters reflected the morning sun and danced as if donning millions of diamond diadems.

"Brother," Surpanakha called.

"Welcome, dear sister of mine," Ravana said as he turned. Then, at a look at her face, he stopped, aghast. With two strides he came over to her and cradled her face on his hands. Tears streamed down Surpanakha's mutilated face.

"Who did this to you, dear sister? Who had the audacity of disfiguring the sister of Ravana?" He roared. Tearfully Surpanakha recounted all that had befallen, naturally with a good bit of exaggerations and carefully omitting her attempt at slaying Sita.

Ravana was silent and ruminative after hearing all what Surpanakha had to say. He became restless and began pacing about his room, like a caged tiger. Then he stopped and turned.

"I want to hear more. Have you come alone? Or is anyone else with you?" He asked.

"No, my brother, Akampan, a minister of brother Khar has escorted me up to this place."

"Where is he now?"

"Waiting outside, brother."

Ravana gave out a thunderous roar calling Akampan's name. Immediately the man from Janasthan entered, quaking all over in fear, for Ravana in rage was terrifying.

"What is it I hear," Ravana demanded as soon as Akampan entered.

"Yes, Your Majesty. Every word you hear is true."

"Do you mean to say that the army of Janasthan exists no more? Nor does my administration in the town?"

"No, sire, nothing exists."

"And all on account of a couple of puny Kshatriyas?"

"They are no ordinary mortals sire. They have divine blessings."

"Huh! Divine!" He paced some more, and then added. "My court sits after breakfast. Be there, you two. I need to make a few very important decisions.

✦ ✦ ✦

10

The Abduction

Ravana's aircraft, the *Pushpak Rath*, whirred on under the level of white fluffy cotton-wool clouds. The flight was going on smoothly except from the occasional bump on an errant air-current. A flight of geese coming in from the opposite direction suddenly screeched in mortal terror at the sight of this strange 'bird' and wheeled away to safety. Ravana sat alone at the controls. This was an ancient machine, originally built by Danava engineers, but confiscated by the Deva half brother of Ravana, Kubera. Ravana had reclaimed it when he drove Kubera out of Lanka. With the help of his father-in-law, Maya Danava, the celebrated architect and engineer, he had mastered the operations in no time and flew it himself, occasionally, on very special missions. Apart from his son, Crown Prince Meghnad and one engineer, no one was allowed anywhere near the controls. Ah! Meghnad was an exception. He had not only learnt the controls, but had mastered it, so much so that he had become proficient in airborne assault from behind cloud cover, and this had made him invincible. In this technique he had also vanquished the great tactician Indra himself, thereby earning the name Indrajit.

The Council of Ministers' meeting had been a walk-over. The enraged Ravana was all for a full-scale military action because an encroachment had been made in his personal fief. The Council had endorsed this move, but Akampan had intervened.

"Your Majesty, I do not think that a military operation is required at all," he had said.

"Then what do you suggest?" Ravana had asked.

"Sire, you are the most valiant warrior in whole of this land. It is not becoming of you to launch a full-scale offensive against two Kshatriya brothers, however valorous they may be. There is a better alternative, I dare say."

"What is it?"

"Sire, from what I hear the elder one is blindly in love with his wife. If you can arrange for the abduction of this woman, then, on one hand you shall earn the respect of all by stealing her from right under his nose and on the other, there is a distinct possibility that Rama will die of heartbreak at the loss of his beloved. Add to it the tremendous expense that will be avoided. And if, sire, Rama has the audacity of coming after you to rescue his abducted wife, then let him, at his own risk."

Akampan's reasoning swayed all and was approved unanimously

Ravana looked down. He was not flying too high, about three hundred *Dhanu*, maybe. He had flown low over the sea, as long as possible, to avoid being seen. Luckily he had not met any boat or ocean liner on his way. He had turned inland at the very last moment. But over land, he had set his course, not for Panchavati, but for the very edge of Dandakaranya, wherein lay the border between the kingdom of Koshala and his Empire.

Maricha was busy with his household chores. He lived in the same cottage that had given him shelter from the wrath of the Koshala crown, but now he lived alone. It was about five years since his mentor had left this world. But by this time he had already mastered the art of magic. After his guru's death, he too had followed in his footsteps and had roamed over the entire non Aryan world. But in a couple of years, he had come back to his cottage to spend time in recluse and to hone his magical skills to perfection. The scene of his mother's head tumbling away from her body still haunted his mind. He was resolved to wreck his vengeance, but did not know how to.

The sun had already completed a quarter of his journey across the sky when Maricha heard his name being called. Who could it be? No one knew that he stayed in this recluse in the forests! Maricha ducked out of the low door of his cottage. The splendid figure resplendent in golden dhoti and a crown flashing gold on his head filled him with awe. The one whom he had idolized was standing in front of him. Maricha fell to Ravana's feet. "Your Majesty," was all he could say.

"Rise, oh worthy son of Taraka, for I have a task of honour for you," said Ravana.

"Emperor, what can I say?"

Maricha was aghast. Ravana had briefed him about the mission and the task cut out for him. He was not afraid for his own life, which he understood now stood forfeit. But it was the abduction part that he could not agree with. It seemed as if he was being relegated to a cheap felon. He tried to dissuade Ravana.

"No, my son, the plan is final. This is the only course that can be taken. But why do you hesitate? It will enable you to take a good revenge on your arch enemy! And I need your magic," declared Ravana, with a tone of finality that precluded any argument.

The midday sun found them hiding behind a bush at the tree line, overlooking the cottage of Rama. Ravana's military eyes took in every details of the defence of the cottage, together with the charred grassland and the circular ditch filled with ashes. His jaws hardened. Then the woman came outside. Ravana tapped on Maricha's shoulder, indicating that it was time for him to move.

Sita had come out into the courtyard to wash her hands. She straightened as she wiped her hands on the *anchal* of her sari, scanning the world beyond the cottage gates, when suddenly she froze. A weird deer had come into view. It was like no other creature she had ever seen. Its coat dazzled golden and flashed in the bright sun, with myriads of sparkling multi-coloured gems. Sita felt ecstatic and jumping up, she clapped her hands in joy. Rama and Lakshmana came out of the cottage to inquire what had made Sita so happy.

"What is it, dear?" asked Rama.

"A deer," said Sita in joy. "See husband, there he is. Golden all over studded with sparkling gems." The golden deer flashed into view once again, frolicking at the edge of the forest. Rama reached for his bow.

"It must be some Rakshasa magic," said Rama through clenched teeth.

"I don't want to know what it is. But I want it as a pet. Please, dear husband, get it for me. You can do it," Sita insisted.

"If you say so, but I don't like this one bit," said Rama, as he slung his quiver over across his right shoulder and strode outside the wicker gate after instructing Lakshmana to stick around at the cottage and not to leave Sita unguarded even for an instant. He had a foreboding that something awful was in the offing.

Lakshmana was jittery. Rama had gone for quite some time now. He was an athletic man. So it would not have been a great deal of a problem to keep up with the deer amongst the trees and undergrowth, which would be deterrent for a fast running deer. This golden deer was something that Lakshmana could not take in. This was preternatural. Rama should have been back long ago. Now shadows had begun lengthening in the field. Sita was getting nervous too. Something was terribly wrong and Sita felt that she was responsible for some misfortune that might have befallen her husband.

"Lakshmana, dear brother, why is your brother so late?" Sita could not contain her anxiety any longer.

"Pray do not worry, dear sister of mine. Your husband is perfectly capable of coping with any situation." Lakshmana sounded braver than he actually felt.

"No, no, my heart tells me that something is wrong. Why don't you go, brother, and see what is holding him back. Perhaps he had injured himself or something and is not able to come back on his own."

"That is absurd. Don't even think about it. And I cannot very well leave you alone at the cottage. My brother had specifically told me so."

"I am not a milksop, Lakshmana. I am a Kshatriyani and can take care of myself. Moreover Jatayu and the bird people are always somewhere around here. What harm can come to me? No, no, you please go and see what's wrong."

At this very moment, a heart-rending human cry rent the air. It was the cry of a man in pain. The birds flew up in alarm over the tree-tops. Then another cry shattered all tranquillity of the forest. "Lakshmana, brother Lakshmana, save me!" It was the voice of Rama crying out.

Ravana shifted in his position behind the tall bush that was efficiently screening him from view. Everything was going according to plan. Maricha had woven a magic of hypnosis and mind control over the unsuspecting Aryans. They were seeing something that was actually not there. There was actually no golden deer. It was Maricha himself, swathed in the skin of a cheetal stag. To the eyes under the spell of a mass hypnosis, that had appeared to be a bejewelled golden stag. It was all illusion. Ravana smirked at the confusion he had helped create. Yes, all had gone very well so far. Rama had left in a hurry, chasing the illusion. Then that cry in Rama's voice! That was a master stroke. Nothing could beat it. He was sure that Maricha was no more. But some sacrifices needed to be made for the greater good. Maricha was expendable. Ravana peered over the edge of the bush. He could see Sita and Lakshmana arguing over something. That was good. Then Lakshmana armed himself and left in a huff in the direction where Rama had gone. But before going he had handed a burning taper to Sita and had pointed to the ground. That was odd. Oh, Ravana would have given a lot to overhear what Lakshmana had said!

After chasing the golden deer for a long time Rama had become tired and irritated. It had been very frustrating. The infernal deer was neither giving him a slip, nor was it allowing him to close in. This could not go on. So he picked up an arrow, aimed and shot it right through the heart. What happened next left him flabbergasted. The fatally injured deer cried out for Lakshmana in his voice as it fell! Gradually the illusion wore off and Rama saw a bearded Rakshasa, swathed in the skin of an ordinary spotted deer, lying there in a pool of blood, dead. It was indeed magic at its best, just as he had feared. Rama wheeled about in his track and sped the homeward way.

Lakshmana was distressed when he heard Rama's voice calling out for him, but he was sure that it was all part of a giant hoax. Nothing could ever happen to Rama. But Sita was disconsolate. She ranted and cursed like an enraged she-wolf, calling him a coward and even accusing him of inaction because he, Lakshmana, desired her and that was why he was hoping that his brother died out there, unaided. This aspersion was too much for Lakshmana to bear. He armed himself in silence and made to leave. Then he stopped and going back into the cottage, came out with a burning taper.

"You remember the Lakshmana Line I hope? Take this taper. Or, better, light a torch with it and keep it burning. If in our absence anyone comes and tries to force entry, set the nearest part of the Line to fire. The flames will instantly spread in a ring all around and will keep burning for many hours, keeping all intruders away." With this, he thrust the taper in Sita's hand and strode away in Rama's wake.

This was the moment Ravana was waiting for. As soon as Lakshmana left, he stood up and draped himself in the saffron garb of an ascetic. From the bag that hung from his shoulder he fished out a begging bowl and taking off his golden crown, he stuffed it in his bag. Then he adorned his forehead with a vermillion streak and stepped out towards the cottage in the guise of a roaming ascetic. "Hara hara Mahadev!" He cried as he came up to the cottage. "Alms for the poor, my daughter!"

Sita came out of the cottage with a bowl full of uncooked rice and raw vegetables.

"Come, father, take it," she invited. Ravana took a step forward, then he stiffened, glancing at the Lakshmana Line and the burning taper stuck in a hole in the ground. Years of guerrilla warfare had left Ravana with a sixth sense. He smelt trouble.

"No my daughter, my vow prevents me from crossing the threshold of anyone's residence. You please come out and give me the alms."

Sita was a woman of a trusting nature. Without a faintest whiff of suspicion of any kind, she stepped up to where Ravana stood asked him to open his bag. Ravana grabbed her arm and pulled her towards him. Sita shrieked. The bowl of alms fell to the ground, spilling its contents all over the place. Ravana threw off his false garb of saffron and stood in his regal splendour.

"I am Ravana, the King of Rakshasas. I have come to take you with me as a hostage for the crimes your husband has committed. No harm will come to you. Do not struggle unnecessarily." He swung Sita up over his shoulders and strode towards the place where he had left his aircraft, well camouflaged by foliage. A shrill call of a peacock shattered the forest calm. This was followed by the cawing of ravens and shrieks of kites. Like ripples rolling away on the surface of a calm pond, when a stone hits its surface, did the bird-calls roll away far and wide. This was strange! Ravana looked around him, alert for any sign of danger. But finding none, he resumed his walk.

Jatayu sat up straight, with his ears cocked to catch the notes of the bird-calls. These were coded signals from the guards who kept vigil on Sita.

"To arms," he roared. "The Rakshasa Ravana has abducted Sita!" Then he stopped to listen again. "They are taking to air! Bring my condor and archers, be ready!" He barked. But the archers were already at action stations and the pet condor had been brought up. The commander of forces had also been listening to the bird-calls with equal attention. Jatayu reached his gloved left hand out. The gigantic condor, trained to kill, stepped up to his perch on his master's hand, with a pair of gimlet eyes fixed upon his master's. Jatayu stoked the silky back of the bird.

"Wait, my sweet brother, I'll show you the kill soon. But let me warn you. Today you'll meet your match."

The bird kept on looking into Jatayu's eyes with a faint, barely audible squawk heard from within his throat. With a powerful, guttural roar, a strange contraption, dazzling in the sun, rose above the trees far away.

Ravana, with all haste, ran up to the *Pushpak*. With his free right hand he swept the camouflage aside and literally flung the struggling Sita on the far seat. Then he tied her securely to the seat, so that she could not escape, nor do herself any harm. Moreover, safety during flight was also to be considered. But Sita was beyond caring. She struggled against the knots that held her down, looked at Ravana with staring eyes and called out for help till she frothed from her mouth. Hastily Ravana pulled some levers and handles and turned a few knobs here and there. The Pushpak sprang to life.

Rama was anxious about the effects of the death cries of the Rakshasa, but his anxiety increased three-folds when he spied Lakshmana running up towards him. He hailed his brother, rebuking him as he came up.

"Is all well Lakshmana? Is Janaki alright? Then why have you left her alone to come running after me like a man possessed? Did I not forbid you to leave camp?" Rama demanded of Lakshmana.

"Brother, pray scold me not, for, almost out of her mind in grief and anxiety, *sister-in-law* ordered me to come after you." Lakshmana was panting.

At this moment a peacock cried out from afar. This was followed by the calls of birds from all around. The calls were closing in like the roar of waves racing towards the shore.

"The Bird-men calling!" cried Rama. "Some misfortune has befallen Sita! Come, brother! Not a moment to be lost!" They sped towards the homestead like a pair of antelopes.

The giant condor swooped in from nowhere like a harbinger of death, beaks parted, talons extended, huge wings blotting out the evening sun. He emitted a blood-curdling screech and went straight for Ravana. Momentarily Ravana was caught on the wrong foot. The aircraft wobbled, almost out of control. The razor sharp talons ripped Ravana's flesh open from shoulder to elbow. Then the bird went for his eyes. Ravana was a man of prodigious strength. With his bleeding arm he warded off the attack and struck the bird away. Then he pulled out his vicious sword, Chandrahash, from the scabbard. The condor attacked again but this time Ravana was ready. The Chandrahash flashed and the poor condor was cleaved into two, the pieces plummeting towards the earth. Sita shrieked! Instantly hundreds of arrows pelted against the under surface of the aircraft's hull. A number of them hit the whirring blades. Ravana, never known for temperance, was enraged now. He wheeled his craft around and peered over the side. A large number of half naked men, adorned with feathers, had gathered on a hillock down below. They were aiming their arrows straight at him. A giant of a man stood like a tower, directing the operations. Ravana could have throttled up and sped away easily, giving them a slip. But he did not. Instead, he hefted a heavy lance that had been stowed in a bracket at hand, aimed at the leader and let it loose.

Jatayu had gone berserk as his favourite condor fell to the earth, cut into two. He ordered to the archers to shoot. Then he saw Ravana leaning over the side of the strange craft. Something glinted and streaked down. Jatayu felt a thud on his chest, followed by searing pain. He fell. The aircraft banked, wheeled southwards and sped away.

Rama was beside himself with grief. The wicker gate of the cottage stood open. A bowl was lying neglected on the ground with rice and vegetables scattered all over the place. Calling Sita's name, the brothers rushed in. No one responded to their call. A strange whirring roar filled the environment. They had heard nothing like this before. They ran outside. The call of birds increased in volume and urgency. The brothers looked at each other. Nothing needed to be told. They were filled with a sense of foreboding. Lakshmana ducked inside the cottage coming out with loads of their arms. They armed themselves to the full as they ran. Suddenly a commotion was heard from the direction of the Bird-men's village. The brothers turned and ran towards the source of the commotion.

A huge condor, cut mercilessly into pieces, was lying at the foot of a hillock. Jatayu's pet condor! A large number of bird-men were gathered on the top of the hillock. All were stunned into silence.

Jatayu was lying on his back. A huge lance was sticking out of his chest. Not much blood was seeping out, his men had assured him. But Jatayu knew that most of the bleeding was internal and that his end was at hand. Already the light was fading from his eyes. He wanted to tell Rama something. But will he come in time? Someone called. Rama had come. He tried to speak but bloody froth emerged from his lips. He raised his right hand pointing southwards, muttering "Ravana...Lanka... Sita," in a barely audible tone. Then he fell back. The sun set.

The Pushpak was whirring along steadily. Sita was sitting there looking over the side. Her body shook with pent-up sob. The ground below was carpeted with green paddy fields, interspersed with wide tracts of forest. A few villages sped by. Tiny houses with tiny people—some of them looked up in awe at the strange metal bird above. Occasional rivers wound along like silver ribbons. Ravana had locked the controls on a southward course. He was intent on tying a bandage over his injured arm by a piece of cloth torn from his *angabastra* to staunch the flow of blood. Tying a bandage one-handed called for such unwavering attention that he did not notice Sita furtively taking off the few ornaments she wore and dropping it on the ground below. They were passing over hilly terrain. She had just spotted a group of five people sitting on a hilltop. They were brown-skinned and very well built and, at least from afar, they did not look like Rakshasas. She dropped the ornaments just as they were flying over these people. They were looking upwards as they passed overhead and she was sure that they had seen her dropping the ornaments. She knew that her husband would be searching high and low for her. These ornaments would tell him that Sita had passed this way.

By the time they were over the sea, the sun had set and it was dark all around. Like a shadow the Pushpak flitted over the sea under a starlit sky. The moon had not risen as yet. Sita drowsed in her seat as Ravana sat erect at the control. Pain from his injured arm racked through his body, though it did not show on his face. He was tired—very much so. But the tiredness too, did not show. It will come later, much later. Till then he could not afford to give way to any physical infirmity. He was Ravana, conqueror of the world. He rubbed his palms over his face. He was not getting younger by the day. Age extracted its own vengeance. He glanced at the sleeping figure beside him. A nubile, comely woman, with a beauty and grace to turn the heads of many. But he was above all those feelings now. Vedawati was about her age when he had met her. She had been the only woman whom he had fallen in love with—madly! But that was in another age, in another world...

Ravana suddenly sat up straight. Far in the horizon was a tiny speck of light. It was the huge fire burning on top of the Trikuta hills, a fire that burned every night to guide the ships at sea, a fire to tell the world that Lanka was awake and vigilant. He made a minor adjustment in his course. The Pushpak reacted beautifully and raced on towards Lanka in glee, like a homing pigeon.

✦ ✦ ✦

11

The Banaras

Five persons were sitting in a shade on the slope of the Malaya Hill in the Hrishyamukh Range. It was near midday and they were feeling sleepy after a hearty lunch. Nearby was the cavern that was their temporary residence. They changed their address quite often as they were fugitives from law.

These persons belonged to a race where all males were very powerfully built. Their complexion was dusky, that set them apart from the Aryans, though they were fairer-skinned than the Rakshasas. Their eyes were brown. Their torsos were bare and they wore short *dhotis* that reached up to their knees. They wore their hairs long and were clean-shaven. They belonged to the non Aryan race of Banaras, who had the monkey as their totem and coat-of-arms. As a mark of their identity, all wore a tail attached to their waist-bands. They were a proud people that had never been subjugated by any other tribe or nation. All of them were fierce warriors, excelling in the use of the mace and unarmed combat. They were of athletic disposition and were excellent rock-climbers. Culturally, they were far more advanced than many non Aryan tribes. Kishkindhya was their capital. Their state was also known by the same name as their capital, but this was nothing unusual in non Aryan states.

Politically the position of the Banaras was somewhat unique. They were one of the two powerful non Aryan people who were on the best of terms with the Aryans. The other being the Snake people or Nagas. At the time of the Aryan invasions, both these tribes had inhabited the fertile plains of the Ganga and her tributaries. But once the Devas had pushed the Asuras out of their strongholds in the valley of the mighty river Sindhu, the Banaras and Nagas found themselves to be in a tight corner. After their cities on the Sindhu bank were destroyed, the Rakshasas had the moved eastwards down the Gangetic plains, incessantly being pursued by the Aryan tribes. The Banaras and Nagas resisted the incoming Rakshasa flood with all their strength, but they had to give way. The Nagas shifted eastwards, while the Banaras moved southwards towards the Nilgiri Hills. The Aryans were enemies of the enemies of both these people. Thus they had become quite friendly.

Riksharaja was a foundling. Long ago the wise Brahma had found him abandoned by his parents. He had taken pity of this small Banara child and had taken him into his household, rearing him up as his own son. As days passed by, Riksharaja grew into a fine young man, well versed in the Vedas and other streams of knowledge together with developing into a valiant warrior. Having been brought up in a Deva household, he was wise to all the military advancements made by the Aryans. After he had come of age, he was given in marriage to a comely Banara damsel. The young couple were happy for a while together, but soon a problem began to surface. It was apparent that Rikhsharaja, in spite of all his physical and intellectual prowess, was sadly impotent. Riksharaja confided this secret to two of his closest Deva friends, Indra and Surya. They feigned sympathy and offered their magnanimous services to their friend. They offered to impregnate his wife as a proxy. In the permissive days of old, this was allowed and legal. The shy girl resisted, but later gave in. It was decided that the couple would move northwards to settle beside a Himalayan lake, where first Indra and later Surya would follow. Bali was born in the first year of their self imposed exile and Sugriva was born the year after. But their mother was constitutionally not very tough. She contracted some infections of her chest in her cold northern home and succumbed to her illness. Riksharaja came back to the Brahma household, the mother and father of two chubby sons.

Brahma was worried about his Banara son. He knew that the Devas, in spite of welcoming him into their society, would always look down upon him. He wanted his son to establish himself as a leader in society. His son had all the qualities of being a good king. So he sent him on to the new homeland the Banaras had carved out for themselves at Kishkindhya, with his blessings. The King of Kishkindhya was old, infirm and childless. He took fancy of the strong and learned Riksharaja and nominated him as his successor. Thus soon enough, Riksharaja became the Banara monarch. He was succeeded by his eldest son, Bali.

Bali was a popular king. He was fun loving and loved his drink well. But he was a just monarch. A man of prodigious physical strength, he put the defence of his state in the top priority bracket. A powerful standing army of Banaras was his strength. This army was always combat ready through regular exercises. Bali never intended to annex adjacent territories, but was fiercely independent. Through the aegis of a tough and battle-ready army he was able to maintain the integrity and independence of his kingdom, Kishkindhya.

Mayabi was the eldest son of the learned, scientist king of Danavas, Maya. Maya, himself, had no great desire of expansion. But his son had other designs. A man of immense physical strength, but sadly lacking in the intellectual capabilities of his father, he was always eager to pick on a fight or two. For years he had eyed the southern kingdom of Kishkindhya. Mayabi was not very sharp of mind, but he was intelligent enough to realise that in a full scale war, his army of the Danavas stood no chance against the well trained Banara commandos. So he opted for an old trick. He despatched a personal letter to Bali challenging him into a duel in a mortal hand-to-hand combat. He was sure of victory. So he ordered his army to take battle-stations at the border with instructions to move in when Bali fell. But he had not bargained for Bali's prowess.

The crowd waited in eager expectation. They had come in their thousands to see the combat of a life-time. An expansive clearing had been readied at the outskirt of the capital as the arena for the wrestling match. A company of the Banara militia maintained close and roving vigil. A gasp, followed by a hush was all that was heard as the challenger entered the clearing. Mayabi was a towering, giant of a man. He wore nothing but a red loin cloth. His torso was bare, displaying proudly a broad, hairy chest, as hard as granite and a pair of terrible arms with bulging muscles. His lower limbs were as massive as a pair of tree trunks. On his head was his golden helmet shaped like a buffalo's head, complete with a pair of massive horns. He looked as foreboding as death incarnate. He raised his massive arms over his head and emitted a roar stunning all.

A great uproar rose from the stands scaring the birds from the surrounding trees into frenzied flight. Their own king had stepped into the arena. Though Bali was not as gigantic as the Danava, his massive frame with rippling, hard muscles, filled all with hope. But this was a fight till death! They were apprehensive for their own happy-go-lucky king.

As Bali entered the arena amidst the great ovations, he beckoned his brother, Sugriva, to come upto him.

"Listen brother," said he in Sugriva's ear. "Whatever happens today, stick close to me. My spies have reported that there has been a massive mobilization of Danava forces across the border. If I die in the Danava's hands, immediately declare yourself to be the king. Seize the Danava, or better, get him killed before he declares himself to be the monarch of Kishkindhya. We cannot barter away the freedom of our homeland. Do you get me, dear brother?"

"Nothing will ever happen to you, dear brother. You are unbeatable," said Sugriva, forcing more cheer in his voice than he felt in his heart.

Bali patted him on his back and stepped forward. He looked around the stands. His subjects were screaming themselves hoarse. He raised his massive arms and immediately all yelling stopped as if by magic. With a sonorous voice Bali then addressed his subjects.

"My dear citizens of Kishkindhya, I am overwhelmed by this love you are showing me. Today, the security of independent Kishkindhya is at a crucial juncture. As you know, this encounter between the challenger, Danava Mayabi, son of the illustrious king Maya, and me, son of the great king Riksharaja, is no ordinary bout of wrestling. It is slated to be a fight till death. I am sure that with your blessings I shall emerge victorious. But if it happens otherwise, I declare that after my death, my younger brother Sugriva will at once don the mantle of the king of Kishkindha, with Prince Angad, my son, as the crown prince." He paused for a while for the uproar to subside, and then added, "Let the bout begin."

In the beginning the contestants appeared to be evenly matched. Then as time wore on Bali seemed to be gradually getting the better of his opponent. Mayabi's aim was to grip Bali in a bear hug as his physical strength was prodigious. But this Bali did not allow. On the other hand he darted inside the Danava's defences and smashed punches after punches all over his opponent's person. They fought on like men possessed, beyond the arena and up into the hills. Soon they were lost from view of the spectators. When they made to follow, the militia stopped them, fearing an uncontrollable stampede and escorted them back to the city. Sugriva found himself to be standing alone in the arena. At first he was a bit undecided about what was to be done. But as grunts and yells resounded in the hillside, he turned and ran up in the direction they were coming from.

Awesome, blood-curdling roars emerged from within a huge cavern. Sugriva sat down on a nearby boulder, laid his heavy mace beside him and waited. Dusk fell. Night descended. Still the roars continued as hollow echoes from deep within the dark cavern. The fighting went on unabated through the night. The next day dawned but still the combatants were at it. Sugriva became restless. The nightlong vigil now began to take its toll. Soon enough he dozed off to a dreamless slumber. When he awoke with a start it was dark all around. Faint growling sort of sound still emerged from within. Sugriva had lost all track of time. Gradually the eastern sky became lighter. With the advent of dawn all had become quiet inside the cave. Suddenly there was a nerve-shattering yell. It was the voice of the Danava. Of Bali, nothing was audible. Sugriva stood up, shouldered his mace and strode to the yawning mouth of the cave, listening hard. Then he drew in a sharp breath. A thin line of dark red liquid was trickling out of the cave. Sugriva was flabbergasted. The yell of the Danava followed by the trickle of blood convinced him that his brother, Bali, had been killed. Frantically he looked about him. A huge boulder was at hand. It was just large enough to seal the cave-entrance. It was heavy and took all of Sugriva's massive strength to roll it off from its moorings amongst the mosses and to seal the cave entrance. Then weeping his heart out, he headed for the capital.

There was no fanfare at the next coronation as the state was in mourning. Sugriva simply took his vow of office and was crowned as king by the Royal Priest at a simple ceremony. Angad, the son of Bali, was declared to be the crown prince, as Bali had desired. Then, as was the custom amongst the Banaras, Sugriva took Tara, Bali's wife as his own and carried her over to his bed-chamber to consummate the new marriage.

Bali tottered to his feet. The prolonged battle had sapped his entire strength. He leaned against the cave wall for a while to catch his breath. In the faint glimmer of light percolating through a few cracks up above he could see the massive form of Mayabi lying there motionless, neck broken, with blood streaming from his nose and mouth. The blood trickled downhill towards the entrance of the cave and Bali stumbled along in that direction. This Danava had really tried his strength. Never was he in so much trouble to vanquish his foe. Even his epoch-making battle against Ravana seemed to be a gentle cake-walk compared to this present fight. Bali stumbled on and on, groping blindly, till he came upon a huge boulder sealing the mouth of the cave. How could this be? He had seen Sugriva following him up along the hill-side. Where was Sugriva? He feebly called out his name a couple of times, then fell in a heap, utterly exhausted.

Bali must have passed out for when he rose again even the faint glimmer of light percolating in the cave was gone. The darkness inside the cave was absolute. Bali's throat was parched and his dry tongue stuck to the drier palate. He could see nothing, but his hearing was sharp as ever. He cocked his ears and listened with all his senses attuned to pick up the slightest whisper of sound that might help him survive in the dark and hostile environment. Genetically he belonged to the toughest race on earth. That, together with the tremendous fortitude handed down to him from the father who had sired him, had kept him alive till now, but he knew that he had to find food and water, mainly water, immediately, or he would die. It was then he heard the faint dripping sound. Water, perhaps rain-water or coalesced dew trickled in through some cleft in the cave, somewhere. Bali located the direction of the sound and crawled on all fours towards it. Sure enough! Water was indeed dripping down from the roof and was gathering in the floor of the cave, before trickling out, losing its way in the darkness somewhere. Bali dropped on the floor to lie prone and drank his fill like some animal. Water works miracles in dehydrated souls. It rejuvenated Bali. He crawled back to the cave entrance waiting for the first light.

Dawn made her presence felt through a thin sliver of golden light coming in through a miniscule gap between the obstructing boulder and the cave wall. A projection of rock jutted from the side wall of the cave and this filled Bali with hope. He placed his back on this projection and planting his feet firmly on the boulder, heaved with all the strength that remained in his mighty body. The boulder rocked, then fell back to where it was. But this slight movement filled Bali with joy. So, it could be moved. He heaved again and again. The boulder began to rock and totter more and more at every heave. Finally with a ripping protest, it tore itself from its station and rolled for a bit, then bounded down the steep side of the hill. Light, fresh air and chirping of birds flooded the gloomy cave. Bali fell on his back and gulped in the fresh, fragrant air. Never before had air tasted so sweet. Then he tottered down the hillside.

At the foot of the hill Bali rested for a while. He knew these hills like the back of his hands as he and Sugriva had spent days in these slopes playing hide and seek in these woods in their childhood. He knew where fruits could be found and water too. Soon he gathered a large number of fruits and sat near a gurgling brook, breaking his fast, immersed in thought. It was now quite apparent to him that avarice had turned Sugriva's head. He had taken advantage of Bali's declaration at the beginning of his duel with the Danava and had himself crowned king of Kishkindhya on the pretext that Bali was no more. To ensure his death he had sealed the mouth of the cave. The more he thought about it, the more agitated he became. His eyes grew red and his breath rasped out hot with suppressed rage. Part of his mind urged him to rush to the capital and to claim back his throne. But part of his mind cautioned him that he was enfeebled by dehydration and lack of food. Moreover he had to take care of the multiple injuries sustained. If he rushed in before he had regained his strength, he did not stand a chance against the legendary strength of his brother. He decided to wait.

Sugriva was sitting in court. With his two queens, Tara, the widow of Bali, and Ruma, his own wife, seated on either sides of him, he sat sedately in the throne, resplendent in his golden crown. Suddenly, like a thunderclap from a clear blue sky, an unexpected deep roar was heard from the gate, reverberating in the palace corridors. "Sugriva, you vile traitor," cried the disembodied voice. Sugriva jumped up in fright from where he sat. The courtiers stood up, petrified. It was Bali coming back from the dead!

When Sugriva came around, it was near evening. His whole body was sore and he had a splitting headache. He found himself lying on a sandy floor of a cave. Four Banaras huddled around looking at him with anxious eyes—his closest friends. They had not abandoned him but had nursed him back to life.

Bali had been merciless. The ten days of enforced rest had worked wonders, flooding his body with strength and his heart with resolve. A red haze had obscured his vision and he did not see Sugriva's pleadings eyes. The roar of blood rushing to his head had rendered him deaf to all of Sugriva's pleas of innocence. He had pulled Sugriva down by his hairs and had rained blows after blows upon him, punching and kicking with all his might. Any lesser mortal would have been dead by the corporeal punishment received, but Sugriva was made of sterner stuff. Still, he could have died at the hands of the enraged Bali, had not Sugriva's minister and closest friend, Hanuman, snatched him from the death grip of Bali and escaped into the hills with his limp body on his shoulders. Hanuman escaped with Sugriva into the Hrishyamukh range, which was out of bounds for Bali due to a curse from Rishi Matanga. The superstitious Bali did not have the courage to test the power of the curse and so this was the only place in Kishkindhya that was safe for Sugriva.

The five fugitives from law now lounged in the Malaya Hill. Sugriva's friends were secure in the knowledge that their hide-out was safe from Bali, yet Sugriva was always restless. What if Bali was barred from these hills? His troops were not! He could easily send marauding bands of soldiers after them! The others, especially Hanuman, were relaxed in this matter. No troop on earth could match the combined strengths of the five. So, while his four friends lounged at their ease, Sugriva sat there, ever alert, with his right hand gripping the handle of his awe-inspiring iron mace.

It was Sugriva himself, who had espied the two climbing figures. All languor left him in a trice as he sat bolt upright. Who could they be? Both were young men who appeared to be Aryans even from afar. Tall, wiry, muscular, they were dressed like a pair of wandering hermits with long hair tied in top-knots, yet both carried long bows and quivers full of arrows. Swords hung from their waist. Who could they be? Were they spies of Bali? Sugriva called for Hanuman in a hushed tone.

Rama and Lakshmana were trudging along the hilly terrain, tired to their bones. For months they had been moving around in the forests in search of Sita. At first Rama had been disconsolate. He was so depressed that Lakshmana was afraid that he would lose his mind. For days and nights together Lakshmana had kept vigil on his brother. He had cajoled, consoled, rebuked, encouraged, even fed and washed his brother while watching over him as he slept, till gradually Rama returned to his former self, resolute and indomitable. Then they began their journey southwards, for that was the direction the Rakshasa had taken, according to the dying statement of Jatayu. Sages they met on the way had advised them to go to Kishkindhya and to look for the outlawed Sugriva, for, according to them, only he could help in their search. So, now they were here, but Sugriva proved to be an elusive figure.

They were plodding on, when suddenly a huge Banara stood before them. He was a giant of a man, with broad shoulders, immense chest, narrow waist and very powerful and muscular arms. He stood directly in their path. Lakshmana unslung his bow in a trice and whisked out an arrow. But Rama restrained him. He had noticed that the Banara was unarmed and that he stood with palms together and a smile of welcome on his lips.

"Hail to you, strangers, greetings from the Banaras. Who could you be, may I ask? To what do we owe the pleasure of this visit?"

"We are two brothers, sons of King Dasharath of Ayodhya, of the Ikshaku dynasty, now deceased. We are on a self exile to keep a promise made. But, my man, who could you, be? You are far from being uneducated. Your command of Sanskrit is exemplary. The use of impeccable grammar, pronunciations, everything shows that you are well versed in the study of the Rig-Veda and Sama-Veda."

"I, my lord, am Hanuman, the son of Pavan. And, sire, could you be my Lord Rama, whose valour can be compared only to the Deva Vishnu?"

"Yes indeed. We, my brother Lakshmana and I, come in search of Prince Sugriva, on some urgent business."

"Then my lords, you have come to the right place. Come, sires, let me escort you to Sugriva's presence." With this, Hanuman raised his right hand as a reassurance to the watchful Sugriva that all was well and led the brothers up hill.

Evening had set in. They were gathered around a small fire in the cave that was the fugitives' hide-out. Dinner was just over, a frugal fare, comprising mainly fruits and vegetables. Now they were sitting together, comparing notes. Sugriva recounted how Bali had become his enemy and he and his friends were outlawed, apparently unjustifiably. Rama related all that had befallen him and Lakshmana, their exile, their battles against Rakshasas and ultimately the abduction of Sita by the Rakshasa Ravana. Hearing the account of abduction of Sita silently Sugriva walked away to the end of the cave, where all his worldly possessions were stowed. He came back quietly, clutching a small bundle. He looked at Hanuman, who nodded his head wordlessly.

"It was almost a year ago. We were sitting outside this cave. It was near sunset when we saw the aircraft you refer to. A weeping woman had leaned over the side and threw these ornaments down. We had no idea who she was, so we had kept these in safe keeping, hoping against hope that someday the rightful owner will turn up and we shall be relieved of our responsibility. It looks as if that day has come."

With this, Sugriva handed the bundle over to Rama. Lakshmana peered over Rama's shoulders as he opened the bundle, tense with suppressed excitement. The bundle contained some ornaments. Sita's they were. Rama sat still looking at the fire, clutching the ornaments to his chest. Uncertain light flickered over him. He appeared motionless as a statue, carved in shimmering bronze. Tears welled up in the dreamy eyes and a drop trickled down each of his cheeks like twin pearls. No one spoke. No word was needed. Rama turned towards Lakshmana. The younger Raghava reached out to grab his elder brother's shoulder, tears rolling down his cheeks unabated. Hanuman looked away into the night. The occasion was too heavy for him to bear.

Not for nothing Rama was referred to as a god walking the earth. For a while he sat still, as if in meditation. Then he re-tied the bundle and handed it over to Sugriva. Neel took it from him and walked away to the corner where it was kept. When Rama spoke again, his voice was rock-steady. He had taken full command of his emotions once again.

"I owe you my life, Banararaj."

"You call me as the King of Banaras, my friend?"

"Yes, I do."

Sugriva sat silently for a while. He was immersed in thought. The he spoke in a low tone.

"My friend, we have much in common. Both of us have lost our thrones unjustifiably and both have lost our wives. Do you know that Bali has held my wife, Ruma, captive in the inner sanctum of the palace and from what I heard, he has been using her as his wife."

"But that is preposterous!" Rama exclaimed. "I am aware of the Banara custom that the dead brother's wives automatically become the wives of the living brother, but here you are very much alive. This is a mortal sin!"

"About your going in search of Sita and then getting her back by force, I am sorry my friend, that is a tall order indeed!"

"Why so?" Lakshmana demanded, his dark eyes flashing darker.

"Because for a mission of that scale seven is a very poor number. We cannot even hope to succeed. But of course, the question would have been different had I been the Banara King. Then I would have had the entire army at our disposal and who does not know about the prowess of the Banaras in the battle-field? But with Bali alive, that is not possible. You could have befriended Bali, perhaps, to this end, but that too shall not serve your purpose. Bali is one of the few men on earth who have vanquished Ravana in a one-to-one combat. But afterwards they have become blood brothers."

"So, what do you suggest now?" Rama asked of his new friend.

"Nothing. With Bali living, we have nothing to do."

"But if he is dead?"

Sugriva looked at Rama with a speculative look. Then he sat up straight.

"All that later. First, let us bind ourselves in bondage of an unbreakable vow of friendship, with this fire as the witness. Of course, if you are agreeable to it..." Sugriva looked at Rama in eager expectation. Rama nodded in agreement.

The friends solemnized their friendship in front of the fire and sat down once again to carry on with their discussions. The Banaras looked visibly relieved at getting the sworn allegiance of the illustrious Ikshaku prince. The onslaught on Bali was planned for the next day.

The Banaras carried Sugriva on their shoulder and ran straight towards their cave with Rama and Lakshmana bringing up the rear, after taking some intricate detours to throw off anyone who might be following them. The sun had set by the time they set their feet across the cave-entrance. Sugriva was groaning and almost senseless with pain. He was bruised and lacerated all over and was bleeding freely from a cut on his right eyebrow. The duel with Bali had apparently not gone well for him. Sushena, the surgeon, hovered over him, ministering to his wounds. He applied dressings on his wounds and poultices over his bruises. The pain subsided soon after he had taken some pain-killing draft. Sugriva then sat up tentatively and looked at Rama with reproach. Hanuman, by this time, had a fire going.

"You are supposed to be my friend," said Sugiva. He was mentally thanking his stars that he was alive at all. "You were supposed to protect me and slay Bali! But you did neither. Here I am, beaten black and blue by the great ape and there is Bali, still in the land of the living."

"I am really sorry, my friend. Both of you brothers are as alike in appearance as two peas from the same pod. Together with that both of you wore loin cloth of the same colour, red. I could easily have mistaken and killed you instead," said Rama as he walked up to sit down beside Sugriva who was more injured in mind rather than body.

The morning sun had found Sugriva stomping haughtily towards the palace gates at Kishkindhya, bubbling with a new found joy and energy. The sentries at the gate bowed low as they recognised him, but very politely had refused him entry. They were doing their duty, they had urged.

"All right, you oafs," Sugriva's ire had known no bound. "You just do one thing. You go into the palace and tell my brother that Sugriva has come and is waiting outside. He demands justice."

Bali had come running out. He seemed to be overjoyed. He extended his hands towards his brother in order to hug him, but Sugriva had stepped back.

"I come not in friendship, brother," growled Sugriva. "I seek redress."

Bali's eyes flashed. He was not known for tolerance.

"Redress, brother? That is a fine word coming from the usurper!"

"Indeed? You think that I am a usurper, do you, you thief of your younger brother's wife? I challenge you to a duel. I demand satisfaction!" Sugriva sounded more confident than he really was.

It was clear from the beginning that Sugriva was no match for Bali. Although Sugriva was a very powerful man, yet his elder brother appeared to be stronger. Had it been a duel of maces, Sugriva would have stood a more than even chance of emerging the victor, for he was really proficient in the use of that weapon, but he had not even half Bali's skill, when it came to unarmed combat. At the word 'go' the two brothers had rushed towards each other like a couple of warring elephants. They had grappled, kicked and cuffed like men possessed. Sugriva had started losing ground in a short while. It was nearly midday, when his knees buckled and he collapsed. Bali had turned in disdain and had walked back to the palace.

The next morning found Bali in his bed-chamber with Ruma, fondling her to his heart's content. He was deriving a sadistic pleasure in treating his rebel brother's wife as a sex-toy, when his equanimity, however, evaporated when a shout of defiance came to his ears. Sugriva it was. Bali jumped up in anger and dressed hastily, almost running outside in a blinding rage. Roaring like a mad bull, he rushed at Sugriva, raining blows upon his body. This day, Sugriva was wearing a garland to make himself identifiable.

Sugriva tottered and fell to the ground in the face of a whirlwind attack. Bali let out an animal roar as he jumped up to finish the combat with a death-blow. But his body jerked convulsively in mid-air and his roar changed to a shriek as he fell to the ground, an arrow sticking out from between his shoulder blades. Blood seeped out to collect in a pool on the ground. Rama stepped out from behind the tree that had hidden him from view.

"Who is it?" Bali rasped, blood frothing from his mouth. "You assailed me from behind. I had no war against you! Tell me, who you are?"

"Your brother, whom you had wronged, is my avowed friend for life. I did what I did to live up to that vow. I am Rama of the Ikshakus."

Bali's eyes widened. He raised his right hand to salute the prince of Ayodhya.

"I have heard of you, Rama. You are valiant in battle. But why did you strike at me from behind like a sneak thief?"

"I was repaying my debt."

"Debt, Rama? What debt?" Bali was finding it difficult to speak.

"Sugriva has made the promise to help me in my search for Sita, my wife, who has been abducted by Ravana, the vile Rakshasa."

"Did you say Ravana?" When Rama nodded in the affirmative, Bali began to laugh uncontrollably, but caught his breath as pain from his chest spread all over his being. "Dear young man, Ravana is my blood brother. Had you sought my help, I would have forced Ravana to give your wife back to you. Had he not listened to my request, I would have dragged him to you by his long hair and would have thrown him at your feet."

Bali fell silent, gasping for breath. At every gasp, more bloody froth bubbled out of his mouth. His eyes roved about, moving over the faces of all. He was searching for someone. His eyes fell upon a lone figure standing outside the circle of men surrounding him. The young man was looking up at the sky. His hands were clenched. Tear flowed down his cheeks unchecked.

"Angad, my son," called Bali. Angad rushed to his father at once. Bali held his son's hand and called out once again.

"Rama," he called. "This is my only son. I am giving him to your care. Take care of him as your very own. You have struck me down in a manner that is typically Aryan. Even then, I respect you. You are an Ikshaku. Ikshakus would rather die than break their promises made. I know that." He was almost inaudible now.

"Rama, my light is fading. I pardon you for your cowardly act. May you succeed in your mission!" His head fell back. The best of the Banaras lay there, dead. Sobbing broke out all around. Sugriva was almost inconsolable. Angad straightened and walked away towards the palace. A wailing broke out from the inner sanctum of the palace. Tara has been informed of her husband's death. Rama, too, moved out of the crowd. Heaviness gripped his heart. His eyes fell on Lakshmana. Lakshmana was staring at him. There was nothing but pain in his eyes.

"Brother," said Lakshmana. He was almost inaudible. His eyes glistened with tears unshed. "Brother, as of today, you have become an ordinary man." The wailings from inside the palace increased in volume. Angad must have reached his mother.

✦ ✦ ✦

12

The Quest

The Banara regular army marched with measured, disciplined treads in their thousands, pushing on southwards. They were now deep into the Rakshasa territory. This was the first time in history that a Banara army was moving over foreign territory on a military mission. Their ranks had been swollen by the thousand odd soldiers from the Riksha tribe, who, with the Bear as their totem, were also known as the Bear Men. They marched under the leadership of the venerated Jamboban. Thus a combined army of non Aryans were marching under an Aryan flag against another non Aryan—another first in history.

Sugriva's spies had spread all over the land to get the final information about the whereabouts of Sita. Soon all returned empty-handed, except for the southern team that was being led by Angad and Hanuman. They had followed lead after lead, till at long last, they hit pay-dirt. They came back after months, but with the definite information that Sita was interned in the island state of Lanka, across turbulent seas. Hanuman had been there on his own and had brought back evidence of his visit to Sita. The task now became all the more challenging. The Banaras had no navy. Theirs was a landlocked state. So the need for navy had never arisen.

Hanuman and Angad had climbed up a hill that stood over a crescent beach of white sand, to get a better view of the seas ahead. They had reached a small hamlet called Dhanuskoti. This was the land's end. The blue sea stretched in front of them as far as eye could reach. If Ravana had taken Sita further south, then he must have taken her across the waters to a place unknown. A hill stood proudly as a silent sentinel over the beach. They decided to climb on top of the hill to get a better view. They stood there silently watching the sea, shading their eyes. The glare of the sun danced on the waves as trillions of brilliant gems. Angad was despondent, while Hanuman was pensive. A sudden voice startled them almost out of their wits.

"Who are you? What are you looking for?" Both of them whirled around and gripped their maces tighter. An elderly ascetic stood there with a quizzical expression on his face.

"We are soldiers of the Banara King Sugriva of Kishkindhya," replied Angad. "We are looking for a lady in distress."

"Lady? Here? Has the sun touched you, my friend?" The ascetic was mildly sarcastic. Angad made to reply, but Hanuman restrained him.

"You see venerable ascetic, the prince of Ayodhya, Rama, is our guest. His wife, Sita, has been unlawfully abducted by the Rakshasa king, Ravana. We are looking for her. Can you give us any lead, please?"

"Ayodhya, eh? Aryan? Now tell me, my dear sir, why should I have any love for an Aryan? And for that matter, why should you? I see from your get-up that both of you are Banaras!"

"Let's leave, Son of Pavan, we can expect no help from one as narrow minded as this one here." Angad began to move as he spoke. He was plainly disgusted.

"Wait, dear prince," Hanuman grabbed his hand. "Sir," this one was for the ascetic. "May I ask you a question?"

"Go ahead, but don't expect any help from me for an Aryan prince."

"I am seeking no help, dear sir," said Hanuman. "I merely wanted to ask if you were originally from the great tribe of Bird people."

"Yes, I am," said the ascetic, absently stroking the two vulture feathers he wore on his head. "But why do you ask?"

"Do you by any chance know the King Jatayu?"

"Know him? What do you mean, sir? Of course I know him! How can one not know his younger brother?"

"Your brother?"

"Yes, that's what he is. I am Sampati, once the king of the bird people. But I had abdicated long ago in favour of my younger brother Jatayu and went on in search of the Eternal Truth. But what do you know about him, and, by the way, how is he now? Is everything alright with my people?"

"The Aryan, whom you are spurning, is the son of the dead king Dasharath, a close friend of your younger brother, who was also the guardian of Princes Rama, Lakshmana and Pricess Sita, while they were residing in the Panchavati forests."

"Was? Why do you use a past tense, Banara?"

"Because your brother, the great warrior king Jatayu, is no longer with us." Sampati let out a blood curdling shriek. The true bird-man showed for a flash beneath the veneer of world-renouncing ascetic. He pulled Angad and Hanuman over to where a number of boulders lay scattered about and took his seat. He beckoned to the Banaras to make themselves comfortable too.

Sampati rose and walked over to the edge of the ledge. He stood there still and erect as if carved from the same granite as the outcrop itself. Silently he gazed across the sea towards the horizon. He appeared to be assimilating all he had heard from Hanuman concerning the demise of his brave brother and the abduction of Sita.

"Come here," he commanded. A shade of the King Sampati of old showed through. Angad and Hanuman rose to move over and stand on either sides of him. Then he raised his right hand to point at the horizon.

"Blue meets blue," he pronounced in a sepulchral voice. "Yonder I can see red mingling with blue." Then he hefted a sigh and resumed in normal tones. "Look there. You may discern a faint dark line where the sea meets the sky. That is the island of Lanka, the abode of Ravana. That is where he has taken Sita. I saw them the other day on Ravana's aircraft. The woman was weeping copiously, leaning over the side."

Angad stood staring at the sparkling sea, aghast. How could they negotiate this huge expanse of water without a single ship? Hanuman's jaws were set. He had to get across. He had to go to Lanka and see for himself that Sita was there and alive. He turned and spoke to Sampati.

"Your Majesty," he began. Sampati stopped him with a look.

"I am no king, Maruti." He turned to look across the waters. "But sometimes I wish that I was one. Oh, how I wish that I could also go along with you people. But now I am old and infirm. In my prime I would have been more than a match for the wily Rakshasa."

"As I was saying, your highness," Hanuman persisted. "I would like to go to Lanka now." Both Angad and Sampati started at Hanuman in amazement. "Can it be arranged?"

"But why, Maruti?" Angad was anxious. "Why do you want to put your head inside the jaws of a hungry lion?"

"Two reasons, both compelling," said Hanuman. "The first is that I want to see for myself that Mother Sita is there, and she's healthy and unharmed. The second reason is that I want to view the defences of Lanka first hand." Sampati slowly nodded his hoary head.

A trill of a peacock's call rent the tranquil environment. Soon enough, the call was echoed from the foothills. A figure appeared like an apparition and stood before them with palms joined together. He was a strongly built man of middle-age. His copper-coloured torso was bare and he wore a short white dhoti and a white turban. There was nothing on him to tell that he was not any ordinary Rakshasa. Only his bird-call gave away his Bird-man lineage.

"You called your highness?" Sea, sun and salt in the air had made his voice rough and a bit hoarse.

"Yes I did," replied Sampati. "Hanuman, my son, this is Parani. He is a fisherman, fishing off these shores. But his boat is a cutter rather than a skiff that other fishermen use. It is a very fast boat. He will ferry you over to Lanka and bring you back. Will you not, Parani?" Parani, not his real name, of course, grinned. His front tooth was missing.

"Your wish, my Lord, is my command."

"Can you take me across at night?" Hanuman demanded.

"Yes sir, I can," Parani replied. He was a fisherman during daytime, but was a deadly smuggler at night. A night cross-over was as simple for him as moving about blind-folded in his own back-yard.

"Is your boat fast enough?" Hanuman persisted in his questioning.

"Try it sir and see for yourself. You shall feel that you are not sailing, but are flying across the sea. You shall be there in no time."

"And the Rakshasa patrol boats?"

"They will have to see me first before they catch me, won't they?" Hanuman was satisfied.

✦ ✦ ✦

13

Lanka

Hanuman was arrested even before he could enter the city. He had safely negotiated the surrounding moat full of some squirming and splashing reptiles, as the draw-bridge was conveniently down and had run unseen towards the walls, some three hundred *dhanus* away, before he froze. The next step he had not foreseen and was caught unawares.

Lanka was probably the only city on earth that was guarded by women. A troupe of Rakshasis patrolled the area outside the wall. They were dark as the night and as enchanting. Scantily clad like the Goddess Kali, their appearance was formidable and all were armed to their teeth. But the alarming fact was that they had guard-dogs with them tied to long leashes. As Hanuman approached the walls, one of them suddenly became very alert. He sniffed the night air and gave a muted, throaty growl and stood stiff-limbed with hackles raised. The guardswoman muttered something to her compatriot. At once they got their spears ready. Hanuman froze and hid himself behind a bush. He knew that he could move stealthily, without making the slightest sound. But he had not bargained for the fact that these guard-dogs would sniff him out.

"Who is there?" the guard challenged. "Come, we know that you are there. Come out, or we'd let the dogs loose!"

Hanuman made a quick calculation. He could easily make short work of the guards and their dogs. But that was no solution. He had observed the guards making their rounds as regularly as a well oiled machine. These two would cover one-fourth of a circle to meet the other team coming in from the other direction. Then they would exchange an encoded message that apparently changed at every round and would turn back. Thus, if he disposed off this team, their absence would be noticed in a short while and general alarm would be issued to apprehend him. That would serve no purpose. So, he decided to surrender in good grace. Raising both hands over his head, he slowly stood up from behind the bush. The guards rushed up to him with their spears pointing straight at his throat. The dogs growled viciously, baring their teeth.

"Who are you? What are you doing here?" One of the guards asked. Hanuman decided to act as an ignorant country bumpkin.

"I am nobody, captain," he answered, cowering in feigned fright. The guard, who was not even a non commissioned officer, glowered at the exalted address and threw her head back to assume a regal posture.

"I have come from the mainland, madam, on a ship, anchored in the harbour out there." A number of well lit ships were clustered at one point far away and Hanuman knew instinctively that this was the harbour. "I work as a cook, madam. Towards evening I went for a walk, having been issued a shore pass. Near to this place I had sat in the shade enjoying the cool breeze, but had fallen asleep. When I woke up it was night and the city gates are closed. My friends are all inside. So I was caught in two minds as to what I'd do. Then I saw the d-dog, madam."

"What has the dog to do with a dog like you?" The other guard was irate.

"I am afraid of dogs, madam. I'll face a lion easily. But dogs terrify me."

"You are not a Rakshasa I see," the first guard persisted in her questioning. "From your appearance you look like a Banara. You could be a spy. Come with us to our officer."

The dimly lit guard-house by the side of the gigantic city gates was a small non-descript affair, furnished sparsely with a table, a chair and a small wooden bed. An earthenware pitcher of water stood at the corner. The officer sat on the chair with her feet planted atop the table dozing to her heart's content. She too, like her subordinates, was very briefly attired, but unlike them, was unarmed. A large dagger and a coiled whip lay on the table in front of her. A conch-shell was there too, no doubt to be blown at the time of emergency. Hanuman was pushed into this room by his lovely escorts.

The captain, a real captain this time, sat up straight, visibly irritated at her beauty sleep being disturbed.

"What is it?" she growled.

"Madam Captain, we have apprehended a possible spy."

"Have you? Now, that's interesting!" She stood up on her feet, swaying a little. She was inebriated. The room felt close and the air stank of stale sweat and spirit.

"Now, my man," she said. "Tell me where you are from and why."

"I'm from Kalinga, my lady. I am a cook on a merchant ship."

"You lie." The voice slashed out. Even the two guards cringed. She reached out for the whip. "Leave us," she ordered the guards. "I have some love to make with my lover boy here. And shut the door behind you if you please." The two guards fled the room with alacrity.

"Now my man," said she, almost drooling with anticipated pleasure. "Thank your stars for the administrations and attentions you'd soon be receiving from Captain Lankini." She cracked her whip menacingly. Hanuman stood up straight, all muscles bulging. Lankini raised her whip to strike, but before she could bring the whip down Hanuman moved. His speed made him appear to be a mere blur. A backhanded slap rang out. The captain of the guards was thrown back against the wall and she lay there stunned, in a most indecent attitude. In silence Hanuman picked up the bed-sheet and tore long strips from the tough linen. He tied her up, trussing her up like a stuck pig. Then he bound a piece across her face for good measure, to keep her mouth shut. He avoided the gag, for there was a risk of the stunned woman choking herself. A small locked door was to be seen on the far wall. Hanuman locked the entrance from the inside and broke the inner door down with a well placed kick. This door led into the city.

Lanka was known as a City That Never Sleeps. Although it was quite late, yet the wide, cobbled streets were still crowded with revellers. Rakshasas were a fun loving people. They loved their jokes, drinks and music. The lilting tunes from the flute and *veena* resonated all around with the resounding beats of the *mridangam*. The drinking houses were still packed with patrons, while some of them spilled out into the streets to weave their unsteady way home. The streets were all cobbled and well lit up by oil lamps in crystal casings to ward off the effects of the elements, set on golden pillars. There had been a gentle shower towards the evening and the streets were still wet. The grandiose street lamps reflecting in the wet surface presented an enchanting picture. Lanka was also known as the Golden City. All pillars were decorated with spiral decors in inlaid gold. The slanting roof-tops had gutters of beaten gold. All this mass of gold everywhere lent an aurous glow to the environs. Hanuman was stunned at the glorious sights unfolding before him.

The city had been built on the hilly terrains of the Trikuta hills. Therefore the whole city showed several enchanting undulations. The central part was the most elevated. The magnificence of the houses and palaces lying sprawled about on the slope showed that they belonged to the nobility. At the highest part was the Royal Palace. The splendour and the grand architecture silently announced that it could not be anything else. Hanuman made a beeline straight towards this place without any hesitation.

Entering the palace was no big deal for a person as resourceful as Hanuman. He clambered over the palace walls and flitting about like a faint shadow, easily gave the sentries a slip. Once over the palace walls, he found himself in a spacious garden. It was dimly lit with decorated lanterns to render it a charm and delusion of the land of fairies. The air was fragrant with the perfume of night blossoms. Here and there were gurgling springs and splashing miniature cataract. The lanterns threw more shadows than light, and this eminently suited Hanuman's purpose. Luckily for him, this time there were no guard dogs about. As he closed in to the palace itself, he stood in the shadows under the eaves and uncoiled a rope from his waist. To one end of this rope he fixed a grapnel that he fished out from within his small bag. He swung the weighted rope in his right hand in ever increasing vertical circles and then let go. The grapnel found good anchorage in the balustrade of the upper floor balcony.

The entire palace was built of marble. The shimmering white of marble walls and pillars, inlaid with precious stones of every kind, together with intricate designs of intertwining vines and serpents made of beaten gold were a feast for the eyes of any visitor. Every bit of furniture was decorated with gold. Even the heavy curtains, billowing in the wind, were embroidered with gold threads. Hanuman was no stranger to palatial riches, having been brought up in the Kishkindhya court and from having travelled far and wide, yet the aurous vistas unfolding their splendour before him struck him dumb. But time was running out fast. He could not afford to stand and admire the architectural and aesthetic beauties. He moved inside the palace, searching every room for any trace of Sita. But he could not find any trace of her amongst the women of the Royal Household.

A dejected Hanuman came out to stand in the top floor balcony. Every room, every corner of the palace had been searched by him. He had even searched Ravana's bed-chamber and the bed-rooms of the queens and the King's concubines, but all to no avail. He was desperate now. Moving out to the balcony he ran his eyes over the palace grounds. Which part could he have missed? Then his eyes fell on the grove of Ashoka trees far to his right. That area had remained unexplored as yet. Scurrying down the palace wall, he sprinted towards the grove.

The Ashoka grove was brilliantly lit by torches hanging in brackets from strategically planted posts. Ashoka trees had been planted in well planned clumps and lines along boulevards. Near at hand an artificial lake could be seen. Hanuman did not wander about but sat perched on the wall surrounding the grove. Plumb in the centre of the gardens was a huge *Shingshapa* tree. This area was the most brilliantly lit. A large group of Rakshasi guards lay sprawled about all around this tree. Every one of them had vicious looking swords beside her. From the tumblers strewn about it was evident that they were all in the grip of drunken slumber. A lone woman sat under the tree. She was a picture of dejection. Sighing every now and then, she wiped off tears with her right hand. Her sari was ordinary and faded. She wore no ornaments at all, except for the thread of her marriage about her slender neck. Hanuman almost whooped with joy. He was sure that he had reached the end of his search. This could be none other than Sita. He went over to her and stood with folded hands.

Sita was terrified. An unknown male standing before her in an attitude of supplication filled her with terror. She was interned against her will in an alien place, amongst alien people. Although she was not badly treated, yet the presence of armed guards about her at all hours was telling on her nerves. She eyed Hanuman with intense suspicion. This could be some new ploy of the Rakshasa king. Though this was a Banara and not a Rakshasa, yet she was much suspicious of him.

"Hail to thee, mother Sita." Hanuman said in chaste Sanskrit as he bent low to touch the ground near her feet with his forehead. Then rising, he said, "Pray, do not be afraid of me, mother, for I bear the tidings from our Lord Sri Rama. I am a minister of the Banara King Sugriva. I am known as Hanuman or Maruti. Our Lord Rama and my king Sugriva are now allied in an unbreakable vow of friendship and brotherhood. They wait eagerly to hear about you. The thousands of a combined army of Banaras and Rikhshas wait to pounce on this island. My Lord Lakshmana, who also sends you his *pranam*, is whetting his arrow-heads and swords in eager anticipation of an onslaught of vengeance against the Rakshasas."

"You could be part of some trick being played by Rakshasas. I don't believe you."

"I knew that you would never believe me. Therefore I shall tell you some tales of my Lord's life that are not known even to chroniclers. These tales are known between you and my Lord only, but my Lord had shared them with me so that I can convince you that I am indeed coming from him."

"Oh Banara, you have almost convinced me. I want to be convinced. But why do my hands tremble so? Why does my heart thunder and race like a war-horse? Why does my entire being break out in sweat?" Sita wept and said after she heard Hanuman's accounts. The eyes of the battle-hardened and pragmatic Hanuman were not dry either.

"Dear mother of mine, I shall now show you something that will convince you absolutely." From his small bag Hanuman extracted a signet ring. It bore the crest of the House of Koshala and bore the inscription of the letter 'Ra'. How many thousands of times had Sita seen this ring adorning the ring finger of her beloved? She wept openly now.

"Oh my son, oh Maruti, you are the dawn to my eternal night of misery. Oh dear, tell me more. Is my Lord well? Does he eat properly? Is he taking good care of himself? Are his weapons kept in their best order? And my brother Lakshmana, whose wrath is enough to send even the Devas scurrying home, quaking with fear, is he well too? Is there really a Banara army out there waiting to come to my rescue? Is your king, the venerable Sugriva, willing to risk his life and kingdom just for a poor woman like me?"

They talked and talked well into the night. Then Sita became overwhelmed by anxiety once again.

"My son, you must leave now. If these Rakshasi *Cheris* wake up and find you here, then your life would not be worth anything at all. Go now, Maruti. May all the gods protect you." As Hanuman made to leave, Sita called out to him once more. From the innermost recesses of her garments she took out a large gem and handed it over to Hanuman.

"Take this, Maruti. Give it to my Lord. This is a family heirloom given to me by my father when I left his abode for my in-laws' place. My Lord will recognise it. It will tell him that his Sita is alive and is eagerly waiting for his arrival."

Hanuman made to leave with Sita's blessings. But as he neared the gate of the Ashoka grove, he stopped. His mission was not complete as yet! True, the main reason of his coming to Lanka had been fulfilled, yet he had not tested the military prowess of the Rakshasas. He made up his mind to provoke the Rakshasas so that the big-wigs came running.

A thunderous roar woke the main Cheri, Trijata up. It will start raining soon, she thought, as she turned over to resume her drink befuddled sleep. Her sleep had been disturbed by the peculiar nightmare she had where she had seen the defeat of Ravana. She had also seen Rama sitting on the Lanka throne with Sita at his side, nodding and smiling as Bibhishan stood waiting with mangoes on a golden tray, wearing the Lanka crown. All this had disturbed her to no end. Then this horrible sound! Trijata sat up, more than disturbed. Dejected, she got up to fetch some water, when the resounding crack of something breaking assailed her senses. What she saw almost drove her out of her mind. A huge man was standing far away, near the gate. He was systematically breaking branches of all the fruit trees. Flowering shrubs lay scattered uprooted in their hundreds. The ornamental hillocks were broken and the boulders strewn about. As she watched petrified with horror, the unknown man uprooted a huge banyan tree to throw it on the wall, which pulverised at the impact. Trijata roused the other Cheris. They grabbed their swords and ran to the intruder yelling at the top of their voice. Hanuman sent them flying with back-handed slaps that landed like sledge-hammers. All this commotion brought the armed guards out running. But these guards, armed with mere clubs were no match for the Banara on the war-path. They lay in a heap, limbs and necks broken.

An irritable Ravana was roused from his slumber by the wailing Trijata. He sat up and irritably asked her to enter. On hearing her tale of woes, he was irritated further. He was roused from sleep to hear a complaint about a Banara breaking branches from trees! Utterly preposterous! He called for his chief body-guard to assign fifteen able bodied men in order to apprehend the miscreant and to throw him into prison. He would stand trial later in the day.

Ravana had not taken into account the prowess of the marauding monkey-man. Nor had the soldiers. Soon all was over and the last soldier to escape with his life, limped over to the palace to report to his superior that the other fourteen men will never again report for duty. Now Ravana was enraged. He splashed cold water on his face began to dress in preparation for sitting in court.

In the meantime, Hanuman had not been idle. He had gathered together about ten or fifteen boulders from the debris of the destroyed ornamental hillocks and stowed them about, not in a heap, but placed in different strategic locations. Then he looked about for a suitable piece of arms. He had come into Lanka, unarmed, save his armoured breast plate, which he had carried in a bag. He put on this armour and, during his search, spied a huge iron bar that served as a bolt for the Ashoka grove gate made of iron sheets. The bar was so big and heavy that under ordinary circumstances, four strong men would be hard put to lift it up. But Hanuman was a man of immense strength and at that point of time, was probably the strongest man on this land. He made short work of this bar and plucked it easily from its hinge. It did not measure up to the vicious mace that he customarily carried, but still it was better than being completely unarmed. He then jumped atop the gateway to the Ashoka grove and sat waiting for the hordes to arrive. And they did arrive soon enough.

Jambumali it was, the son of the Prime Minister, Prahastha. He stormed in with twenty men, all on horseback. But he too had made the fatal error of underestimating the strength of Hanuman. Seeing his foes thundering in, Hanuman, with his blood-curdling battle-cry of "Jai Shree Rama" jumped down from his perch. He met the charging cavalry men head-on. With three clean sweeps of his vicious iron bar he accounted for all the twenty one cavalier youngsters. The rider less horses returning to their stables told the sad story to all. Ravana went berserk.

It was a full scale military operation, from the look of it. Ravana, now on a cautious note, had assigned five of his captains, Birupaksha, Yupaksha, Durdharsha, Praghosh and Bhashkarna, to attack the indomitable Banara, with full strength. He had cautioned the five captains that this was no ordinary person. They had to be always on their alert in order to apprehend the miscreant alive, if possible.

Hanuman heard them long before they could be seen. A full scale army on the move makes quite a din. Hanuman relaxed. He knew exactly what he would do. Guerrilla warfare was his pet subject and he excelled in the art.

The army made quick time as it moved in. Once on the boulevard that made a straight run to the Ashoka grove, their troubles began. The road, though wide enough, was not meant for an army on the rampage. It was lined on either side by tall trees, set close together. The boughs hung low to meet their fellows on the other side to make a perfect tunnel to protect against the elements. But now they deterred the soldiers on elephants. They had to crouch low over the backs of the animals and were, for the large part, unsighted. The whole army had to move along this road. It could not be bypassed, as woodlands stretched far and wide on either side, precluding the free movements of all. So, there was jostling for space and tempers began to run high. Foot soldiers, cavalry and chariots moved in like waves of the sea, with the elephants bobbing up and down like ships of war. Soon, the orderly march became relegated to a forward surge of unruly mob, with no semblance of any discipline. Men got themselves entangled with horses. Spear shafts got in the way of chariots. Added to all this, the trumpeting giants demanded privileged passage. The captains jostled with each other and with the soldiers, in their eagerness to reach the miscreant first, in search of glory. This added to the confusion. The night was dark, so the soldiers carried enough torches to light up the darkest corners, but the light that emanated fell far short of Hanuman's perch. Thus, while Hanuman remained unseen to the soldiers, they themselves presented as well illuminated targets.

The experienced eyes of Hanuman identified the five captains easily enough. One was riding an elephant and was a bit to the rear, while the others were on chariots. One of them marched at the head of the army and he was being pushed further up by the foot soldiers who were afraid of being trampled underfoot by the pachyderms. This captain made an eminently suitable target.

Hanuman waited till the soldiers came within range. Then he alighted from the top of the gateway. He walked to the nearest boulder and picked it up. It was bigger than a human head in size and was immensely heavy. He hefted the boulder up, balanced it over his head, arched his back to get maximum leverage and lobbed. The boulder arched high up and then, reaching the highest point in its parabolic curve, raced down towards the earth. Yupaksha, on the lead chariot, never knew what hit him. Neither did the soldiers. They heard the sudden 'Splat' and saw their leader Yupaksha toppling backwards from his chariot, his head transformed into a pulp. The superstitious soldiers had not seen or heard the boulder. So this appeared to them some sort of eerie black magic. They faltered, only to be pushed by their brethren coming up from behind. Thus more jostling, pushing about, yelling, abusing and fisticuffs ensued. In the confusion a foot soldier slipped and fell, to be run over by a chariot. This added to the confusion. The soldier, who had been run over, belonged to the platoon that was, till very recently, being commanded by the just deceased Yapaksha. This evoked ire of the soldiers as the offending chariot was that of another captain, Durdharsha. The soldiers surrounded the chariot demanding redress. The stationary chariot was now a sitting duck for the rocky missiles. While all this was going on, the soldiers saw a huge boulder whistling through the air to land on Durdharsha's head and crushing it instantaneously. Panic prevailed. The foot soldiers in the front turned and started running back. They ran directly into the horses of Birupaksha's cavalry. The horses shied, neighed and reared up. The fleeing soldiers, in their intense panic, lost their heads when they found their way obstructed. In the meantime, a couple of boulders fell on them from different directions squashing more soldiers to pieces. The soldiers were convinced that this was a sort of black magic they had never seen before. They thought that the miscreant had split up into a number of forms and were attacking them from different sides. They were good soldiers in broad daylight. But where magic was involved they were reduced quaking imbeciles. In the melee another captain got killed. The leadership was being decimated. Smelling grave danger Birupaksha ordered his charioteer to drive straight to where all this confusion was centred. But at this moment the soldiers fleeing in panic began hacking at their compatriots who had obstructed their path. A riot ensued and men began to fall right, left and centre. A number of hands grabbed at Birupaksha's chariot. The horses panicked and wheeled about. The hapless Birupapaksha was thrown off his balance and he toppled over from the chariot. An onrushing elephant squashed him underfoot. Praghosh, seeing all this, urged his mahout to march his elephant forward outside the messy area. Hanuman now vaulted down from his perch and faced his enemy for a one-to-one confrontation. Praghosh seeing the enemy for the first time yelled in anger and hefted a huge spear from its bracket on the elephant back. He threw, but Hanuman twisted to one side and it missed clean. By the time Praghosh picked a second spear up, Hanuman was over to the side of the elephant. He grabbed the trappings in one hand and with a battle cry vaulted on to the back of the animal. He swung the iron bar and Praghosh's head, despite the helmet he wore, was cleaved into two. Hanuman pushed the body over, grabbed the mahout from behind and bodily threw him off from the elephant's back. Then he wheeled the elephant around himself and ran the animal down towards the fleeing soldiers. Near the fleeing ranks, he vaulted down from the elephant's back and goaded the frightened animal towards the mass of humanity. It was total rout.

Hanuman went back to his station to catch his breath back. He knew that more worthy warriors would enter the fray now and he made himself ready for the next ordeal.

Prince Aksha, the youngest son of Ravana, was a close friend of the deceased Birupaksha. He was there in his father's court-room, fully garbed for battle. Ravana was pacing the hall up and down with unrepressed angst when news of the rout came in. Aksha came up to face his father.

"Father, may I have your permission to go to battle against this marauding Banara?"

"You my son! But you are too young to face him. This monkey-man is as strong as he is wily. I fear your security."

"But father, how long will you be able to protect me for? I am a warrior, the proud son and the proud brother to the most celebrated warriors of this land," Aksha said, glancing at his elder brother Meghnad.

"Brother," Meghnad said gently. "This is not the moment of hot headed action. We have lost enough men already. All were the best of men. Now guile is needed. Why are you so eager for the fight?"

"Bother, Birupaksha was my friend."

A lone chariot thundered down the boulevard. The pair of white steeds could be vaguely made out in the feeble light of a crescent moon. Hanuman was astonished in seeing, that after all the ordeals a single charioteer was coming to get him. The chariot trundled to a stop close to the gate. A young voice called out.

"Whoever you are, please come out and show yourself. This is Prince Aksha, the youngest son of the Emperor, who is challenging you to a face-to-face combat. Show your face, you coward!"

"No one calls me a coward and lives, young man. But you go back. You have long years ahead of you. I don't want the blood of a brave young man on my hands. Be gone!"

"My closest friend has been slain in your hands. I demand reprisal!" Aksha was already fitting a vicious looking arrow to his bow.

"Go home, boy, you shall get plenty of time to fight me. Later, maybe, but not..."

Hanuman never got to complete the sentence. He was unsighted, no doubt, but he had not taken into account that Prince Aksha was very much proficient in the use of the *Shabdabhedi Baan*. Prince Aksha raised his bow, drew and shot in one fluid movement. Hanuman could thank the stars that he was wearing the breast plate of his armour. Three sounds in rapid succession cut through the still night air the twang of the prince's bow, the whine of the flying arrow and the clang of metal hitting metal. Hanuman was thrown off his feet and he fell to the ground from his high perch with a resounding thud. For any ordinary person, the fall itself would have been curtains, but not Hanuman. He was of an iron constitution. Soon after his fall he sat up once again, gingerly shaking his head to clear the cobwebs from his brain and ringing ears. He was bleeding from a laceration at the back of the head.

Prince Aksha's lack of experience saved the day for Hanuman. Had the prince stayed put on his chariot, waiting to shoot the living daylights out of Hanuman when he came for him, Hanuman would have had no escape. But the prince, in his enthusiasm of youth, thought that his foe was dead or dying. With a vault he alighted from his chariot and ran with a naked sword, to where Hanuman had fallen. His sole aim now was to decapitate his foe and to present the severed head to his father on a golden platter. Hanuman jumped up as Aksha aimed the sword with a mission to kill. Metal clashed on metal and sparks flew. He had parried Aksha's stroke expertly with his iron bar. Aksha sliced, cut and thrust with an expertise that made Hanuman applaud his training. This kid was an expert swordsman, one of the best he had ever met. Suddenly he seemed to stumble and loose his balance, to fall backward. Aksha did not understand that this was a ploy. He jumped up to aim a killing stroke. This was the moment Hanuman was waiting for. The prince's guard was gone and his whole body was exposed. With all his might Hanuman threw the iron bar at the face of the prince. The lower jaw cracked audibly and teeth flew out as Aksha fell into a heap. But he was a real hero. After a momentary pause, Aksha jumped up with a yell and made to grab Hanuman round the waist. This time Hanuman went for the kill. He grabbed the long hairs of the prince with one hand and with his waist-band in his other he hefted the prince above his head, whirled him round and round, and threw him into the granite wall of the Ashoka grove. Aksha's head caved in and blood, brain and gore splattered all over the place. Hanuman let out an almost animal cry of victory and leapt up to his seat atop the gateway to tend to his wounds. A couple of frightened night-birds cackled as they flew away.

Hanuman's primal cry spread through all corners of the city and beyond. The eternal flames burning on the top of the Trikuta Hill wavered. Ravana, waiting tensely in his court, started at the cry. He faced towards the ornate ceiling, both hands clenched in fists in a futile attempt to control his surging emotions. A cry of severe anguish escaped his lips. "Aksha..." he cried and collapsed on his throne. The cry of a lamenting father reverberated throughout the hall and echoed in the deserted corridors, dashing against the cold pillars of marble. No one spoke. After a while Ravana raised his face and looked around. The courtiers gasped and stepped backwards in abject terror. The eyes were bloodshot. The teeth were clenched. Every muscle in the powerful frame stood out. His lips moved. A single wish escaped the parted lips. "My chariot," he uttered, rather, whispered. But this whisper sounded like blowing gale bent on total destruction. Prahastha, the Prime Minister, the maternal uncle and a long time associate of Ravana, stepped up to the left side of his King and placed a comforting hand on his shoulder. Only he could do it. He too had lost a son that fateful night. Ravana did not look at Prahastha, but gently warded him off. With his right he picked up his terrible sword, the Chandrahash and strode on towards the door. Suddenly he found his way barred. Through a scarlet haze he saw his eldest son, Meghnad, standing in front of him.

"Father," Meghnad stood firm in his path. "It is not becoming of you to go to battle against a puny Banara. Yes, I concede that he had been lucky so far. I lament the death of our soldiers. I lament the loss of my dear brother. But have some confidence in me, father. I wish to go forth to meet this Banara. May I have your permission, Sire?"

"You don't understand, Meghnad, this is no ordinary Banara. In my time I have seen many great Banaras. But this Maruṭi far surpasses them all. Is he really a Banara? Or is he some famed Deva like Indra, Agni or Pavan in disguise? No Meghnad. I cannot allow you to go on such a misadventure. I have to go myself."

"Father, have I ever brought you shame and disgrace? Do you not think that I am dependable? Then allow me to go Sire,

I give you the word of honour that before the night wears off, I shall bring him before you bound and shackled."

Meghnad put his forces together. From the elite Imperial Guards he chose twenty of the strongest and most disciplined men.

"My men, we go on a dangerous mission tonight. But follow my directions. I give you my word that the soil of Lanka will not drink a further drop of Rakshasa blood. All of you follow me on foot, but maintaining a distance of at least twenty dhanus with my chariot. Each man take weapons of close combat only. And a coil of rope each. Now bring Nagpash to me."

Nagpash was a wry young man, of lanky built. He was an expert with the lasso or lariat. He was Meghnad's sidekick for many years. His expertise had earned him his name. People now had forgotten that he was originally called Nagpal. To this man Meghnad gave some specific instructions.

The eventful night was in its last quarter. The watch over Lanka rang the hour. Hanuman relaxing in his seat stifled a yawn. Sleep was not at all welcome at this juncture. He knew that warriors of the topmost order will come in now. But he was ready for all ordeals. Then they came. It was a single chariot, drawn by four horses, as black as night itself and, therefore, almost invisible. A handful of foot soldiers followed, jogging along in a tight formation, but maintaining a fixed distance from the chariot. Hanuman sat up, intrigued. The chariot came within hailing distance and stopped.

"Maruti," a baritone called. "I know that you are there. This is Meghnad, the eldest son of the Emperor, who is addressing you. You have put up a valiant show tonight, and as a warrior

I salute you. There has been enough of bloodshed. Now it is time to talk, to discuss things. My father, the monarch of Lanka, wishes to meet you in person." Meghnad stopped as he felt the chariot floor move. Nagpash, who was there on his chariot, had slipped away. Meghnad called out again.

"Maruti, I come in peace. See, my men are stationed far away. I bear no arms. Please speak, if you hear me."

"Valiant Meghnad, also known as Indrajit, yes, I have heard of you. Tales of your valour have also reached Kishkindhya, from where I come. But let it be known to your father, that there will be no discussion, no parley, until he releases mother Sita first. Tell him that otherwise Shri Rama will come with the fearsome Banara army and will raze Lanka to the ground."

Even as Hanuman spoke, Meghnad could hear a faint whisper of a swishing sound cutting through the still night air. Nagpash was getting ready to cast his deadly lariat, dyed black for camouflage. Meghnad wanted to keep Hanuman talking. For then only Nagpash could cast with lethal precision, for the Banara could not be seen in the darkness.

"As you say, Maruti," Meghnad replied. "I shall not force you to come with me. But could you please tell me, why you destroyed the Ashoka grove?"

"It was a ploy to bring to bring you all running and I was successful in my..." Hanuman broke off as suddenly an unseen lasso dropped upon him to tie his massive arms to his trunk. He heard Meghnad order, "Pull!" For the second time that night Hanuman fell from his perch. As he fell the soldiers swarmed all over him tying him down with hemp ropes and leather thongs. His hands were tied, but to his satisfaction, Hanuman noticed that they were tied in front of his body.

Never before had Hanuman seen such a personality in his life. This was a born leader, thought he. Such immense strength, such controlled violence! Had his hands been free, he would have been hard put not to salute his main adversary. Through the veneer of a resolute jaw-line, a heavily moustached countenance, an immensely powerful physique draped in the best of red silks, Hanuman saw his blood-shot eyes concealing tremendous pain. How could such a towering, majestic person stoop so low so as to abduct another's wife? Hanuman shook his head. Something was not adding up.

Ravana too was appraising his foe. Here was a Banara, but such a Banara as he had never encountered before. There was great strength in the massive frame. That was evident. This man must be in pain, thought he, given the bruises and lacerations all over his body. Here was the man who had been responsible for the death of hundreds of his soldiers and commanders. This was the man who had taken away his youngest son. Yet, strangely enough, he felt no animosity towards this prisoner. The eyes haunted him. How could anyone have such a calm and confident look even when standing face to face with death! Such depth only comes with knowledge and wisdom. Ravana was eager to know more about this person. He signalled Prahastha to begin.

Prahastha stepped forward and, with a bow to his King, began the interrogation.

"Banara, who are you? Where are you from? Who had sent you?"

"Mr. Prime Minister, that is who you are, are you not, Prahastha, the renowned Prime Minister of Lanka?"

"Yes, that is who I am. You have guessed correctly."

"Prime Minister, sir, I have a submission to make. I want to talk directly to His Imperial Majesty alone, and to no one else, whosoever he might be."

Prahastha drew in his breath to speak, but was deterred by Ravana's raised right hand.

"I find this strange, dear Banara," said Ravana. "You are an intruder, a prisoner. You have no right to address the crown. But you do. Why?"

"It is so because Sire, I am no ordinary intruder or criminal. I come as the emissary of His Highness King Sugriva of Kishkindhya."

"Speak," said Ravana.

"Sire, King Sugriva has sent this message to you, through me, Maruti, son of Pavan, also known as Hanuman and a minister to His Highness the King. Sugriva has reminded you that you are as a brother to him, as you had been a blood brother to Bali, recently deceased. So, he sends you this brotherly message that it is not becoming for an Emperor of your stature to steal the wife of another man. We know the truth, even if others do not. You are a much greater person than the Aryan chroniclers and sages have painted you out to be. Do not demean yourself by keeping Queen Sita a hostage any further. The Princes of Ayodhya, Rama and Lakshmana, are at present, guests in Kishkindhya. King Sugriva has sworn eternal friendship with Prince Rama. If you do not release mother Sita then Rama and Lakshmana will attack Lanka with the huge Banara army at their back. Spare Lanka of the destruction and tears. Release mother Sita."

Ravana sat quietly for a while. Then he sighed and stood up.

"Maruti," said he. "I do not consider this message coming from the King of Kishkindhya at all, for I do not recognise Sugriva as the king. Bali is sadly no more. So, the rightful king should have been his son, who is not a minor any more. Moreover, my brother Bali had been murdered in the most despicable manner, by the same prince that you are speaking so highly of. No negotiation is possible in these matters, and that is final. Lanka is ready to face all consequences." Ravana paused and paced about. Then he stepped up to Hanuman.

"Maruti," he resumed. "The Rakshasas and the Banaras have been foremost amongst the non Aryan forces in this land. We were civilised, boasting of great cities and culture since long before the Aryan Devas invaded our beautiful country. They robbed our homeland and us, both of our peoples, are now cornered and hard pressed to retain what is rightfully ours. Why should the Aryans incite a war between the Rakshasas and Banaras? We, non Aryans should take a united stand. Come Maruti, let us join hands to wipe off this Aryan menace from our land altogether. We can do it." Hanuman did not speak. He marvelled at the insolence and at the vision of this remarkable man before him.

"Hanuman, your so called king threats me with annihilation. Fine enough. We Rakshasas had always been at the receiving end of Fate. A final battle, a real show-down was always on the card. I have hastened it for I want the last war to end all wars to be fought on my terms, on my grounds.

"Now, what is to be done with you? You have behaved like a miscreant and an intruder and you have to face the consequences.

"Prahastha, you and other ministers first decide what is to be done, then let me know."

Ravana turned to leave. As he was on his way out, he stopped and looked at Hanuman.

"Do not worry about Sita. No harm has befallen her till date, and never will." With this he left the room.

All hell broke loose once Ravana left. Some shouted, "kill him." Some said, "flog him." The ministers bent their heads together and conversed in low and serious tones trying to decide Hanuman's fate. At last, when nothing could be finalised, they decided to send a messenger to the King. Since his childhood, Hanuman was trained in meditation. Using the same approach, he had cut off all external stimuli and had decided to wait. He knew exactly what he would be doing, no matter what the verdict turned out to be. Like a *yogic* specialist he had used a specific technique when he was tied down. He had simply got all his immense muscles to bulge out when he was tied. Now that he stood relaxed, all the ropes hung loose. A shrug was all that was needed to free himself from bondage.

Within a short while all who were seated, stood up, as the Royal Usher announced, to the trill of trumpet, the arrival of the Emperor, signifying the fact that the official court would sit in session. The sun was rising as Ravana entered with his train; Hanuman was astounded at the sea-change that had come over this man. It appeared that Ravana had taken a hurried bath and a change of clothes in between. His hair was wet. His arms were freshly anointed with red sandalwood paste. He wore a dress of golden brocade. His angabastra was also embroidered with threads of gold. In his left hand he carried the sword Chandrahash and in his right he carried his sceptre of office. In the light of the torches that still blazed to ward off the gloom of the court-room, Ravana seemed to be dressed in a garb of fire.

The courtiers resumed their seats after Ravana seated himself on his golden throne. The umbrella-bearer took his station behind the throne with the huge white umbrella, adorned with gold. Two comely damsels stood on either sides with fly-whisks made of the tail hairs of yak. The uniformed sentries drew the massive mahogany doors shut. The court was now officially in session.

"Prisoner," called the Emperor in his deep baritone. "Do you plead guilty of intruding uninvited in the territory of sovereign Lanka, or do you not?" The court scribe scribbled furiously.

"I come, Emperor, uninvited," replied Hanuman, with his back straight, looking into Ravana's charcoal black eyes. "But I come as the emissary of King Sugriva, of the sovereign territory of Kishkindhya." Ravana nodded, as he expected nothing else as a reply.

"But you are guilty of destroying State property, killing men on official duty and waging an undeclared war on Lanka. Or are you not?"

"I am guilty on those counts, Emperor, but am not ashamed of what I did." Ravana nodded once again. Then he turned to Prahastha.

"What has the Council of Ministers decided about this prisoner?" Ravana asked.

"Sire," replied Prahastha. "We could not arrive at a conclusion in this regards and therefore we leave the matter in the hands of Your Majesty to decide. There are some amongst us who favour a capital punishment as a spy, while there are others who favour a lenient stand."

Ravana sat in silence looking at Hanuman. Then he sat up straight.

"I have decided and this is my decision. The prisoner is to be..." He broke off as his brother Bibhishan leapt up to his feet. Then he continued. "...honourably released as he is the official envoy of King Sugriva. You were saying something, Bibhishan?" He asked, looking at his younger brother. Bibhishan reddened and sat down slowly.

"No Sire, I have nothing to add."

"Maybe you had thought that I would order the prisoner's death. And you wanted to remind me of the International Law regarding the immunity of official Emissaries. But, anyway, I remember those laws, I dare say," Ravana said with a faint, indulgent smile touching the corner of his lips.

So, this was Bibhishan! Hanuman looked at him in disdain. This was the reputed younger brother of the powerful monarch. He was supposed to be a theoretical genius and an Aryophile. He was dressed all in white and had the white streaks of tilak adorning his forehead. A sacred thread peeped out from underneath his white silk angabastra. This man, thought Hanuman, was proud of his lineage and professed himself to be a Brahmin like his father, even though the Rakshasa or for that matter all non Aryan societies were essentially casteless.

Meghnad stood up waiting for his chance to speak. Ravana looked towards him and nodded.

"Sire, that was on the first account. But there is another part in his offence, the destruction of life and property, I mean."

"Yes, Meghnad, on that account he shall be punished. The Banaras are very proud of the false tail that they wear on the back of their waist bands. I declare that this Banara's tail be burnt prior to his release."

Akampan, now promoted to be a courtier, approached the bound Hanuman with a blazing torch, to inflict the punishment. Then it was all pandemonium. With his now famous battle-cry of "Jai Shri Rama," Hanuman slipped out of his bondage. Then he exerted his phenomenal strength to the thongs that bound his wrists together. The seasoned leather thongs snapped off as if made of the weakest twine. He snatched the torch from the astonished Akampan and hurled it towards the curtains. The curtains caught fire immediately and an inferno resulted, as one curtain after another burst into flames. Hanuman did not wait to see the results of this conflagration, but plucking two more torches from their brackets in the wall, leapt with them beyond the reach of the flames towards the closed door. Knocking the door over with a kick, he leapt into the corridor. His next few kicks knocked the sentries unconscious, and he ran down the corridor, setting fire to all combustible articles that came into his view. When he emerged into the garden outside, the entire Royal Palace was blazing like a funeral pyre, with flames roaring out of all windows. The fire had already reached the upper stories and adjoining wings. Shrieks of female voices now added to the din. Hanuman leapt over the wall and ran up to the next palace. He ran, jumped, sprinted and leapt, setting fire to one house after another and soon enough the entire aristocratic section of the city was ablaze. At this juncture a steady wind blew in from the sea as if conniving with Maruti in his bid to set the entire city to fire. Fire leapt from one house to the next. Lanka was equipped with all civic amenities except a fire-fighting capability. People ran here and there, many carrying buckets full of water. Men yelled, women wailed, horses neighed and dogs yelped. In the confusion Hanuman slipped off towards the sea, with a glance over his shoulders. The area of the Ashoka grove appeared to be located far away from the burning city, so Sita will be secure.

On his way out, Hanuman found two iron machines standing like sentries atop the two main towers of the main seaward gate meant to cast projectiles of different types at the enemy far away. In the interest of the landing forces these had to be destroyed or at least, tempered with. With inborn agility, Hanuman shinnied up the first tower. He grabbed the contraption with both hand and began to push. The machine budged but did not topple over. But Hanuman was not a person to give up easily. He pushed again. His muscles knotted up tight. Veins stood up along his limbs and temples. But still he did not give up. At long last the machine tottered, and then moved further, ultimate crashing down on the moat below. The moat was something that had escaped Hanuman's attention at first. It was teeming with marsh crocodiles, each one of them of gigantic proportion and suitably well toothed and angry. The heavy machine had fallen directly on the top of a couple of these reptiles putting paid to them. The water frothed all over with rushing and churning animals. It appeared as if they were not averse to cannibalism. The water frothed red. Hanuman shuddered and leapt over to the next tower. Soon, this machine too fell in the moat, accounting for a few more of the animals. Then Hanuman jumped down and ran straight for the sea-side.

Hanuman ran across the sandy cove and jumped into the cutter. Parani had already slipped off the moorings with a grin.

Behind them Lanka was an inferno. For a city built of marbles and sand-stone, it surely was burning well.

Angad was standing on top of the hill with Sampati, looking at the southern seas with immense anxiety. The sun was rising, but an unnatural orange glow lit up the southern sky. Their anxiety knew no bounds. Hanuman was due back long ago. What could have befallen him? But they could do nothing about it. So they waited.

The sun was quite high in the sky, when Angad's young eyes first caught sight of the moving spec in the sparkling waters. It raced towards where they stood. Soon the shape was apparent. It was the cutter, cutting through the seas at a speed which was almost unheard of. Angad jumped with joy and raced downhill to the beach.

The Banara platoon was lining the beach in a grand reception party as the cutter flowed smoothly into its berth. All were yelling at the top of their voices. All discipline had gone down the wind in their ecstasy in seeing Hanuman returning from Lanka in one piece. Hanuman waved from afar. The Banaras, headed by Angad splashed in to the knee-deep waters to help him disembark.

"How was the trip?" asked Angad. "Did you find mother Janaki?"

"Yes, I saw her, talked to her and now," Hanuman paused and turned for a glance southwards. "Now Lanka burns." He added with a smirk.

+ + +

Book II

The Saga of Ravana

1

The Cinders

Ravana sighed and turned back from his window. A pall of ominous smoke still hung over the city. The afternoon sun could barely reach down to comfort the citizens. Ravana shook his head in exasperation. It was unbelievable. A single Banara had wrecked such havoc! The morale of the Lankan had never fallen so low. Ravana called for his team of body guards. He had to go for a tour of the devastated city and that too, on foot. The citizens had to see him standing beside them in the hour of their need.

The fire had taken a long time to be brought under control. It had begun at the Royal Palace and had spread to engulf the whole of the Aristocratic district. Soon however, almost the whole of the city of Lanka was ablaze. The citizens and soldiers alike had joined hands in the fire fighting. By the time the flames were brought under control, more than half of the city had been gutted. There had been casualties too. The Royal Infirmary was overflowing with the number of burn patients.

Hands reached out in supplication. Families had been rendered destitute all of a sudden. The acrid smell of burnt flesh assailed olfaction. Ravana marched throughout the length and breadth of the city, returning to the palace only after the sun had set. Prahastha was standing on top of the stairway, hands akimbo, fuming.

"What is this supposed to mean Dashanan?" The Prime Minister addressed his King and his nephew by his given name, when meeting in private or when emotionally disturbed. Now this emotion factor had got better of his strong sense of propriety.

"What is what, dear uncle?" asked Ravana.

"You should never have gone out into the city without proper escort in the given circumstances."

"I fail to get your point, uncle. My subjects have suffered. It is my bounden duty to stand by their sides in this hour. Had I not gone, I would have been guilty in my own eyes. That I cannot allow, can I?"

"Whatever it is, it was sheer foolhardiness. Do you have any idea Dashanan, any idea as to how your own people are blaming you today for their present debacle?"

Ravana's strong shoulders slumped. He said nothing but strode up the steps past his uncle to enter his private chamber beside the court-room. This was one of the few rooms in the palace that had miraculously escaped the ravages of fire. He sat down on his low couch. Prahastha followed him. Without looking at him Ravana asked.

"And you uncle? Do you feel the same way?" He looked up slowly to meet the eyes of the Prime Minister. This was one person, whose opinion he valued most. Prahastha sucked in his breath. Never before had he seen so much pain in anyone's eyes. The eyes told him all. He drew a low stool up to the couch and sat down.

"Dashanan, what I feel is not important. What should be done is more important. Lanka has never before faced such crisis as today. I am afraid Dashanan, very much so."

"Why is it uncle? Come tell me. Don't hesitate."

"Dashanan, a single monkey-man has wrecked such havoc today. No, I am not speaking of the fire alone. That was sheer luck. Had the wind not fanned the fire, the damage would have been minimal. I am thinking about the military aspect. How many men did we lose last night, Dashanan?"

"You know better."

"Yes, I do. But let the numbers be. Men can be replaced. But the captains? Can they be replaced that easily? Both of us have lost our sons in the onslaught. But to what avail? Do you still need to hold Janaki as a hostage?" Ravana was silent. So Prahastha continued after a pause. "Be rational Dashanan. You have taken the poor girl in your custody as revenge against the disfigurement of your sister. You have made your point. Now is there any sense of carrying the thing on further? What more have you got to prove? Do you know that people are saying that you are infatuated with her? They are saying that you lust for her. But I know you better. So you must have your reasons.

"One Banara had caused this mayhem. Now thousands of them will come swarming over. Then what? Don't sit silent, nephew. Say something."

"Uncle, can you call the council to meet me at its earliest? I want to answer all your questions in front of the council. The members deserve to know. And yes, also make sure that

Mehgnad attends this meeting. It is important for him to attend. He is the Crown Prince. This will be part of his education."

Prahastha left. Ravana sat there alone in his chamber, pensive, forlorn. An attendant had come in and asked hesitantly whether she will light the lamps. But Ravana waved her away. He needed the solitude. He needed the darkness. He wanted to reach within himself in order to assess where he had gone wrong.

He was ambitious. There was no denial of the fact. But his ambitions had never been concerning himself alone. He had wanted all the Rakshasas, nay, all Asura tribes to come in terms with themselves. They had a glorious past once upon a time. But now all was enshrouded in a veil of self denial. He wanted all of them to shake off that lethargy. He had wanted to build an empire, but not for himself alone. But what had it all come to? Cinders that now stood lamely representing the Rakshasa will for self-determination! Nothing else! He felt a foreboding of doom. But there was no backtracking in this game of dice. He has thrown his hand and now could do nothing about how the dice fell.

So, people are blaming him today. They are saying that his lust is bringing about his downfall. He did not deny that the woman Janaki was beautiful. He did not deny that he had felt a stirring of something unidentifiable deep within himself. But was it lust? Could anyone stop him from taking her once he had her so much within his power? What did they know of lust? He had enjoyed its share since long. He knew that whatever he felt for Sita was far away from lust. He had felt certain tenderness towards her. True, when he had first abducted her, his all consuming sense of retaliation has blinded him. But with time, seeing the sorry, defenceless state of the woman, his protective instinct had taken upper hand. His feeling for her now had a certain filial quality in it. They were blaming him for falling in love with her. What did they know of love? They had never known Vedawati. Ravana sighed. That was the only true love of his life. He had not become Ravana then.

✦ ✦ ✦

2

Ravana's Love

"Vedawati, where are you?" Ravana's voice rang out in the forest. A laughter cascading through the air like a cataract broke out from somewhere out there. Did this woman care for nothing? Not even her own safety? Running about in the forest like this with the least regards of wild animals or marauding tribesmen! Ravana was becoming anxious now.

"Look my love; don't run away from me like this. You almost gave me a heart attack!" Ravana was serious.

"But you said that your heart does not belong to you anymore? Then how can I give you an attack?" Vedawati had feigned innocence.

Ravana stretched out in the shade beneath the ancient banyan tree and put his hands behind his head. He looked upwards. The sun was peeping through the tiny gaps in the leafy canopy, throwing an intricate lattice-work of enchantment where they lay, side by side. He sighed and shut his eyes in contentment. Vedawati reached over and ran a blade of grass tenderly over his eyelids.

"Soon you will be gone. You are on a campaign. You cannot abandon it halfway just because this slip of a girl. You have an empire to build, dreams to fulfil. I cannot tie you down."

"Come with me to Lanka, my dear."

"And what of your wife, Mandodari?"

"What of her?"

"Won't she be annoyed?"

"Why should she? She is the Chief Queen and she will remain so. Then why should she mind?"

"I don't know Dashanan. Everything is so uncertain now. You see, I am from a different ethnic group altogether. I do not even know whether I shall be able to adjust in your household."

"Enough of this. I am taking you over to Lanka with me to wed you as my lawful wife."

"You know, Dashanan, I had been in command of myself for long, ever since my parents died. But now, nothing seems to be right anymore."

Ravana reached over to pull her head down on his strong chest. The poor girl! She had suffered so much in life. Now, at least she deserved better.

Her father, the famed ascetic and philosopher Kushadhwaj, brother of the guru of the Devas, Brihaspati, was a choosy person. He had brought up his daughter well. Even at a very young age she was quite learned and had mastered the Vedas with ease, earning the name, Vedawati. She was beautiful as well as accomplished. It was a rare combination indeed. Suitors had flocked to her house, but none matched up to the expectations of her father. These suitors were mostly from Deva families, as could be expected, but other races could not keep themselves away as well.

One morning Vedawati had gone for her bath in the river nearby. On her way back she had stopped just outside her house, alert to the possibility of danger. A gleaming chariot was drawn up in front of the front gate. A giant of a man, in regal garb alighted and walked over to where her father stood at the entrance and touched his feet.

"Maharshi," said he. "I am Shumbha, the King of Danavas. I come to you today as a supplicant. I ask for your daughter's hand in marriage. I shall give her all comforts imaginable. She shall be my chief queen and shall rule my domain sitting in her throne beside me. Pray refuse me not, for I am not a person who tolerates refusal."

"Away, you debauch of a person! Do you think that I am not aware of your misdemeanours? I have heard of you and I refuse to give my daughter to you as your wife."

The Danava was enraged beyond measure at this refusal. He drew his sword and placed the tip on the throat of the elderly Brahmin.

"I told you Brahmin, that I am made of different mettle. I never stand any refusal. Call your daughter now. I shall take her away with me."

"I shall not," replied the intrepid Brahmin. "Not even at the pain of death. I shall not give my daughter away to a drunken debauch that you are."

What happened next was a blur. From her hiding behind the bushes Vedawati saw the Danava howl with rage and swing his huge sword. Her father was decapitated in a trice. Her mother wailed and came rushing out. With a primitive growl like an enraged ape, the Danava picked her up and hurled her away. She lay in a heap, unconscious. Shumbha then turned the house over looking for her and Vedawati ran away for her life towards the river, hiding in the reeds all day long. When she returned towards the evening, even the burning pyres had died out. Her mother could not bear the shame and had mounted the same pyre as her deceased husband as a *Sati*. People hailed her as a true, pious wife, but Vedawati found her to be a self-centred woman. Not a thought of her youthful daughter crossed her mind as she went for suicide. Then on, Vedawati had lived the life of austerity and this was how Ravana had found her. From that day Vedawati's life had undergone a tumble head-over-heels.

"No, Dashanan, I can't go with you now. You have a campaign to complete and I can't accompany you like a camp-follower, you know that. But I shall wait for you. Come, on your way back and I shall go with you to Lanka as your queen."

But that day never came, thought Ravana with a sigh. Breaking off his campaign, he had come to Vedawati's place, but she was nowhere to be found. Later an elderly Brahmin had told him that when Ravana had gone, Vedawati was so very overwhelmed with shame at having her virgin body being used by Ravana that she lit a huge pyre and had entered it, pronouncing a curse upon Ravana that she will come back and in her next life she would be the cause of his death. Ravana had sent the old man sprawling and had left the scene, dejected.

When he was trudging back to his camp, he was accosted by a small Shudra kid, hiding in the shrubbery. He revealed the real story of Vedawati's end to Ravana.

After the occupying Rakshasa army had departed, the local Brahmins had come to Vedawati. They had accused her of an illicit relationship with a Rakshasa. A Panchayat was held and it had decreed that Vedawati would be burnt on a stake. Vedawati had never renounced Ravana as he was given to believe.

The entire Aryan settlement was razed to the ground and all the Brahmins were put to sword. But that did not quench the all consuming fire that burnt within Ravana's breast even now.

"Sire," Prahastha called. "You are sitting in the dark! Shall I call for a lamp?"

"No. I had refused it. I prefer sitting in the dark now. Have you got in touch with all the council members? Are they coming?"

"Yes they are coming. In the meantime I shall go home for a while to freshen up. It has been a long day for all of us. You take care of yourself Dashanan."

Prahastha departed. He had called him by his childhood name, a childhood that was lost forever.

✦ ✦ ✦

3

The Early Days

"Dashanan, Dashanan, where are you?" His mother was calling. He was out there on a hillock near their home playing 'the king' with his two younger brothers, Kumbhakaran and Bibhishan. Every morning they used to come here to play. Their games were sort of rough and tumble types and Bibhishan was generally at the receiving end. He was the quieter, studious sort amongst the brothers. These games were not very appealing to him. Even then he joined because he did not want to be left out.

"Coming, ma," yelled Dashanan. The brothers came running to their home in the forest. Their mother Kaikasi was doing her household chores. Their little sister Surpanakha was sitting with a bowl of puffed rice and was more snivelling than eating.

Their small hut was in a clearing in the forest, close to a small hillock. They lived frugally, for their father was an ascetic known as Rishi Bishraba. He was a very talented learned man, but not very wise to the ways of the world. Books, scripts, scriptures, prayers, meditation and the yajna fire ruled his life. They were always hard up. But their mother with an uncanny acumen kept them fed and clothed. Their father was often absent from home, going to towns and cities on several assignments that they were too young to understand.

Their mother gave them their breakfast of some unidentifiable cereals and fruits. They were all growing children and their demand of food was great. This was more true with Kumbhakaran, because, although he was the second amongst the children, was of a bigger build and the greatest strength. Just as they were finishing their meal, a sudden droning sound filled the air and through the clouds descended a strange contraption they had never seen in their life before. At first they had thought that it was a bird. But later, as it descended closer, Dashanan saw that it was a strange vehicle that flew through the air as a bird. It was metal covered and glinted in the morning sun. Kaikasi gave the strange craft a cursory glance and went about in her works.

"Mother, what is it?" Dashanan whispered, absolutely overawed.

"That, my child, is the Pushpak Rath. It travels through the air very fast and belongs to your half brother Kubera, who rules over Lanka. It means that your elder brother has dropped in to visit his father."

Kaikasi was right in her deduction. Soon enough, a tall, well built figure opened the wicker gate and strode in. He was resplendent in golden silk and brocade, adorned with gold ornaments of all sorts. His appearance spoke of such affluence that looked almost indecently out of place in the shabby environment. Dashanan and his brothers looked on agape in awe. Their sister was too young to bother about such things. Kaikasi wiped her hands at the end of the dull sari that she was wearing and welcomed her step-son.

"Come, my son, come in," said she.

Kubera cast his eyes about and asked,

"Father is not in?"

"No, my son. He has gone away to the city on some errands. But please be seated, will you? I'll serve you some refreshments. Here, Dashanan, Kumbhakaran, Bibhishan, meet your brother. Come up here."

Kubera wrinkled his nose in disgust.

"No Anarya (non Aryan) Rakshasi can ever be a mother of mine, nor any half breed my brother. I go now woman. Please tell my father when he returns that I had come looking for him." With this he wheeled about and departed.

Kaikasi stood there, shoulders slumped, two drops of tear rolling down her cheeks. Little Dashanan sided up to his mother and looked up to her.

"Mother, why was he so rude?" Kaikasi wiped her tears away and looked at her son.

"He is not at fault, my son. He had no mother to teach him good manners."

"But he calls father, 'Father'. It means that you could be his mother. But he did not want you. Mother, what is Anarya, and what is half breed?"

"My son, your father and Kubera are Aryans. They are fair-skinned and tall. We are Rakshasas, being dark and therefore Anarya or non Aryan. You are half Aryan and half non Aryans. So he called you half breeds."

"Is it a bad word?"

"No son. It is your proud heritage, for you inherit the best of two worlds. You are an Aryasura and so are your brothers and sister."

At this Dashanan held his head high. He was proud of his new identity. He was proud of being an Aryasura.

It was not often that Dashanan came across their father at home. Whenever he was at home, the children were supposed become invisible. He did not like to see them play around the hut. The children too, avoided him for fear of being scolded. Furthermore, he had a tendency of making the children sit down in front of him with books and things. Dashanan and Kumbhakaran were totally averse to study. This sort of study entailed learning the Vedas by heart without delving into their meanings. But these two brothers found Nature to be a better teacher. They learnt from the trees, the wind, the stream flowing nearby, the bees, birds, animals, everything. But Bibhishan was made of a different mettle. He loved sitting by his father, lapping up the difficult *shlokas*, wallowing in Aryan philosophy, helping him with the yajna fire.

That night Bishraba had come in late, just as Kaikasi was sitting down for her meal. He was tired and hungry from a long walk homeward. As there was no other food ready at home, Kaikasi gave him the plate she had readied for herself. The Rishi fed himself to his satisfaction, burped and sagaciously declared that despite all her negative points, it had to be admitted that she was a good cook. Then they had gone to bed. The children had all gone to sleep in the other room, so, with impunity the Rishi mounted her. He always did, every night when he was at home. His lust was insatiable. This had worked to Kaikasi's advantage many years ago. She had wanted good learned sons. So she had made the Rishi fall for her charms. It was lust all the way, with love taking a back-seat. Now it was all lust for him and duty for her. She had never minded this role, for she knew that this was her lot. But at heart she knew that she could not be content at remaining a passive Rishi's wife all her life. She had high hopes for Dashanan. She was a Rakshasa Princess herself. She wanted her son to rule the world. But as things were drifting along now, she knew that her dreams would never be realised. If her father could come to her place, even if it was just for a few hours, she would have discussed her son's career with him.

As if divining her thought, her father, the Rakshasa erstwhile king, presently deposed, Sumali came over to his daughter's place. Bishraba was, as usual, absent from home and the elderly Rakshasa spent long and fruitful hours with his daughter and grandchildren. They went for a long walk in the evening. The air was balmy and fragrant. They walked up to the hillock nearby and sat down to rest near the top. Kaikasi had gone back earlier with her daughter, on the pretext that much remained to be done at home.

Dashanan sat beside his grandfather plying question after question at him. He wanted to know all about his identity, his heritage, the history of his people, everything. Kumbhakaran was not much interested in such talks. He ran about the hilly slopes after the flitting butterflies.

Early at the dawn of civilization, a group of neo-civilised people had pledged that they would protect the waterways. This pledge had resulted in their being called "the Rakshasas", from the root word of 'Raksha', to protect. In keeping with this vow, they built their first cities on the immense waterway, River

Sindhu. This was long, long before the Aryans had come into this land as marauders and invaders on horseback with their iron weapons. The Protectors were now hard put to protect their own homes and hearths. They lost their homeland and were pushed away first towards the east along another great River Ganga, then later southwards as the Aryans occupied the Ganga basin as well. The first invading Aryans were from the Deva clan.

Down south, the Rakshasas were not disturbed too much and they thought that they could now settle down and be masters of their own lives. With this view, they made their capital on the island of Lanka. A great city was built on the slopes of the Trikuta Hill, bearing the same name. The Rakshasas had been a great people with scientists, architects and engineers of their own. They had built great cities once upon a time. But now, they had lost all in the Aryan invasion. They had no other option but to give the commission of building the new city to a Deva architectural firm, of the Vishwakarma School. This proved to be their undoing. They should have known that the Devas shall never rest before they totally vanquished the Rakshasas. Soon enough, with this objective in mind, they struck at the capital. Lanka, at that time, was ruled by a triumvirate of three brothers, Malyaban, Dashanan's grandfather, Sumali and Mali. The Deva army was led by the great warrior Vishnu. Lanka was besieged for days. Then it became apparent to the Rakshasas that they could not hold the city for long. The Vishwakarma architects had given away all secret doorways and passages, in fact all about the defence system of the city to the Devas. Mali volunteered to hold the fort with a handful of picked soldiers, while Malyaban and Sumali vacated Lanka in the dead of night, with the rest of the Rakshasas and all women and children. They travelled at night through the dangerous tracks of rain forest, hiding at day-time, till they reached the uninhabited northern coast. A number of skiffs, cutters and country-boats waited there to ferry them across the dangerous waters to the mainland. Not all could make it. Most of the country-boats could not wear the turbulent sea and capsized. The people crowded there were either drowned or devoured by the sharks and barracudas that were on the prowl for such eventuality. When the party, or what remained of it, reached the mainland, they hid themselves in the caves of the Eastern Ghats. To confuse their enemies they called these caves Patal or the Underground Kingdom. Mali and his soldiers fought bravely, but were killed by Vishnu's army to a man. Kubera was installed as the king in a Lanka devoid of Rakshasas.

"So you see Dashanan, Lanka is ours by rights," said Sumali. "I can never forget the day when we had to vacate our beautiful city in the dark of night to save our skins. I sometimes think that I should have stayed back to fight for our homeland. Maybe, like brother Mali, I would have been killed. But at least I would have died with self-respect."

"Grandpa," said Dashanan gravely. "That would have been useless. You are alive, that is good. Who would have told me these stories if you would have been killed?"

"Right you are grandson. That is a good, valid point. But you know something? I feel in my heart that someday I shall return to Lanka once again. I live for that day."

"Yes Grandpa, you surely will someday. But when you go, please take me along with you."

That night Sumali had a long talk with his daughter. They were discussing their future. Sumali had begun to see a faint glimmer of light at the end of the dark tunnel.

"Dear daughter, I see great promise in Dashanan. He has everything in him to be the saviour of our race we were waiting for."

"But how can you be so sure, father? He is still so young!"

"Some leaders of men are born, Nikasha," said Sumali, calling Kaikasi by her pet-name. "They need to be recognised early and nurtured. Your son is a born leader. Now, it is up to us to see that he is nurtured properly."

Shukracharya had come to visit them within the next few days. It seemed that Sumali had acted. He was the greatest Guru the world had ever produced. His only drawback was that he was an Asura by birth. Due to this reason alone the Devas proclaimed that their Guru, Brihaspati, was the greatest. But this did not deter them from the fact that they sent Kacha, the son of Brihaspati to Shukracharya, to learn the art of surgery, in order to save lives. Shukracharya was the past master of all branches of learning, be it philosophy, astronomy, mathematics, science, socio-political studies, law or military strategies.

It was a cool autumn evening when Shukracharya turned up at their dwelling. It was one of the rare occasions when Bishraba was at home. Both the sages embraced each other like long-lost brothers, although, in reality there was no love lost between them.

"You, what?" Bishraba was incredulous and appalled, as if he had never heard anything more preposterous in his life.

"Yes, Bishraba, I want to take your sons under my tutelage."

"Listen, all this is fine, but I could hardly afford your fees, my friend. I heard that you charge astronomical sums."

"Yes, I admit that I am expensive, but you needn't bother about your money. I won't charge you anything."

"Still..." Bishraba was not convinced at all.

"No more arguments please. Then it is settled. Please call your sons. I'll take them along with me to my place."

"Just a moment. I don't think that it would be wise to send all my sons away at the same time. You see, most of the times I am away. If all sons go away together, my wife would be disconsolate. Why don't you take two of my sons with you? My third son can then stay at home and look after his mother. I give you my word that I shall take care of his education my own self."

It was ultimately decided that Dashanan and Kumbhakaran would go with Shukracharya, while Bibhishan was to stay at home, under the tutelage of his father.

Dashanan and Kumbhakaran stayed with their guru for about ten long years. During this period they learnt all about philosophy, law, science, mathematics and military strategies. During their training period, Shukracharya also trained them in the use of arms of different kinds and unarmed combat as well. At long last their stipulated education was complete. Shukracharya had asked for his fees or *Gurudakshina* to be paid in two parts. The first part was a fee of one silver coin per head and the other part, to be paid within the next five years, was a handful of sand each, collected personally from the beaches of Lanka!

That morning, as Dashanan and Kumbhakaran were packing their meagre belongings prior to leaving the Gurukul for good a young student came running up to them.

"Oh, it's a great thing that I could catch you before you'd gone," he panted. "The Acharya is looking for you." He stopped to catch his breath. Dashanan and Kumbhakaran nodded and followed the young boy to their Guru's abode.

"Come in my boys," said Shukracharya, putting away his quill and ink. He was jotting down some notes in dried palm leaves. "Two things still remain undone before you go home. Come with me."

The Acharya put on his angabastra and wooden slippers and with long, purposeful strides, walked on ahead with his two students following close behind. Dashanan had tried to ask where they were going, but had received only a grunt for a reply. Their feet carried them along narrow jungle-paths, till they came upon wide, undulating plains. The northern sky gleamed clear blue and above the line of evergreen trees, the silvery range of the snow-clad Himalayas rose in majestic splendour. Out there in the distance, beside a free-flowing, crystal clear mountain stream, amongst boulders, large and small, stood a cottage. A hermit's abode it was, by the look of it. Shukracharya strode on towards this cottage.

An ascetic, a sagacious old Brahmin, resplendent with a thick mane of silver hairs and a flowing silvery beard to match, came out to greet them. Shukracharya bent over to touch his feet in obeisance. His students too, did likewise.

"This, my boys," Shukracharya declared, "is the greatest of all Acharyas and the giver of justice to all. He is known as Brahma. As you can see that by birth he is Aryan. But in real life he is far above such narrow minded division as per caste, creed or class. Through his qualities alone he has earned the respect of Aryans and non Aryans alike.

"Acharya Brahma, these are my students. They have recently completed their studies at my Gurukul. I would request you to work on their horoscopes and to see what the future holds for them. I have high hopes, you see."

Brahma looked at the two brothers with gimlet eyes. Dashanan felt as if even his innards were being examined.

"Come here, son," called the old man. "Sit beside me." He patted on the skin of a blackbuck spread out as a seat, beside where the sage himself sat on the skin of a tiger.

"Rakshasa, I see."

"Yes, sire, and proud to be so. Dashanan is my name. Son of Kaikasi."

"And Bishraba. Grandson of Sumali."

"Yes, sire."

"Hmmm..." Brahma sat silent for a while, gazing at Dashanan's eyes in deep concentration. Then he sighed, took a chalk and drew some intricate diagrams on the earthy floor, counted and calculated, then straightened up. After that he meditated for some time, during which the others dared scarcely breathe.

"Shukracharya, mark my words. This ward of yours will make his name in the world. A day will come when the earth will shake under his footsteps. He will be a leader of his race. But dear boy, beware of the Kshatriyas and one other non Aryan tribe, the Banaras, for they bear you no good." Dashanan touched the floor with his forehead and stepped back, as Kumbhakaran stepped forward. Brahma looked intently into your eyes.

"Shukracharya, I see a devoted soul, devoted to his brother, for whom he may lay down his life. But his own life would be, for the better part, not be utilized well at all. He will float in his own world for the better part of the year, but on other days his elders will feel that it is good to have him around. I can tell you nothing more."

The sun had dropped into the western sky when they left Brahma's dwelling. Contrary to what Dashanan had thought Shukracharya began to walk further north. When they reached the foothills, the western horizon seemed to be on fire. They began their upward climb. Their path was arduous as the terrain was difficult. Often they had to climb from boulder to boulder in places where no track was available. Ferns abound in the places they negotiated. The air was heavy with the perfume of flowers and moist foliage. At places huge evergreen trees with moss on their trunks obstructed their way. But they trudged on. At long last Shukracharya stopped, saying, "We are there." Dusk had descended and it was quite dark. Shukracharya pointed at a huge boulder leaning against the side of the hill.

"Move this boulder for me, will you?" Shukracharya said.

Dashanan applied both his hands on the boulder and Kumbhakaran applied his back to it, to push with all his strength and body weight. They ground their heels and braced and pushed. Both fell flat, Kumbhakaran on his back and Dashanan on his face. At the slightest push, the boulder had slid sideways effortlessly, while Shukracharya laughed like a child. It was a master-piece of engineering feat, well camouflaged. As the boulder slipped off, the yawning mouth of a cave was revealed. Shukracharya entered the cave and called them in.

It was pitch-dark inside. Dashanan could not even see his own hands held in front of his face. The he heard the scraping of rock on rock. The Acharya had taken out flints tucked in some unknown place. Soon a torch flared up. With a nod of his head, he strode forward into the cave.

The cave ran straight into the bowels of the mountain. After some time, it turned sharply to the right. Then it split into three possible paths. Without any hesitation whatsoever, Shukracharya took the left hand path. It climbed upwards and was strewn with chunks of stone and boulders as if in times gone by, the area had been hit by an earthquake. After a long time, the meandering, narrow passage opened into a chamber. Shukracharya raised the burning torch above his head. At once their eyes were dazzled. The light from the torch had lit up a cache of arms. Rows upon rows of armaments of all kinds were stowed in racks hewn into the rocky face. Sukracharya gestured at the weapons.

"Take your pick," said he, his voice reverberating in the close confinement of the cave. "All are made of the best quality of iron. They belonged to Tarakasura, the Asura king, who was vanquished by Kartikeya. Now I give it all to you. Take what you fancy and leave behind the rest, to be used later at your will. I give these arms to you, Dashanan. To be used as you think fit."

They spent that night in the cavern, to leave at daybreak. Shukracharya had a small store of emergency food-stuff in the cave, like beaten rice and lumps of hardened molasses, stored in stone jars to keep them safe from rodents. This satiated their hunger, while a mountain stream flowing through a crack in the cave wall quenched their thirst. They talked well into the night, well, Dashanan and Shukracharya did, while Kumbhakaran made himself comfortable in a corner and soon began snoring. They talked about many things, mostly about how to establish a new order for not only the Rakshasas but also others of the Asura race. Dashanan was now filled with a new resolve. He will raise an army of the Rakshasas to resist the Aryan expansive tendencies. But, for that he needed a head-quarter. He needed to win Lanka back.

Bishraba was at home when the two brothers arrived. The arms they carried seemed to irritate him and he said as much to his wife in *sotto voce* to his elated wife. Dashanan overheard it, but said nothing. They had been away from home for about eleven years. Dashanan wished to avoid any confrontation with his father for his mother would then be distressed. She was so happy at their return... he did not wish to destroy her happiness.

Bishraba was not a man to let up in anything. Over dinner that night, he was not even discreet.

"Those weapons, boys, I don't like them around at home. This is a Brahmin residence and I wish to keep it that way. I sent you off with Shukracharya to get some real education. But look at you! You come back laden with weapons, I don't know, you got from where, looking like dacoits."

Kumbhakaran's head snapped up at these words. He was the quiet one at home. But now his eyes flashed, but a look from Dashanan quelled him.

"Those weapons, father, are gifts from our Acharya. For your information, let me please remind you that we were trained on all the subjects that you specialise in, including Veda and philosophy, and that also we received full training in the use of arms and in Military Strategies."

"But what use are arms at a Brahmin residence? No, I shall not have that. You better give them to some eligible Kshatriya prince, while you, for yourselves, get ready to help me in my line of work as good sons of a Brahmin. I shall arrange for your sacred thread ceremony at the earliest."

"It is of no use, father. You say that we are sons of a Brahmin. Yes that we are. But we are sons of a Rakshasi too. A gem of a mother she is and we are proud to be known as her sons. Your society, father, calls us half-breed. Let it be so. We are proud to be Rakshasas. As Rakshasas we renounce your offer of a sacred thread ceremony, father. We Rakshasas have no caste."

"Is that how you talk to your elders? Is that what Shukracharya taught you?" Bishraba stood up, thoroughly enraged by now. Poor Kaikasi could only look once at her son, then at her husband, on the verge of tears. Dashanan finished his meal at leisure and stood up.

"I do not wish to belong to your society, father. Your society is only meant for the pure Aryan blood. A half caste like me will be a pariah, a source of embarrassment for you. It was your eldest son, Kubera, the usurper, who called us half-breeds, and that name still rankles father."

"Kubera, usurper! What do you mean?"

"Yes, he has usurped the kingdom of Lanka that rightfully belonged to the Rakshasas. But let him enjoy the pleasures, father. For it would not last him long."

"You dare to call my eldest son, a usurper and that too standing in my house, eating my food?"

"Yes father, I dare to. But would you rather not have us sharing the same roof as you? Come on father, tell us that!" Dashanan dared his father.

"Yes. I would rather not! And listen Dashanan, you may consider yourself to be too big, but for all I care, if you stay here you shall have to abide by my wishes and live by my rules. And that is final!"

Dashanan turned on his heels and looked at his mother. Seeing her tearful face, his resolve tottered. But then, he reminded himself that he had a tryst with destiny. Kaikasi stood up as he approached her. Dashanan cradled her face in his hands.

"Mother," said he, his voice almost breaking. "My heart weeps for you. On the very day when you thought that once again you have all your children around you, you lost your eldest. I go now mother. Don't weep for me. I shall send for you when I stand on my own feet. Take care of my brothers and sister."

"If you go, the door of this house will be shut for you forever." Bishraba thundered.

"Mother, tell your husband that I do not care about any of that. Also tell him that father or no father, no Aryan can never raise his voice at me, and never will. The Rakshasa Dashanan has spoken!" Dashanan's voice held such a majesty that his father wilted.

Dashanan went back to his room to get his meagre belongings together. He armed himself with all weapons that he could carry and made to step out of the room, when he saw his brother Kumbhakaran arming himself too.

"You too, brother?" Dashanan asked with astonishment.

"Why? Do you think that you can take care of yourself alone?" Kumbhakaran gave a wry smile. "Don't ask ridiculous questions, brother!"

Touching his mother's feet, hugging his younger brother Bibhishan, ruffling the hairs of his little sister Surpanakha, and taking leave of his mother, Dashanan took a burning torch in his hand to light up his way and stepped out of his childhood place. Kaikasi stood at the doorway for a long, long time. The dancing light grew smaller and smaller still, till it became a mere speck in the distance. It seemed as if the light was going away from her own life. Thereafter all blurred as tears overcame her self control. Bishraba was nowhere to be seen.

✦ ✦ ✦

4

The Making of a King

The slope of the hill was teeming with people. Almost all of them were able bodied young men and they were hard at the task of going through military drill. Each group of twenty were led by a sergeant. A captain oversaw the training of five such groups. The total training process was being overseen by an elderly warrior. Prahastha, the commander, and the maternal uncle of Dashanan, might have been a middle aged man, but physically he was fitter than most of the young men in training. Dashanan as the commander-in-chief, moved through the ranks supervising the training of individual groups. There were groups practicing with their swords. Those who could not be issued swords were making do with sticks. Some were wielding spears and javelins. Others were practicing unarmed combat. Far away in the plains the cavalry units were going through their paces, while on another side of the plains the archers had set up their targets and were honing their shooting skills.

After leaving their father's place the two brothers had set off at a brisk pace towards the south. They had to travel through hundreds of *Kosh* of hostile Aryan territory and they wanted to be across the Vindhya and Satpura range of mountains as early as possible. The area they now were in was held by the Kurus. Soon they would be crossing a part of the Koshala kingdom where the Ikshaku kings ruled. They would be more or less safe once they entered the Dandakaranya forests. There many Rakshasas and other non Aryan tribes were said to live. If needed, they could find sanctuary there.

Six days into their forced march, the drumming of hooves made them instantly alert. Immediately the brothers looked for cover, but there was very little cover in the plains they were negotiating. So they crouched down behind a tree and got their bow and arrows ready. Suddenly a very familiar voice boomed out.

"Don't shoot. Dashanan and Kumbhakaran, this is your grandfather Sumali. I am coming to take you along with me."

Six horsemen were riding up trailed by two pack horses and two spare rides. As they closed in, Dashanan's heart jumped with joy. The lead rider was indeed their grandfather. His burly figure was recognisable from quite some distance.

Just as he heard through his network of spies that Dashanan and Kumbhakaran had left home, Sumali had taken five of his most trusted warriors and with spare horses had ridden hard to reach them. He was very much anxious about their security. He had spies also in Lanka and he was aware that Kubera was capable of any amount of mischief in order to keep his throne safe.

Thereafter the journey was pleasant and relaxed to a degree. They gave wide berth to the area that was controlled by the Bird People because their allegiance towards the Aryans was not to be trusted.

Later they crossed the Kishkindhya kingdom, where the elderly Riksharaja was the king. They were given safe conduct through this area, although no hospitality was offered and none was asked for.

Soon enough the ground became uneven and undulating. Boulders were strewn about here and there. They were reaching the Eastern Ghats where the city within caverns, or Patal was their destination.

They flocked in their thousands. The Rakshasa grape-vine had been buzzing over the last few months. News had spread amongst the Rakshasas all throughout the land that Dashanan had come to relieve them of their miseries. People began to view him as some sort of a messiah. Fragments of information strayed into Aryan ears and they became restive. But precious little they could do about it. The area where they had made their headquarters was a tough terrain and so remote that anything short of a full-scale military operation would be futile. Kubera was becoming fidgety. But the information that most of the Aryan kings received was that the Rakshasas were regrouping. This, to their mind was harmless. What they did not know was that firstly, this regrouping thing was actually misinformation that had been judiciously spread around to lull the Kshatriya spirit. Secondly, the Rakshasas were not only regrouping, but were recruiting as well. Together with that, they had started intense and vigorous military training. As things were progressing, the Rakshasas soon would have the finest commando unit in this land and the Rakshasa army, a definite force to reckon with.

Dashanan was walking up the slope of the hill with purposeful strides. He was highly satisfied with the training process. It seemed as if whatever he had learnt at the Gurukul was being put to good use. Midway up the slope, however, his steps broke. A huge cheer from the trainees made him stop. He turned around and looked towards the north. Then his lips quivered in a faint smile. He too felt like cheering this head off.

A long caravan of ten wagons was winding its way over the fertile plains. It was escorted by about fifty horsemen, all armed to their teeth. The first horse was a huge battle charger. The rider was a giant of a man. Kumbhakaran it was. Dashanan yelled for his mount. His horse was ready and it was a twin of the charger that led the caravan. Both were very big, magnificent animals, coal black in colour and were of Kambojan origin. Dashanan vaulted on to the back of his horse and thundered down the slope to meet his brother. Kumbhakaran had been despatched with a small platoon and a caravan to retrieve that cache of arms that their guru Shukracharya had presented them with and Kumbhakaran had delivered. Now he was coming back with enough arms to equip the whole army. The much awaited campaign could begin now.

Prahastha was sceptic. That, of course, was nothing new. He always was one. He played the Devil's Advocate in the Council meeting that night.

"We are planning to take Lanka. That's fine with me, gentlemen, but are we really equipped for it? We know that Kubera has a well equipped army, comprising all four sections, the foot soldiers, the horse, the elephant and the chariot. We can never even hope to match his strength. There is a saying that attack when you are stronger. Go for truce when your opponent is stronger than you. We should not give way to emotions."

Malyaban, the elder brother of Sumali, was presiding over this meeting as he was the senior most person around. He turned and addressed Dashanan.

"What do you say, Dashanan? Prahastha's statement has some solid reason. It is true that we lack the elephants and chariots. How can we face them in battle?"

Sumali shifted in his seat.

"Dear brother," he said, addressing Malyaban. "Frontal battle against Kubera's army is out of the question. Dashanan has something else in mind."

Dashanan rose and walked over to the very edge of a ledge that overlooked a deep gorge. His unseeing eyes were focused on the horizon, beyond which lay the city of his dreams, Lanka. After standing there, motionless, for a while, he turned. His eyes unconsciously swept over the hills around. The entire slope was dotted with fire. His soldiers were having their evening meals. Soon the fires would be extinguished one after another, when they would fall asleep. Everyone depended upon him to provide the right answers. He had to deliver. He would never get a second chance. But, like any born leader he instinctively knew that he should give that much of his plan that the others needed to know. Of course, now he had to convince them that he had something hidden up in his head. He strode back to his seat, but remained standing addressing the gathering.

"We know Kubera's advantages, his strengths. But we have one great advantage and that is surprise. That is our main strength. But we have to keep in mind one great weakness of Kubera. He has no navy to speak of. This may seem strange, given that Lanka is an island state, but it is a fact that he has no battleships. That can work in our favour."

"But how?" The elderly Jambumali interceded. "We have no navy too."

"I agree. But Kubera cannot stop us when we invade Lanka from the sea."

"What exactly do you have in mind, Dashanan?" Prahastha asked.

"Listen very carefully, uncle. I shall lay the whole plan down before you now." He took a large piece of rock in his hand and placed it in the centre of the gathering, right next to the bonfire. He then took his dagger out to act as the pointer. He crouched down to sit next to the rock. The fire played on his features matching his inner fire. He was on the verge of a situation that could make him or break him. This was the most important meeting in his life.

"Let us take this rock to be the island of Lanka." He marked a point on the rock with a piece of burnt wood. "This is the Trikuta Hill and this is Lanka the city. In the dead of a moonless night, we cross over and land here at the south east part of the island, here." He tapped the desired point with his dagger's tip. The dagger caught the light of the fire and flashed in an unholy gleam. "We then cross the swamps and forest tracks to attack the city from this side. It is the least guarded area, as it is on the far side, away from the sea. Kubera knows that an attack will come. But he will be expecting us to attack from the sea. We shall circumvent him and catch him by surprise. If all goes well, then we shall be able to capture Lanka with the minimum bloodshed." Kumbhakaran was the first to give his whole-hearted support to the plan. In fact he was already aware of it as his brother had discussed every aspect of the plan with him, even before he had left to get the cache of arms from the Himalayas.

"This is the best plan we have ever discussed," said Kumbhakaran. "I am totally in its favour."

"But Dashanan," Malyaban asked. "How do we cross over?"

"Not 'we' grandfather, say 'you'. You are not going. After we take Lanka, we shall call you over."

"What!" Malyaban exploded. "Do you think that I am now too old to fight? I could still show some of you young whippersnappers some tricks!"

"I am sure of that, grandfather, and I do not think that you have grown old. You shall stay here to command our reserves and to oversee the horses, for we won't take them over too. We are taking a circuitous route and the sea journey will be much longer. It won't be too good for the horses."

What Dashanan did not elaborate was his plans after they reached the city of Lanka. They did not need to know now, he thought.

All were silent for a long, long time. Heads bowed, all the Rakshasa stalwarts pondered on what they had just heard. Each was immersed in his own private world. Dashanan still sat crouched beside the fire. The flickering fire-light played on his features and shadows flitted across. Sometimes his visage appeared to be downright cruel, sometimes tender. If he could seize Lanka, he would seize the world. The words "Half breed" kept ringing inside his head in a silent cacophony. Dashanan thought, 'What was his mother doing now? Probably she was still weeping her heart out for her lost sons. Father would surely make her life miserable, he being an Aryan and she a mere Rakshasi, a despicable species to be spat upon'.

Malyaban was internally rueing his age. Although he did not admit it, yet he felt that age was catching up on him. What he would not have given to feel an elephant under him and a lance, pulsating like a living creature in his right hand. He had lived a long and fruitful life. He desired nothing more than spending the rest of his days in recluse, if they managed to wrest Lanka from the grip of the Yaksha king.

Sumali was also thinking about Kubera. Here was a proud Aryan, a Brahmin by birth, ruling the half-caste Yakshas in the kingdom of the Rakshasas that he had seized by default. How could such men claim to be better human beings? Sumali had heard that Kubera was amassing a huge wealth, at the expense of his kingdom. Business people were having a field day in Lanka as all trade was exempt from taxation. The Governmental exchequer was being maintained by the tax the common people paid—the artisans, the small shop-keepers, the soldiers, the craftsmen, the farmers and others. Many Rakshasas had stayed back, not in the city of Lanka, but in villages scattered all over the island. They had not wanted to leave the land they had worked so hard to wrest from the tropical rain forests. But now they were paying the price. A steady trickle of Rakshasa refugees now came to Patal asking for sanctuary. These were the people who could not bear it any more. They needed help. But those who were languishing out there needed help more. He straightened his back and looked around him. He had decided to give his consent to Dashanan's rather far-fetched plan.

Kumbhakaran kept looking at his brother in astonishment. True, he had heard it all before, but now, surrounded by his own people on the war-path, all seemed possible. He was really astounded by the little part Dashanan had held back from the others. 'Does he hold something back from me too?' He asked himself. For some unknown reason, suddenly he missed their younger brother Bibhishan. Ah, Bibhishan, had you been here you would have learnt some self-respect. Possibly their venture would fail. Possibly they would all die. But death with the head held high was infinitely better than grovelling at the feet of some who tried their level best to establish that they were better people than Rakshasas. You should have been here, brother.

The old minister Jambumali was apprehensive. A military operation of this scale needed money, a huge amount of money. And this they did not have. But there was more than enough cached out there in Lanka. He wanted the whole affair of invasion to be completed and that too at the earliest. He knew which way his vote would go.

Prahastha was sceptic as usual. He wanted to know more details of the invasion plan. He knew that a well planned project ensured its success, much more than anything else. He wanted this project to succeed. He had a lot more at stake in this adventure than he had led others to believe. His elderly parents and wife had been left in his village home, back on the island, when he himself had fled. Yes, he had fled to save his neck. That was true. But an intact neck was needed to fight another day. His family he was forced to leave behind, because of the advanced age of his parents. The voyage by sea would have wrought havoc up on the longevity of the elderly couple. But now he was eager to return to Lanka. And he wanted the plan, whatever it was, to succeed. He wanted to make sure that it would succeed.

The younger commanders, Birupaksha, Makaraksha, Biparitaksha, Durdom, all were itching for action. They wanted to plunge into battle. They were all for Dashanan's plan. But, of course they could not speak their minds before the seniors have spoken. So, they waited their turn.

As was expected, it was Prahastha who broke the silence first. Noisily he cleared his throat. Then he looked around at the silent, tense faces and said:

"Dashanan, in principle I agree with you totally. But there are many things which need be taken care of at the very outset. All doubts should be cleared. I don't know whether there is any one amongst us, here who would say no to an invasion of Lanka. But to make the mission successful, we should make it as flawless as possible."

"Do you have a question in mind, uncle?" Dashanan asked.

"Just now you pointed out that Kubera has no navy. Fine enough. But nephew, neither do we! What can be done about it? How can we cross over?"

Dashanan smiled and clapped his hands. Five men materialised at once, as if out of thin air. The assembled men started at this apparition.

"These men will ferry us across, dear uncle. They are smugglers, used to making night runs in the Lanka waters. All of them have cutters that can comfortably hold twenty men each. There are ten such cutters waiting."

"Do you expect to overcome Kubera's mighty *chaturanga sena* with just two hundred men?" Sumali exploded. "This is preposterous!"

"This number is more than sufficient grandfather. They will not be ordinary soldiers. But they will be trained commandos, handpicked by myself."

"Well that is settled then?" Kumbhakaran yawned as he spoke. "Then let us break up tonight, shall we? Tomorrow we have a tough schedule ahead of us."

"But one thing needs to be settled," Jambumali remarked. "When do we attack?"

"In a week's time the monsoon returns to Lanka. Most of the nights are rainy or cloudy. There will be no moon. We attack then." Dashanan stood up as he spoke. The prolonged crouching on his heels was giving him pins and needles. "Grandfather," this time it was Malyaban he addressed to, "Can we break up now?"

"Yes, of course. But if any one has any other question, he better speak out now." Short-sightedly he peered at every person's face. "So that is settled then. We attack in a week from now."

The meeting broke up. All went where they were bivouacked. All, except three persons. These three persons stealthily moved away unnoticed. One of them was Dashanan. Reaching their camp site, he kept on walking beyond the camp, into the woods, till he came up to a cavern. Here was his secret weapon he told no one about.

The interior of the cavern was dark. Dashanan stood motionless at the cave entrance all senses attuned to catch the faintest whisper. But he heard none and smiled in satisfaction. Putting two hands on both sides of his mouth he emitted a sound that was a perfect hoot of a tawny owl. Almost immediately, this hooting was repeated, but twice and from within the cavern. Dashanan then mumbled the passwords. "The moon rises in the south." From the interior of the cave, but quite audibly came the reply, "It never does. Come in Commander-in-Chief." Dashanan boldly entered.

As he stepped across the threshold, a torch flared up deep within; twenty nubile Rakshasis were assembled there, all in different postures of relaxation, all equally scantily attired. A large collection of arms, all very useful in close combat, were strewn about. These women were Dashanan's secret weapons. They were led by a ruthless captain called Lankini. This was actually a code name. What her real name was, no one ever dared to ask. She was as merciless as she was voluptuous. Everyone of the Ladies' Brigade was a superbly fit soldier that no one knew about. They were part of an elite troupe, handpicked and personally trained by Dashanan, and were absolutely loyal to him.

"The attack begins next week," Dashanan said in a low voice. Lankini nodded. She was expecting something like this. "I go now," Dashanan declared and turned to go.

"Don't break my heart, Commander. Look I'm all eager for you." Pingalakshi, a ravishing beauty, coquettishly remarked. Underneath her flippancy, she had really fallen in love with this handsome young superior. A tinkle of laughter from all girls rolled around. Even Lankini smiled.

"Don't waste your time and energy, woman," Dashanan smilingly replied. "There are many things to do and a city to be taken."

"Ohhhh!" wailed Pingalakshi in mock anguish. Dashanan smiled again and left. He had imposed the discipline of celibacy upon himself till Lanka was taken. Afterwards? Well, who knows?

A shadow separated from the group returning from the meeting, and took a deviation as they reached camp. Soon after this shadow, another shadow flitted away in the first shadow's wake. The one who followed was a giant of a man, but extremely agile and fit for his bulk. As he moved, Kumbhakaran showed no sign of fatigue or sleepiness he had shown at the meeting. He moved soundlessly, from cover to cover and shadow to shadow, never for an instant losing sight of his quarry. The quarry moved up the hillside and reached a tiny cave near the top. There he lit a taper and scribbled some message on a thin piece of cloth. Thereafter he reached out. A cage rattled. He took out a sleepy pigeon and tied the cloth to her right foot. "I'll release you at dawn tomorrow," said he as he replaced the pigeon in her cage and turned, blissfully unaware of the fact that every action of his have been watched and every word heard by an unseen shadow mingling with other shadows. Then he turned to leave, blowing the taper out before he left. Biparitaksha's features were well lit up as he did so. Kumbhakaran did nothing. He was specifically instructed by his wily brother not to do anything. He knew what was in that message. There all details of today's plans were jotted down for Kubera's eyes. But all plans were part of a giant ruse. Dashanan had a totally new set of plans that he had not discussed with anyone, not even with him, because he had a habit of talking in his sleep, a habit that had persisted since his childhood. Kumbhakaran had nothing to complain about.

A week passed by in a frenzy of activity. Prahastha was perpetually sweating these days. He was always seen to be running about with a sheaf of dried palm leaves on which he kept his notes. He was always muttering numbers under his breath or shouting at others over something. Jambumali repeatedly counted money and took stock of everything. The training sessions were intensified and Dashanan was often nowhere to be seen. Kumbhakaran knew where he was, so he did not fret, but appeased others with inconsequential observations if people questioned Dashanan's absence from the scene. Meanwhile, Kumbhakaran kept his eyes to the sky. Every second day, a pigeon was seen to fly towards the south from a neighbouring hilltop. Kumbhakaran smiled to himself, as tension mounted. He turned and moved away from the direction of the camp. He had to meet a huntsman on the far side of the hill. That huntsman hunted with hawks.

It was the day of the invasion. Dusk had fallen. Contrary to expectation, there was no rain cloud to be seen. The visibility was wonderful with a radiant moon coming up early. But whatever happened, preparations were in such a stage that cancellation of the programme was unthinkable. They were proceeding, come what may. Ten cutters were lined up in a cove near the beach-head. Men, well armed, got aboard the cutters in quiet and disciplined file. Arms and provisions were piled in. The silence that prevailed was almost electrifying. Kumbhakaran climbed in aboard after all his select band had got in. Silently their cutter moved ahead. The invasion was on.

The cutter was sailing fast through the choppy seas. All men were sitting rock steady in their assigned seats, each immersed in his own thought. Only one was fidgety. Kumbhakaran moved over to sit beside him.

"Nervous, Biparitaksha?" he asked. Biparitaksha gave a nervous smile that was lost in the darkness. He was sitting in a shadow. The others gave a cursory glance in their direction.

"Do you like pigeons Biparitaksha?" Biparitaksha paled, although his pallor too, was unseen in the dark.

"Why do you ask?"

"No, just thought... I love pigeons. They are so lovable. Flying high in the sky, they make you almost want to fly with them. They are useful too. Carry vital messages..."

"I know all that. I don't like pigeons."

"That's too bad. I love them so much that I always have a few about me." All men in the boat were now looking at them. They had understood that something was amiss. They had heard iron in the voice of Kumbhakaran. Kumbhakaran reached down and, from under his seat he pulled out a pannier. He fished inside it and took out a pigeon. It was beautiful and white with black specs perfectly visible in the pale moonlight. It was dead.

"This poor pigeon is dead. Hunted down by a hawk. It is sad. No? Aha! I find something tied to his leg. Can you untie it for me please? You can't? Well, Durmukh, can you help me please." A young Rakshasa called Durmukh, a group captain, untied the thing tied to the leg of the dead pigeon. He spread it open.

"Sir," said Durmukh. "It is some sort of a message. But I can't read it in this dim light."

"That's a problem indeed," said Kumbhakaran. "Kalantar, can you light a taper please. Just for a while. No one can see a light here." Indeed nothing could be seen all around except the dark waters and a wan moon bobbing on the waves. A few scattered dark smudges told of the presence of the other boats in their vicinity, all speeding towards Lanka in a close formation. Kalantar lit a taper. Durmukh read out loud.

"'All is set. Off this evening.' That's all it says. What could it mean?" He asked looking all around.

"Ask our friend Biparitaksha. Perhaps he can enlighten you, because over the last few days he had been flying pigeons all over the place." Kumbhakaran's eyes flashed a luminescent red. "But I think it is meant for our friend, little King Kubera. Biparitaksha, for one who does not like pigeons, you are the most peculiar. Aren't you, friend? Because you keep a whole lot of them as pets!" Kalantar's taper blew itself out.

Biparitaksha emitted a snarl that was more feral than human and leapt towards Kumbhakaran's throat. Iron flashed in his hand in the meagre moonlight. The Rakshasas gathered around scattered. Biparitaksha was fast, but Kumbhakaran was faster. His left hand shot out to grab Biparitaksha's throat. With his right hand he plunged a long and thin blade into Biparitaksha's chest, just underneath his left breast. Biparitaksha died with the faintest of a chocking sound. No one spoke. Kumbhakaran absently pulled his blade out and wiped it on the clothes of the dead man. Four Rakshasas lifted the corpse up and swung it over the side. Immediately there was maelstrom in the waters. The sprays all but drenched the Rakshasas standing close to the side of the boat. The waters smudged dark and then as suddenly as it had begun, all was quiet as triangular fins encircled the boat. This area of the strait was infested with sharks. The boat shot forward. Kumbhakaran sighed and took out a conch-shell. An ashen faced Durmukh sat still. Biparitaksha was his controlling officer.

"You knew that he was a traitor, didn't you, sir?" He asked of Kumbhakaran. Kumbhakaran sighed.

"Yes I did."

"Then why did you allow him to send all those messages? Why didn't you kill him long ago? He has put this entire mission in jeopardy!"

"Your Commander-in-Chief is wilier than you credit him to be, my young friend. No, he did not put us into jeopardy. In fact the traitor had unknowingly helped our mission. He had forwarded everything he was fed with. The real plan, no one knows except a handful like Prahastha, Sumali and me, and of course, the captains of these boats. But enough is enough. Now it is time for us to shift into the real working plan." With this Kumbhakaran stood up in the boat, put the conch shell to his lips and blew. The sonorous tone spread all around.

Hearing the blowing conch shell from afar, Lankini, standing upright, holding onto the mast, straightened.

"There she blows. Now all others will turn back in the main run from their detour. Faster if you can, dear man," she called out to the captain. "We have to be there before the others." She and all her soldiers were dressed like ordinary village damsels. Many carried baskets with them. But these baskets were filled with weapons of all kinds. Lankini called out again. "Sir, you'll hear a second conch-shell blowing from further out there." She pointed behind her. "Put in all you can muster when you hear that, will you?"

Dashanan was standing in his cutter far behind the main body of the cutters. He had lagged behind on purpose. When he heard Kumbhakaran's conch-shell blowing, he just nodded. Prahastha standing by his side took out his own shell and blew. A large mass of cutters left their moorings and sped forward to join the advance body. These contained a number of additional soldiers, not known to any but a select few. Dashanan's ruse had been working perfectly till now. He expected that with the misinformation that he had so judiciously planted, the beach-head at Lanka where they had planned to disembark would be practically deserted as all the defensive forces would have gone over to the south-eastern coast of the island to anticipate the move of the landing parties. Dashanan's cutter leapt forward like a war horse. The invasion proper started now.

Lankini's boat was the first to reach the island. They were way ahead the others, but this was exactly according to plan. As their cutter ground to a halt, the captain silently lowered a small boat over the side. The girls shinnied down ropes hung over the side and were ferried across the shallow waters of the lagoon without getting their saris wet, and this too, was according to plan. The beach was, as they had expected, deserted. All the security forces had been sent to the south eastern coast in a wild goose chase. The girls now broke the shell of silence that they were cocooned in, so far. They began chatting, laughing and singing all at once. They picked up their basket and ambled over to the city of Lanka, hips swinging and gait, provocative.

The walls of Lanka loomed up ahead, in front of the girls, dark and foreboding in the pale glimmer of moonlight. A deep moat encircled the city. They were well aware that this moat teemed with crocodiles. The draw-bridge was up, so they were denied entry. The girls were unperturbed at this. All this they knew. They just lined up near the edge of the moat and yelled at the top of their voice. A number of sentries came running, spears at the ready. Seeing a bunch of comely damsels they visibly relaxed.

"Hey, you girls," called out one of them. "Who are you and where did you spring from?"

"We are Lankans. We had gone to the mainland for some festival, but you oafs have drawn the bridge up. Come on. Put it down fast. Don't you dare keep us waiting." Lankini replied in a loud voice.

"Will you spend some time with me? Then I'll put it down." This was followed by some ribald jokes.

Suddenly Pingalakshi caught her mid-riff and sat down groaning. Lankini ran to her, laid her down and yelled back at the sentries.

"Look, you baboons. My friend is having a severe tummy ache. If you do not lower the bridge fast, I am going to report to the Kotwal. He is my cousin twice removed."

This proved to be the ultimate weapon. The bridge came down grating and clanking. The girls crossed over and the sentries closed in, fussing over Pingalakshi, who had to be carried across. They were more solicitous than necessary. Anyway, they carried her over to the small guard-house set beside the huge main gate. There they lay her down on the single cot kept against the wall. Some ran to fetch water; some started fanning her, while one was intent on stroking her tummy.

"It's quite alright. I'm better thank you." Pingalakshi mumbled and made to sit up. The tummy-stroking sentry was very concerned at this. He grabbed her shoulder and pushed her back.

"It is alright. You just lie down, shut your eyes and take some rest. I shall look after you."

"Men, dear men, please don't crowd around. Just let her have some fresh air and she will be perfectly alright." Lankini was insistent and she practically shooed everyone outside.

Only the attendant of Pingalakshi and the captain of the guards remained.

All the other girls were seated cross-legged on the ground outside. The sentries were seemingly besotted by their coy looks. Duty, now, was the last thing in their minds. A horde of rampaging elephants charging towards them would not have driven them away from their pots of honey. Even those sentries who were patrolling the top of the rampart had climbed down. They did not want to be left out of the fun. After all who in their right frames of mind would dare invade this great, invincible city of theirs? One of the girls took out a flagon from her basket.

"Now, who wants a drink," she asked. "I am frightfully thirsty and I am going to drink some. Anyone cares to join?" An instant clamour arose and hands shot forward demanding a share of the beverage. The girl, Neelakshi, was resourceful enough to have brought a number of earthenware tumblers. The drinks were poured and handed around. A fresh flagon materialised. The heady smell of strong alcoholic beverage, together with the girls in their vicinity had turned all heads. Soon heads began to loll and the guards toppled over one after another like so many rag dolls. The strong spirit was liberally spiked with the most potent of opiate hypnotics. The girls were transformed in a trice. They leapt up and pulled out lengths of rope by which they securely tied the sentries down, and pulled them into the shadow of the wall, away from prying eyes. They then proceeded to arm themselves.

In the meantime, Lankini was being fussed over by the captain. Lankini acted like a bashful female but flirted unabashedly. She too took out a flagon from the basket she carried. The captain quaffed off cup after cup of the deadly beverage, with his eyes transfixed at the deep cleavage that had opened up before his eyes. Soon he too was in the land of dreams. Lankini whipped around to see what the other man was up to.

That kind and caring gentleman had, by this time, found Pingalakshi's body too enticing to overlook. As Pingalakshi apparently slept, he was gradually beginning to bend over the top of Pingalakshi's supine form, when he stopped in the midway. A sharp dagger-tip was an effective love-stopper. Lankini's voice grated harshly as she whispered close to his ears.

"Enough of play, big man. Now let her tits go, or I'll slice of a bit from your proud manhood." Pingalakshi's eyes snapped open. She sat up straight, adjusted her clothes, pushed the would-be-lover off from her and jumped off the bed. Not a vestige of pain could be seen anywhere on her visage in the flicker of the lamp burning in a corner. Now her dagger joined Lankini's pressing at the throat of the amorous man.

"Apart from the men outside, how many of you are there? Answer me!" She pressed the tip of the dagger into the man's throat. The man drew in a sharp breath as a trickle of blood ran out from where the dagger had impinged.

"Two more. They are on the farther side." He waved a hand showing where they were. Lankini nodded at Pingalakshi. The latter ran outside to where her fellow girls were still busy at dragging the drugged sentries closer towards the wall. She signalled to Neelakshi and three others. The girls rose and came up. All were the darkest complexioned ones. They stripped completely. Then, taking a dagger in hand, they melted within the shadows.

By the time Lankini had finished tying the amorous sentry together with the drugged captain and gagging the former, the squad of four was back. Their daggers were dripping blood. Lankini raised her eyebrows inquiringly.

"Disposed. Had to kill them." Lankini nodded and turned to the only conscious man available. She gestured towards the small iron door that led into the city and asked.

"Where are the keys?"

Fear does open gates faster than any key. Lankini took the keys from the waist of the stoned captain and unlocked the gate. Then she opened the gate a mite and peered into the city. Lanka was asleep.

"Now we wait. Let the others catch us up."

Although the city's main defences had been breached, the girls took no chances on the off chance that there might be patrolling sentries on the walls. They lined up against the wall in the darkest of shadows and sat down to wait. Dark complexioned, they simply melted in the dark shadow becoming almost invisible where they sat. The first boat following them floated in silently. The raiders shinnied down knotted ropes as the cutter slowed down a little distance away from the beach. They stepped into the water and sank down, before striking out for the coastline without splashing about. They did not advance towards the city when they landed, but crouched down close the water line, waiting for the other cutters to come in. The cutter that had brought them in, did not lower anchor, but was away in a trice. More soldiers, this time with horses, had to be transported. Moreover the first line of cutters could not block the passage of the cutters that followed. Soon the entire beachhead was teeming with Rakshasa soldiers all of whom crouched down to wait in total discipline. Ultimately the last boat arrived. Dashanan the Commander-in-Chief, alighted along with Prahastha and their faithful group of body-guards. Dashanan unsheathed his sword and pointed towards the city. This was the signal for the soldiers to move into attack formations, and they advanced stealthily under the leadership of Kumbhakaran. Lankini detached herself from the shadows and went up to Kumbhakaran and saluted.

"Welcome Commander. The gate has been secured."

Kumbhakaran returned the salute and signalled by hand signal only, that they were to form columns of two-by-two and enter Lanka through the small gate in the Guard House. At a signal from Lankini, her detachment moved up and joined the formation.

The Rakshasa soldiers were all taken by surprise at the sudden appearance of a number of damsels in their midst. But all were them were too well trained to let their amazement show. Lankini opened the small gate in the guard-house and the columns of soldiers snaked in to melt into the city.

The captains knew their job. On entering the city, they split the soldiers up into two groups. One group, under Kumbhakaran, turned towards the heart of the city where the business centre and main habitations were clustered. There they again split into two. The main group, comprising of the best combatants, were led away by Kumbhakaran towards the army barracks, to secure that area. The rest did nothing but to merge in the shadows and wait for their call to secure the residential areas. Intelligence had been of top order and all of them knew the exact lie of the city, its weakest spots and the strongest points of possible resistance. The other group, comprising mainly of commandos and the women troupes, swung across towards the higher grounds wherein lay the Royal Palace and the aristocratic district. This group was led by none other than Dashanan himself.

It took Kumbhakaran much less time than anticipated to secure the army barracks. The main reason was that the larger portion of the army, including the cavalry and the elephants and gone away to the other side of the island on a wild goose chase. This was a masterpiece of misinformation. Within a few moments the scattered groups of guards was all disarmed, tied down and the sleeping soldiers put under arrest. The barracks fell without a sound and without any bloodshed. At a nod from Kumbhakaran, six archers lit fire arrows and shot them upwards towards the sky.

The city group was waiting for these fire-arrows. As they saw them snake upwards, they came out into the open and began patrolling the streets. The taverns were closed down and the late night revellers packed off towards home unceremoniously. The city fell, again without bloodshed.

Dashanan was anxiously scanning the sky, from his crouched position of concealment in the shrubbery that ran along the perimeter wall of the Royal Palace. He knew that all was proceeding according to the meticulously prepared plans. Even then he could not cut down his heart rate, which seemed to be racing like a wild horse. Seeing the fire-arrows streaking upwards, he leapt up to his feet, unsheathed his sword and bayed like a wolf. This was the signal for all out attack. Hundreds of ropes snaked upwards from within the shadows. The grapnels found their grip on the palace ramparts and hundreds of dark-clad figures shinnied silently up the ropes to drop on to the palace grounds, without a sound. Then they converged on to the palace itself.

By this time a smaller detachment of soldiers moved away from the palace and spread out in the whole of the aristocratic district of the city. Every house therein, was put under guard and the inhabitants put under arrest.

In the meantime, Dashanan moved into the palace, followed by his commandos, as lithe and as silent as a group of black panthers. Then first blood was spilled. The Imperial Guards stood not a modicum of chance against these trained commandos. They were the pick of the Yaksha soldiers. But years of inaction as palace guards had robbed them of the required alertness and combative skills. Now their waist-lines had grown and most of their prowess was centred around the parade grounds, taverns and in bed. But they put up a fight, nevertheless. Clashes of iron soon rang out in the palace corridors and blood was spilled. Bodies of the Guards lay scattered about in remorseless abandon as the Rakshasas sprinted up the stairs to the Royal bed chamber.

Kubera was in bed with one of his concubines, blissfully unaware of the happenings all around. He was so engrossed in his thrusts into the maiden form crushed underneath his massive bulk, that he did not hear the muted scuffles coming from outside his closed doors. As he climaxed, the door crashed open. Kubera turned to see his own half-brother standing there with blood splattered all over him, holding a naked sword in hand. Kubera jumped up and went for his sword hanging in its scabbard from the bed-post. He cut a strangely comical figure in his obese nudity.

"I wouldn't, if I were you, brother," cautioned Dashanan.

"What do you want? Don't you know that it is a culpable offence to enter the King's room without permission?"

"I don't need any permission from the likes of you," Dashanan replied with utter disdain.

"Guards!" called the naked king.

"There's no one to hear your call, dear brother. Now you get dressed and come with me. We have some matters of state to discuss. And you," this was to the pretty girl, lying there, watching the proceedings with wide-eyed amazement, drawing up the bed-sheets right up to her neck to cover her bare torso. In the present circumstances, the blood-splattered bravado of the manly Dashanan had aroused in her carnal interest. "You scoot." Dashanan was brief and to the point. The girl let go of the bed-sheet and padded over across the room, proud in her nudity, disappearing into the inner sanctum. Kubera dressed in silence. He was escorted under guard to the court-room.

Rows of flaming torches in the brackets in the walls dispelled all vestiges of darkness from the court-room. Dashanan was sitting on the throne and Kubera was standing in front of him, unarmed and unfettered.

"Dear brother of mine, Lanka, as you can well understand by now, has fallen. I have a specific proposal for you."

"I do not negotiate with a usurper," replied the deposed king.

"Usurper, brother? Why? That's the best joke I heard tonight!"

"Yes, you are that and don't call me 'brother'."

"Ah yes. You are an Aryan! How can a Rakshasa be your brother? But that's a different and inconsequential issue, citizen

Kubera. The main thing is that, as a king I could have you thrown into the dungeon, or let you be trampled underfoot by a war elephant. But I do not want to take recourse to either of these options. I shall set you free. Leave Lanka before sun rises today, along with a hundred of your chosen companions. You are never to set foot upon this realm again. That is an order."

"But how shall I leave? By my Pushpak?"

"Forget Pushpak. You shall leave by sea in your own barge. Get yourself ready to be gone. Oh, yes, your queens will accompany you. Let it be known that Dashanan is magnanimous."

"But what will you do with the Pushpak? You won't be able to pilot it!"

"I am a quick learner," replied Dashanan with a smile.

Thus Lanka fell to the Rakshasas. Kubera left in the wee hours of morning with his henchmen and all his queens. The first thing that Dashanan did next morning, was to send a fleet messenger to the Yaksha forces assembled at the other end of the island, ordering the commander to lay down arms at the feet of the new king as the old king had fled the capital. He knew that these soldiers will surely surrender as sans Kubera they were now like a rudderless ship. After that he set about in consolidating his victory. Celebrations were muted and retaliation banned. Those amongst the Yakshas, who wanted to leave the island, were allowed to do so. Prahastha was of the opinion that these men should be thrown into the dungeons for life or better still, be done away with. But Dashanan would not listen. He did not want his kingdom to be built on rivers of blood. His aspirations ran much higher than worrying about a few stray soldiers.

Dashanan had about him a very knowledgeable, wise and loyal group of counsellors. With their help, he set about to build a new Lanka—a Lanka that would be a sanctuary of learning, knowledge, free thinking, valour, equality and brotherhood. All discriminations regarding caste and creed were done away with. Employment and education became universal. Lanka thrived to become the crown jewel of the non Aryan world. It was Dashanan's ambition to recover the lost glories of the Rakshasas and other non Aryans and he was singularly successful in achieving it. The tax burdens were eased and people plied their trade with easy minds.

Within a very short time Dashanan consolidated his hold on the island kingdom. But the most pleasant surprise that lay in store for him was the coming of his younger brother and little sister, well, not so little anymore.

Bibhishan's coming was godsend to Dashanan. Bibhishan was a good tactician in civilian matters and he was invaluable as a financial advisor, though at times it seemed as if he was a bit stingy. But the austerities that he advocated and imposed were needed for the fledgling kingdom. Dashanan understood this and did not interfere with his brother's ministrations. Lanka began her march towards prosperity.

If Bibhishan proved himself to be an asset, Surpanakha proved herself to be a disaster. Dashanan had no idea that she was a nymphomaniac. She had grown up to be voluptuous teenager, hankering for sex. Dashanan had received some reports about her problem, but gave little credibility to them. But one day, he saw her going about it, with his own eyes. It was with a captain of the guards that she had indulged with carnal excesses in a less frequented corner of the palace corridor. But as luck would have it, Dashanan had chosen this route as a short-cut to the court-room. As he turned round a corner, muted animal sounds drew his attention. Then he saw his little sister having it out with the guards' captain. The captain was transferred to a remote border outpost in the mainland and a woman body-guard was appointed for Surpanakha as her chaperone. But Dashanan realised that he should give his sister away in marriage at the earliest.

But no problem could compare with that created by his trusted general Kumbhakaran. Kumbhakaran was basically a man of action. In peace time he fidgeted about, not content in living without excitements. Dashanan had given him a responsible post; that of the commander of armed forces. But Kumbhakaran found that it was a pen-pusher's job. He sometimes went out for hunting expeditions, but soon found that there were not many predators around in the jungles of the small island state. In order to ward off the tremendous boredom, Kumbhakaran began to indulge in drugs like opium. His hours became irregular. Often he had to be carried back home by soldiers. Dashanan was caught in a quandary. There was none whom he could trust more with the responsibilities of the post held by Kumbhakaran. Yet, this problem was bad for the morals of the armed forces. Dashanan had no way out, but to relieve him of his post. He tried very much to get his brother to quit the addiction, but all to no avail. Kumbhakaran's level of indulgence increased to such an extent that he could not exist without the effect of drugs.

"Brother," Kumbhakaran told him one day. "I have become a total liability for you."

"Don't take it that way," Dashanan chided. He loved this brother of his more than he loved himself. "Why don't you kick this obnoxious habit and come back to the mainstream. You have always been my right hand and you know it." Kumbhakaran shook his head.

"Brother, I have gone so far that I cannot stay away from it. What I would suggest is that you take another extreme course of action." Dashanan's eyes narrowed.

"What is that?"

"You get a bed-chamber for me built away from the palace, on the other end of the grounds. Let me stay there in peace. I give you my word that once in a while, I shall come back to you with a clear head to help you in any way you need."

The deal was struck and Kumbhakaran removed himself from social life. Dashanan sorely missed his brother's presence at his side.

✦ ✦ ✦

5

Matrimonial

Prahastha had made the king's life hell. Almost every day, he pestered Dashanan about the necessity of marriage. A king needed a queen at his side. This brought him credibility and rendered stability to the kingdom. That was what Prahastha said. At last he gave in to the wish of his Prime Minister. He consented to marriage. Emissaries were sent to all non Aryan kings in search of marriageable daughters.

Lanka was now stable. Dashanan's rule, based on justice, equality and a positive work-culture soon made the kingdom one of the most prosperous one in the whole country. But this stability made Dashanan restive. He was a soldier, a man of action. He decided that he had to do something. He wanted to march out on the war-path, but his army was not ready as yet. So, as the next alternative he elected to go hunting and that too in the mainland. When he went hunting he wanted to match his wits and strength against the most ferocious of predators to be found on the mainland.

Dusk was setting in. Dashanan, alone and on foot was following the tiger he had wounded a short while ago. A brief lapse of concentration had ended in his less than lethal shot. So, he followed it the whole day, more out of compassion. He wanted to finish what he had started. He did not want the animal to survive maimed and in agony.

At long last he could find his quarry. The tiger had taken shelter in a shade on the bank of a rivulet. Dashanan crept stealthily up to where the beast lay. Silently he fitted an arrow to his bow and drew. The tiger, out of some unfathomable survival instinct, turned his head and looked at him. As he leapt up to attack, Dashanan let his arrow fly. This time he did not miss.

Then, on his way back, Dashanan foolishly lost his way. It was so dark that one could not even see the fingers of one's own hands. Fortunately, Rakshasas had an uncanny sense of direction, so Dashanan at least could proceed in the direction of the camp. But Dashanan missed a bifurcation *en route*. So he walked on and on, blindly and utterly helpless. Now he rued the fact that he had not come on horse-back. His horse could easily have homed in with unerring precision.

At long last he came upon a clearing in the forest. Right across, on the far side of the clearing, was a palace. Never before had Dashanan seen such a splendour carved in marble. In the faint light of a crescent moon hanging limply from a star-lit sky, the palace seemed to glow in its own illusory internal radiance. Gripping his great bow in his left hand and his right hovering near the hilt of his sword, Dashanan crept up to the mysterious palace.

The palace appeared to be deserted at first sight. A wide flight of steps led up to the front foyer. It was an immense pillared hall. The hall, as such, was bereft of furniture, but the pillars were worth seeing. They were made of marble and were intricately decorated with wreaths of golden vines and flowers and fruits of lively gems of diverse colours. All light came from concealed lamps, strategically placed. A fountain, flowing with the faintest of tinkling musical note, adorned the centre of the room. Its water was illuminated by a well concealed light source, which wove a magical wave of changing colours. In stark contrast with the pillars and walls, the floor was shining black, seamless marble. The walls swept up to a marble dome that was all but obscured by a strange mist that emanated a pleasant, refreshing aroma. The air was refreshingly cool and appeared to be silently circulating throughout the hall.

"May I help you, sir?" A voice said from behind him making him almost jump out of his skin. Dashanan turned to find a liveried footman standing there with half a smile on his lips. The man was obviously of Danava descent. He was tall with a powerful build. His complexion was dusky, almost like burnt copper.

"Whose palace is this?"

"It belongs to the Danava king, Maya."

"Ah, that explains the wonderful architecture." The name of Maya was not unknown to Dashanan. Maya was a great architect and a scientist *par excellence*. Though he was often compared with the Deva architect, Vishwakarma, there was actually no comparison. Maya was by far, way better than his Deva counterpart. This was mainly because he was very innovative.

"May I know who you are, sir? I shall let our king know about you," the footman said.

"Tell him that the Rakshasa king Dashanan of Lanka would like to have the pleasure of King Maya's acquaintance." The footman conjured up a cushioned stool for Dashanan to sit upon and disappeared into the inner recesses of the palace.

Dashanan did not have to wait for long. In a while King Maya came in with long strides. He was a big man, almost matching Dashanan's stature and Dashanan was no dwarf. Maya came in, all smiles, and embraced Dashanan.

"What a pleasant surprise!" said he.

"The pleasure is all mine," replied Dashanan.

"You have come alone, I see," said the Danava king. "That's unusual."

"Actually I had come for hunting. I had gone alone after a tiger I had foolishly wounded. By the time I finished him off, night had fallen. Then I lost my way. I had no idea that I was heading into your realm. I apologise for my intrusion."

"Oh no, that's nothing, my boy," said Maya, slapping Dashanan on his back. "Come, let's go inside the palace. You freshen up first and then we talk. It is not very often that I get the chance of talking to a civilised person in this wilderness, and I am not letting this chance go."

For a man of his build, it was strange that Maya was a vegetarian. To Dashanan's enquiring glance, he smilingly told him that he was vegetarian by choice and a teetotaller, for he believed that a surfeit of meat and alcohol addled the brain and muddled the senses. This statement was enough to fuddle the senses of Dashanan, so he concentrated on his roasted pea-fowl and the excellent wines.

"Your Highness," said Dashanan, after finishing his third course in silence. "I am curious to know something, if you don't mind."

"Not at all, my boy. Ask anything that comes to your mind."

"You are far from your own capital. Why so? Why do you prefer to stay in this recluse, so far from your relatives and friends, without many attendants?"

"That, my son, is a long story." Maya sat for a while, apparently collecting his thoughts. Then he said, "My boy, I have made many mistakes in life. But there's one mistake that surmounts all.

"You see, I had married outside my clan. That was a grave mistake. I should have stuck to Asuras. But, no! I had to go out of my way to court an Apsara, who, you know, are of mixed Aryan descent. True, their blood contains traces of the non Aryan, but still they, the Apsaras and Gandharvas have a greater proportion of the Aryan in their blood.

"Hema was an Apsara I had fallen madly in love with. That was about twenty three years ago. I was then an arrogant young man, at the height of my confidence that I was the best architect on earth. There was none who could compete with my scientific discoveries. I considered myself better than even the Deva scientist Vishwakarma. It was then I met this Apsara called Hema at Indra's court. She was a dancer there. I had been staying with the Devas for a stint, trying to coax the truth of aerodynamics from Vishwakarma. Hema was enthralled at my bearing and verbosity. She too fell in love with me, and we got married. A whirlwind love followed and over the next successive years she bore me a daughter, Mandodari, and two sons, Mayavi and Dunduvi. But, gradually, she became very fidgety. I could make out that she was getting upset by our ways. She considered the Danavas were not civilised enough." With this he stopped, looking outside the window, vacantly into the night, communicating with his own inner self. Dashanan dared not break the fragile silence.

"Thirteen years ago," resumed Maya, "she decided that she could take it no more. She was from the danseuse sect, who could not stay away from the stage and her ankle-bells. She decided to return to the Deva capital. She wanted to resume dancing. I did not stop her from going. I could have, but didn't. I had seen her spells of depression. I loved her too much to sit back and let her suffer. So I let her go. She left, never to return. I brought my children up by my own hands. I got this recluse built and stayed back here in semi-retirement. I had considered following the path of ascetics, but my responsibilities towards my daughter, as yet unmarried, held me back.

"So, that's my story. I hope you'd forgive me for boring you stiff with my tale of woes."

Before Dashanan could reply, a faint tinkling of ankle-bells and a whiff of some exclusive perfume distracted him. A damsel with an ethereal beauty and celestial grace floated in.

"Meet my daughter, Mandodari," Maya introduced her. Dashanan was smitten. Mandodari looked at Dashanan and found him staring unabashedly at her. She lowered her eyes.

The next morning, Dashanan had a request for Maya. He asked for his daughter's hand in marriage. Maya was elated and he gladly agreed.

There was elation in Lanka and celebrations galore. Their king was getting married! What could be better news than that? People in the street had nothing else to talk about. The owners of the pubs treated the last customers with free drinks. There was singing, dancing and frolicking in the streets as never before. Lanka went mad with joy.

In the midst of all this joy, Dashanan was pensive. He missed the fellowship of his brother Kumbhakaran. These days Kumbhakaran was never seen in public. Only rarely he appeared sober enough to come to attend court. But when he did he showed a quick grasp of all matters regarding state affairs, only such occasions were rare. Dashanan talked matters over with his minister and mentor, Prahastha. Both decided that perhaps the best thing would be to get him married. So, envoys were sent far and wide in search of possible brides, not only for Kumbhakaran, but for Bibhishan as well. As for Surpanakha, Dashanan had decided to marry her off to the king of the Kalakeya clan of Danavas, called Bidyujjihwa.

The envoys returned within a few months with news of several good matches for Kumbhakaran and Bibhishan. Dashanan decided upon the great granddaughter of the famous Danava king Virochan, called Bajrajwala, as a wife for Kumbhakaran and Sarama, the daughter of Shailoosha, the king of Gandharvas, as a wife for Bibhishan. Dashanan was well aware of the affinity of the Gandharvas for the Devas, yet he voted on this match because of Bibhishan's likings for the Aryan ways of life.

Four royal weddings in tandem! The Lankans went crazy with joy. The celebrations that followed were nothing like Lanka had ever seen before.

Dashanan's father-in-law, King Maya, gave him a special gift that he had devised himself. It was a unique missile launcher that worked on the principle of compressed air. He had also designed special missiles from a new alloy that was stronger than iron, but much lighter in weight. The entire contraption could easily be operated by a single person. He stayed back for about six months in Lanka. Within this time he taught Dashanan how to operate the Pushpak and the basics of navigation. Dashanan soon became an expert pilot. Maya, in this period, also designed several other war machines for Lanka's defence. These he installed over the gates of the city. Specially trained sentries manned these machines day in and day out. Lanka now became the most impregnable city on earth.

A year went by and soon the Rakshasas had another reason for rejoicing. Queen Mandodari had given birth to a handsome, strong little boy. As he was born, the little prince almost brought the roof down with his hearty cry. He was so vociferous, that his father smiled and said, "The little one's cries are thunderous. Let him be called Meghnad." Meghnad grew up to be a great warrior and brought pride to his race.

Dashanan was becoming restive. Years of inactivity now began to tell upon his patience. One morning he stood on the roof of his palace to welcome the sun. The city of Lanka, still half asleep stretched out before him. The gold plated roofs of the golden city dazzled in the morning sun. Beyond the ramparts lay the beach, the same one he had landed on years ago, with his army. Far away the blue sea sparkled like a million diamonds in the rays of the rising sun. It was a sight that inspired all to do great things. Dashanan turned and sent his body-guard along to fetch his minister, Prahastha. He wanted to take his minister's advice before he called a meeting of his council of ministers. He wanted to launch a fresh offensive. He wanted to take the war to the threshold of his main enemy, the Aryans.

✦ ✦ ✦

6

Under the Golden Flag of Lanka

The trumpets trilled. The drums rolled. Golden Rakshasa flags fluttered in the breeze. The heavy tread of foot-soldiers shook the earth. The cavalry trotted out of the stables, followed by the chariots with clattering wheels. Elephants trumpeted to add to the cacophony. Orders rang out. The Rakshasa army was on the move.

Ravaṇa stirred in his couch. Night was closing in on the scorched city. The ministers were late. He felt a stirring of restlessness. Memories of past glory had made him restless. But what glory? To what end? In his campaign he had faced reverses too. Unfortunately for him, these reverses had mostly been in the hands of non Aryan kings alone. The Aryans, not one of them, could withstand the ferocious discipline of the Rakshasa army on the march.

Dashanan had received the first jolt in the kingdom of Varuna. The land was green and peaceful. Coconut palms teemed and the whole area was overrun by watery inroads from the sea. The palace itself was almost in a recluse, surrounded by moats and waterways. The gardens were studded with fountains and crisscrossed by streams. The Varuna army, led by his ministers and sons, had stood no chance against the vastly superior Rakshasa army.

Dashanan had seated himself on the grand throne vacated by Varuna. The throne was made of ivory and was studded with cowries. A gentle tinkling of running water from the myriads of fountains decorating the hall of Varuna's court, added serenity to the environments. Varuna was nowhere to be seen. He had reportedly gone over to the far away Himalayas to attend a music conference with Brahma. These days he was seldom seen in his own kingdom. He had recently been upgraded to a Deva status and given the charge of all waterways. His eldest son now stood in chains, in front of Dashanan.

"Why did you oppose me?" asked Dashanan. "I had not expected it."

"Why hadn't you?" Varuna's son arrogantly asked.

"My campaign is against the Aryans. I am not interested in warring against non Aryan kingdoms."

"We are Aryans," came the haughty reply.

"No you are not. Look back into your genealogy, my boy. Don't forget your past. Only over the last few centuries or so, your forbearers have been dallying with the Aryans and specifically with the Devas. But that does not make you a true, blue-blooded Aryan!"

"What do you mean, sir?" The lad was indignant, though a bit confused now. Dashanan sighed and looked about him. The Varuna contingent was huddled together in a corner of the hall. There he espied a figure in deep red silk and sporting a flowing beard and shoulder length hair, both silvery in colour. Dashanan stood and with palms joined together, asked him to come forward.

"You are the Royal Priest, I believe," he observed.

"Yes, I am. I am Bishwambhar, a Brahmin."

"I think you have an idea about what I am speaking about. Don't you?"

"Yes I have."

"All right. Then you can correct me if I am wrong." He turned to face the young prince. "Now, dear prince, listen carefully to what I say. Varuna is your family name. A thousand years ago, or maybe more, one of your forefathers resided in a flourishing city on the bank of the River Sindhu. He was a sage and one of the wisest men around, enjoying a god-like status in his community. For some unfathomable reason, the invading Indra left him as well as his wife and son unharmed. He abducted them, and kept them hostage under his own protection. There Varuna befriended the Brahma, who was a great philosopher in his own rights. The subsequent Indras were careful to integrate parts of the local religious practices that prevailed into their own religion and the ancient Varunas were given a god-like status. But your ancient people were a proud lot. They remained aloof till about a couple of hundred years ago. Possibly regular marriage into the Aryan families had diluted the ancient non Aryan trait in your blood. They conveniently forgot about the friends and relatives who had been slaughtered. They became part of the Aryan society and were integrated into the Devas." Dashanan stopped and looked at the priest. The elderly man bowed his head and said nothing. The young prince fidgeted.

"I am a Deva, and I shall die a Deva," said the prince arrogantly.

Dashanan absently looked outside the window. The green coconut trees nodded their heads in unison, as if calling out to him. He was thinking of Vedawati. His love had made him mellow. He waved a hand for the prince and his retinue to be taken away. He then appointed a governor for the province and ordered his army to march. He was going back to Vedawati.

But Vedawati was dead! Dashanan's world seemed to come apart at this news. He put all Brahmins to sword and had the entire village torched. Then he flew out with his army to ravage all Aryan kingdoms that lay in his path. Swords flashed, blood poured, cities destroyed, all in revenge. The golden flag of Lanka flew proudly over the greater part of this land. Koshala fell under the marching Rakshasa feet, as did Anga, Kashi, Matsya, Malla, Madra, Kuru, Panchal, and such other states. The golden flag flew over kingdoms as far north as that of Gandhara.

Dashanan was worried. The blockade was going on for about a week now, but the opponents had not relented a wee bit. After overrunning the Kinnara state, the Rakshasas were heading towards the Himalayas when suddenly their path was obstructed by a strong contingent of the non Aryan Nibatkabaj Danavas. The Nibatkabaj were renowned for their phenomenal physical strength, iron hard resolution, straight-jacketed discipline, and wily improvisation. All these factors, so lacking in any of the Aryan armies faced, together with the fact that they were non Aryans, caused Dashanan to hesitate about a full-scale onslaught. But, now, it was an impasse. Their forward movements were blocked and retracing steps would cost much in the ways of planning, resources.and prestige. This, Dashanan could not afford at this juncture. So he started to devise other means to surmount the problem.

"Sire, I have come to know the name of the one person whom the Nibatkabaj respect very much." The spy looked about him furtively, as he reported to his king.

"Who is he?" Dashanan asked.

"The Brahma."

"A Deva? Then he will spurn my offer for sure."

"No, Your Majesty. From what I heard, Brahma is different from other Devas. He is very logical and impartial. That's what people say, my Lord."

The spy had been correct in his assessment. Brahma had seen at once that Dashanan wanted no bloodshed and he agreed to intercede with the Nibatkabaj on his behalf. The meeting with the Danava chief had been very fruitful The Danava had seen eye-to-eye with Dashanan's view of non Aryan solidarity. But they had certain obligations, he said, that could not be surmounted. For generations together, the Nibatkabaj had stayed cheek-by-jowl with the Devas. Initially there had been a great deal of hostilities, but now peace had returned. The military supremacy of the Danavas had forced the Devas to sign a treaty of non aggression with them. Though it was done many centuries ago, both the sides had kept their end of the agreement. They had obstructed the Rakshasas' path, because it led straight on to the Manas Lake and the Kailash, the realm of the Shivaites.

"Do you know the history of Lord Shiva?" the Danava asked, while he was chatting with the Rakshasa chief. Dashanan sipped the exquisite Madhwi that the Danava chief had brought in and nodded in the affirmative.

Centuries ago, during the heydays of Asura civilisation, religion was very simple. Fertility was worshipped with Pashupati being the male driving force and the Mother as the female. They had been the precursors of the concept of Purush and Prakriti which would evolve in the later days. The chief priest was the most powerful man in the realms and was known as the Shiva or the Constant. He was faithful to this name and was the most respected person in all the city-states. With time the Shiva was deified and had merged with Pashupati. When the Aryans came in and drove the Asuras out of their birthplace, their nascent religion absorbed the Pashupati-Shiva as their own. The Devas were in need of an iconic figure and what could be better than Pashupati? They called the Shiva, Devadideva, or the Deva who was the original Deva, and Mahadev or the greatest Deva of all. Shiva continued to be worshipped as a god by the Aryans and non Aryans alike and true to this tradition, the subsequent Shivas all maintained equal distance from these two peoples, although personally they stuck to their non Aryan ways. The present Shiva stayed far away from civilization in his recluse in the Himalayas, beyond the Manas Lake, near the Kailash peak. His own army was exclusively non Aryan and was known by the name of Pretas. His wife, deified as Prakriti incarnate, was also a non Aryan woman, the daughter of a king from a mountain tribe and was known as Parvati. The sanctity of their place of residence was maintained by the Preta army in the mountains and the Nibatkabaj in the foothills.

"If you want to pay your respect to the Shiva and his consort, I would suggest that you go there alone and on foot. I shall arrange for a team of guides to take you into the mountains. Let your army wait here till you return, and enjoy our hospitality," the Danava offered. Dashanan gladly accepted.

For seven days they had been climbing into the hills. The path was arduous and the terrain very difficult. But Dashanan was physically very fit and kept pace easily with his four guides, all of whom were mountain people and as sure footed as mountain goats. The view was exquisite. Snow encompassed most of the landscape with stark peaks surrounding them on all sides. They passed a few lakes on their way, where the waters were, miraculously, not frozen, in spite of the severe cold. The guides said that this was due to the blessings of the Shiva. Dashanan was sceptic. He did not believe in the supernatural and knew that there had to be some scientific reason for this phenomenon, most probably volcanic.

This was the wrong time of the year to visit these parts. Winter was at hand and the cold increased with every passing day. Way back they had left the last of the hamlets and the greens behind. Even the conifers had dwindled away. No birds or animals were to be seen anywhere. On the seventh day, the weather became inclement. Dark, foreboding clouds closed in and it began to snow heavily. The wind howled. A blizzard began blowing. The guides felt that it was foolhardy to proceed further and they took their shelter in a cave, where they lit a fire, cooked their meal and, after an early dinner, fell into their bear-skin beds. In the wee hours of morning, Dashanan and his guides were rudely awakened by a thunderous roar. The entire hillside shook, as if by a stroke of a giant sledge-hammer. "Avalanche!" cried the guides in alarm. A snowy ledge from somewhere up above had broken loose and had dropped down to bury them alive.

Dashanan groped his way towards the mouth of their cave. The fire they had lit had burnt down to mere embers now and it was almost completely dark. The mouth of their cave was sealed off by a mountain of snow. There was no escape. Dashanan ran his hand over this snowy seal and could detect no opening. Then, suddenly, a cold breeze wafted in from somewhere. There was a chink in the block, large enough to permit entry for one hand. All of them began scraping and digging around this tiny hole with their weapons. But it was almost an impossible task. Dashanan's sword snapped into two. The guides fell back, exhausted, their hands bleeding with their efforts of digging out an escape route. In the first light of dawn entering through this hole, Dashanan saw that his companions had given up hope. But he was not the one to give in that easily. He went back to the small opening and tried to peer outside. The blizzard of last night had stopped and the sun had risen, causing the snow to sparkle in blinding flashes. He put his mouth close to the opening and bellowed, "Help!" His sonorous voice filled the cavern and could be heard echoing all around the bleak environment. He shouted again, and again, and yet again.

After the blizzard had stopped, the Shiva put together a scouting team of Preta volunteers under the leadership of his general, Nandi, to scour the mountains in search of any living being trapped in the night's snow-storm. They had now come down from their lofty quarters to their winter camp beside a hot spring. At first light the platoon of volunteers set off to scour the hills.

It was Nandi, who first heard the faint cry for help. His hearing ability was far above any average person. He called in his troopers and they set off towards the part where the sound had come from, yelling at times to keep in touch with the victim of the blizzard.

"It was your roar that saved the day for you," Shiva smilingly said. They were sitting around a blazing fire. Dashanan and his companions sat huddled in their bear-skin blankets, now sufficiently recovered from their ordeal.

"I am told," Shiva continued, "that your tremendous roar or 'rava' set the mountains trembling. I, therefore, rename you, 'Ravana'. Through this name, bestowed upon you by me, you shall declare your Shivaite status." Ravana prostrated himself in front of the great ascetic in acceptance.

"It has also been brought to my notice that your sword is broken. I shall gift my sword Chandrahash to your care. Use it judiciously to protect the downtrodden and it will serve you well."

After spending a couple of days with the divine couple, Ravana and his retinue left for the plains. Nandi and his team of hand-picked guides showed them the way down to their camp in the foothills. The Danava chief ran up to hold him in a close embrace. Prahastha, standing close behind him, smiled. They had all given him up for dead. The Rakshasa army waved the golden flags and shouted, "Hail Ravana, the Emperor of Lanka!" In response, Ravana unsheathed the sword Chandrahash from its scabbard and held it aloft. The vicious blade flashed in the glare of the sun. The Nibatkabaj Danavas took up the cry, "Hail, hail! The cry increased in crescendo and rolled onwards to spread all over the land, from the mountains to the seas; from shore to shore! The days of Aryan supremacy were gone! The golden days of non Aryan rule had returned!

✦ ✦ ✦

7

Charged with Treason

Ravana stroked the bejewelled scabbard housing the Chandrahash. Till date he had never had the occasion of unsheathing this weapon of destruction, in anger. But things appeared to be changing now.

Someone knocked. Ravana straightened and ordered the intruder to enter. It was no intruder. It was his Prime Minister, Prahastha, entering with his senior minister, Saran.

"Your Majesty," Prahastha addressed him formally. "All are here."

"Ask them to enter. And Uncle, first ask the maid to light the torches."

The maid came in immediately and the torches were lit, lighting the cosy chamber up like daylight in their splendour. Ravana's seat was upon a slightly raised platform. In front of him a number of chairs were arranged in a close semi-circle. All filed in, led by Prahastha. Saran brought up the rear. They paid their homage to their king and seated themselves in their assigned seats, with the two nearest chairs being occupied by Prahastha to his right and the Crown Prince, Meghnad, towards his left. Ravana scanned the faces before preparing to speak. They all were tense, expectant. Bibhishan was pale under his tan. Meghnad's jaw was set. Prahastha was frowning with his eyes focussed on eternity. The minister of finances, Jambumali, was sitting in a corner, contemplating his fingernails. The younger generals, together with Nikumbha, the celebrated son of Kumbhakaran, were all eagerly waiting for him to begin. Saran's face was devoid of any expression. It was at this juncture, a heavy tread resounded in the adjoining hall. The doors of polished teak, studded with knobs of gold, swung open to reveal a huge, powerful figure.

"Hail to the King of Rakshasas!" The sonorous voice boomed. Ravana almost jumped up with joy. Bibhishan scowled with chagrin.

"Kumbhakaran, brother! You have come!" said Ravana.

"Yes, brother. I came awake this afternoon and heard about the present crisis. How could I not rush to your side?" Kumbhakaran gruffly replied.

"Welcome brother, but why don't you come in and take your seat?" Kumbhakaran entered with heavy, measured tread and seated himself. He looked as powerful as ever. Only now his waist-line had grown up to more than the desired girth. His eyes looked puffy and were red-rimmed and there were pouches under his lower lids, pouches that were not there before. Ravana cleared his throat and began.

"My friends, the enemy is at our door. This time we have to fight to save the sanctity of our golden city of Lanka. Never before, in the history of the present rule, had the Rakshasa stronghold been under threat of invasion. I have called you all in to get your views in this matter. Now, speak!" Ravana ordered. Prahastha was the first person to speak.

"My king," said he, "the question is not whether we should resist any invasion or not. The question is whether we should fight at all or not. We have all seen the havoc a single monkey-man had wrought upon our city. We have lost a large number of men and commanders. All damage had been brought about by one man, in a single-handed effort. He had broken down our defence system as well. More such monkey-men will soon be swarming all over us. Will it be prudent to allow them to enter our city perimeters? Or should we opt for peace and hand over the hostage to the Ayodhya prince?"

"Are you afraid, Prime Minister?" Meghnad obtusely asked. "If you are, then let me assure you that your prudence is unfounded. Hanuman had caught us unawares. We had been guilty of underestimating our adversary and had paid the price."

"No, prince, I'm not afraid," replied Prahastha. "I'm not the one to be moved easily to fear. You know that as well as anybody. Don't confuse my prudence with fear."

"I know all about your valour and military life, Prime Minister. That's why I was a bit stunned to hear you advocating for peace. But I get your point. Even then, I am afraid that I can't see eye-to-eye with your views. When the enemy is breathing down your neck, my view is to take him on and tear him to pieces." Meghnad declared. The younger generals cheered him and echoed his sentiments. Bibhishan cleared his throat and asked for the floor. Ravana nodded, instantly alert.

Kumbhakaran sat up straight. Both of them knew their brother well enough.

"I say, Your Majesty," began Bibhishan. Why was he always such a stickler to formalities? Thought Ravana. This was an informal cabinet meeting!

"I think that you have erred when you had abducted the wife of Rama of Ayodhya. You had acted out of a rash impulse of retaliation at the disfigurement of our sister. This was unbefitting act for a person of your stature. Moreover, I think that you too, have underestimated the adversaries. But now you know better. What I suggest is that you hand over Rama's wife back to him ask for his apologies. Ramachandra is merciful. He will surely pardon you and Lanka will live to see another day. Otherwise all are doomed." Bibhishan sat down. The instant uproar that followed threatened to disrupt all discipline.

"Silence," roared Kumbhakaran and immediate silence returned. He turned to face his king. "Brother, I am distressed at the fact that you had abducted another man's wife, whatever may be the reason. You had always held women at great respect and this act has made you fall from grace. I am sure that Aryan scribes will have a field-day in vilifying your character. But, even though you seem to have acted out of impulse, I somehow feel that your continuing to hold her hostage has some inner meaning, not yet apparent to any of us. Whatever may be your reason, I think that we are not the persons to question your judgement or defy you. You are our king, chosen by us to lead the people. If your decision is war, then it is my decision to back you up to the hilt. Now, we have to decide where and when regarding the ensuing war and nothing else, for as I see it, war seems inevitable now."

"I think we should jump the enemy right in his lair," declared Meghnad. "We should cross over to the mainland and attack them when they are stranded on the beachhead."

Ravana now held up his hand to stop the flow of conversation.

"One by one I shall try to answer all the points raised. First let me tackle the last question raised. No, prince Meghnad. Attacking the enemy on the beach at mainland would not be a very good idea. There will be very little room to manoeuvre, and we would probably be caught out at sea, sitting ducks to their raining arrows and other missiles. On the other hand, if we allow them to cross over, the reverse may be true."

"It is a pity that Hanuman has destroyed our defence mechanism atop our gates," Meghnad murmured.

"Yes, it is true," admitted Ravana, "but it would be foolish to sit and cry over that. Now I come to brother Kumbhakaran's question. Yes I admit that I had acted out of impulse and that it had cost the life of good Maricha. But my decision to hold on to the hostage was based on some sound reasoning. It is political. Surpanakha's disfigurement was a minor issue. The main issue was the extermination of my governor Khar and his army. Today the saffron flag of Koshala flies atop the governor's palace at Janasthan. Could I allow that? I want this war and if it is to be fought, let it be fought in our own back-yard, where we are the strongest."

"I am with you all the way, brother," Kumbhakaran said. "But had you bargained for the Banara army from Kishkindhya?"

Ravana left his seat and walked over to the window opening towards the city of Lanka. The city was dark. The merry nightlife that Lanka was famous for, was missing. But no more flares from the conflagration could be seen. Lanka was gradually coming in terms with herself. The mention of Kishkindhya had brought back nostalgic memories. His heart ached for the deceased happy-go-lucky, jovial king of Kishkindhya, Bali, his blood-brother. He still remembered the good days spent in Kishkindhya.

They were on their way back after their campaign in the northern states. Ravana had no intention of waging a war with the Banaras. His reason was simple. They were not Aryans. So, he had pitched camp outside the borders of Kishkindhya and had sent an emissary to the court of Bali, extending his hand in friendship. The very next morning, the emissary had returned with an honour guard of a hundred Banaras, led by the king's brother, Sugriva. King Bali, Sugriva informed, would be very happy to welcome the Rakshasa emperor to the capital. He was also happy that the emperor had come in peace and not asking for war, not that the Banaras were not ready to withstand any onslaught, he had added. For seven days the Rakshasas had enjoyed the Banara hospitality. Food and drink there were in plenty. There was song and dance too. Then, after seven days, Bali had accosted him.

"My friend," he had said, "It is a pity that I did not have any chance of matching my strength with yours. Your power is legendary. I would like to challenge you to a bout of friendly wrestling. If I lose, I shall be content to be a vassal of Lanka. Now what do you say?"

"And what if you win?" At this response Bali had thrown back his head and laughed the famous laughter of his.

"If I win, I shall ask for your everlasting friendship."

"But that you have got already," Ravana had replied.

"No, no, dear friend, I have something else in mind," Bali had said with a smile.

They had battled for three days, without result. Bali was extremely powerful and a wily competitor. Ravana, on the other hand, was not as strong physically, but was very intelligent and a highly skilled and agile wrestler. Near the end of the third day, Ravana had fallen with a resounding crash. Bali did not lose the opportunity of pinning him down. After the bout, when both of them had taken their bath, he had taken Ravana to the family temple. There, in front of the deity, not only they had sworn eternal friendship, but Bali had taken his dagger out to slit his own forearm open. Then he had pulled Ravana's hand and had slit his forearm too. He then had let his own blood run out to mingle with the flowing blood of Ravana.

"Now, both our blood run as one. From today onwards I declare that we have become blood brothers," he had said.

Ravana turned back and faced Kumbhakaran.

"The presence of Banaras under Sugriva has only served to strengthen my resolve. Bali had been my blood brother and I intend to avenge his dastardly killing." He resumed his seat. Bibhishan stood up.

"Your Majesty, brother, pardon me for saying this. But you have slipped away from the basic principles of kingship. Through your foolhardy action, you have put Lanka's independence in jeopardy. Today the Rakshasas, as a race, are being forced to face the consequences of your haughty, headstrong action, born out of base lust that you are foolish enough not to admit. This is not only my opinion, but the opinion of the man on the street. There is still time. Hand mother Sita over to her rightful husband and beg for pardon. I shall see that you are pardoned."

"This is treason," Kumbhakaran's roar reverberated round the room breaking the stunned silence that followed Bibhishan's impassioned speech, to smithereens.

"Treason, brother?" Bibhishan whipped around to face Kumbhakaran. "This is no treason. I am merely criticising our king who is proving to be a traitor to the Rakshasa people! In his blind, senseless hatred against the Aryans he is forgetting that we are carrying half Aryan blood in our veins. We are closer to the Aryans than most of the people in Lanka. We are Aryasuras."

"This is enough!" Ravana's whisper cut through all debates going on. This whisper was more menacing than all roars put together. Prahastha shifted uneasily in his seat. He had seen that look in Ravana's eyes before and it boded doom. Ravana sat still as a statue carved out of granite. Only his eyes flashed fire. His left hand gripped the scabbard and his right hand gripped his sword, Chandrahash, with such strength that his knuckles had turned ivory.

"Yes, I agree that this is treason." He continued in a whisper. "Had anyone else had the temerity of speaking this way, his head would have rolled off his shoulders this instant and his blood, spurting from the severed arteries would have sprayed this whole room red. But I spare you, not only because you are my own brother, but because internal bickering would show us in no glorious light in these turbulent times. Begone, you traitor! Remove yourself from my sight before my patience fails! You are no longer welcome in Lanka! Away with you, you cowardly stooge of Aryans!" Ravana's whisper rose in crescendo as he spoke, till his voice was thundering in the closed confines of the room.

The silence that followed could be cut through with a sharp-bladed knife. The footfall of Bibhishan sounded ominously loud as he crossed the expanse of the room. As he reached out for the door-handle, Ravana's voice cut across like whiplash.

"While you go, bear in mind, that this exile is applicable for you and your close cronies as well. But do not, I repeat, do not try to drag your family away along with you. I cannot bear it if you put your wife, my sister Sarama and my nephew, young Taranisena, who is more than a son for me, through the rigours of your treacherous, uncertain future. Now go!"

All remained silent till the measured treads faded away down the hall. Then Kumbhakaran spoke in a low, gentle voice.

"Do not grieve, brother, for having amputated a gangrenous limb. My only regret is that he goes away to join the enemy camp with all our secrets locked inside that scheming head of his."

"I doubt it, brother," said Ravana. "He will not fall so low so as to join the enemy of the Rakshasas."

"Kumbhakaran is right, you know Dashanan," said Prahastha. "I am sure that he will join our foes. If we face defeat, it will be through his treachery alone, and not to the valour of Rama and his army. He lusts for the throne of Lanka. Still, I would say good riddance."

Ravana felt sad and aged. His eyes smarted. But he could not afford to give in to emotions. He had a kingdom to rule and a war to wage. He brought his mind back to the subject of Lanka's defence. Discussions began afresh. Ravana gave the orders to mobilise. Drums boomed and bugles trilled. Lanka was going to war.

✦ ✦ ✦

Book III

The Saga of Lost Hopes

1

Devastations Begin

Makaraksha stood there, weeping silent tears. It was strange, somewhat incongruous, that a powerfully built warrior, would stand there, weeping. The buzz of a bumble-bee against the court-room's window seemed indecently loud. No one uttered a word. The ministers and courtiers sat there in stunned silence. The war had been going on for quite a few days now. Every day the Rakshasas had dealt telling blows, but had suffered a lot in return. One after another eminent generals had entered the battle, never to return. Lanka was gradually being depleted of all her valiant warriors. The great generals, like Mahaparsha, Vajradangshtra, Birupaksha, Atikaya, Vajrahanu, Taljangha, all were dead. With them had died Rakshasa soldiers in their thousands. Every household of Lanka had suffered the loss of at least one of its male members. The wails of lamenting women rent the air of Lanka day and night. The citizens stayed indoor for the better parts of the day and when they moved out, their eyes looked vacant, their movements, purposeless, and their smiles lacklustre.

Ravana looked up towards the messenger Makaraksha. He could not believe his ears. Veerbahu, his son, was dead! How could it be possible? No, no. He must have heard it wrong! Why! Veerbahu was the best warrior Lanka ever had, apart from perhaps Meghnad and Kumbhakaran!

"Messenger, did I hear you correctly? Veerbahu is dead you say? You are sure?" He asked Makaraksha the third time.

"You heard me correctly, Your Majesty. Prince Veerbahu is dead," Makaraksha sobbed as he replied.

"Now, messenger, pull yourself up. Tell me, how he died."

Makaraksha wiped off his tears and pulled himself together.

"Your Majesty, it breaks my heart but still...

"The prince had led a formidable force into battle today. The Rakshasa officers under his command were giving a superb show of themselves, but then three Banara generals moved in for the kill. Hanuman, Sugriva and Angad were unstoppable, Lord! They were ruthless, killing at will. With their lethal maces, they looked like Yama, the God of Death! Veerbahu had all the while been standing there on his chariot, on the high ground beyond the gate, observing proceedings and directing operations. But when he saw that his forces were being decimated, he ordered his charioteer to drive straight into the fray.

"Like a mad elephant churning through the reeds did he enter battle, my Lord. The enemy soldiers were simple blown away like chaff in a winnowing wind. The speed at which he drew and released arrows was to be seen to be believed!

Hundreds fell around him. The Banara generals saw disaster and they moved in upon the prince all together. But in the rain of his arrows they were so gravely injured that they retired." Makaraksha paused and asked for some water, which was brought in immediately in a golden goblet. He took a long drink and resumed his reporting.

"Then came in their Commander-in-chief, Rama. He thundered in with Lakshmana and the renegade Bibhishan covering his back. The battle that ensued would require a bard to describe, Lord, I possess not the gift of words. Well, sire, like a lion springing in on his prey, the buffalo, Rama sprang on to our prince, gnashing his teeth in rage. A vicious battle followed. Veerbahu, I sadly say, was a wonderful warrior, but was no match for a great archer like Rama. Even then, he gave a good account of himself. But all his arrows were being dextrously deflected by the Kshatriya prince, while his own arrows pierced prince Veerbahu in a number of places. Our prince began losing a huge amount of blood, which was flowing down all over his body like rivulets. But still he continued fighting. Rama was amazed and he called words of praise for our great prince.

"Then, Your Majesty, I am ashamed to say what followed. Bibhishan came up and handed over a divine missile to Rama. Verrbahu realised that his end was near. He picked up a javelin for a final throw at the Prince of Ayodhhya. But that javelin never left his hand, sire. Rama took aim and fired. Like a serpent's tongue, the missile streaked out, struck our prince on the breast-plate of his golden armour, passed clean through his chest and buried itself in the earth." The messenger stopped, panting.

Ravana looked outside the window. There was still a few hours of daylight left. A keening arose from the inner sanctum of the palace. The news of Veerbahu's sad demise must have reached his mother, Queen Chitrangada. Ravana rose from his throne.

"Prime Minister," he called out to Prahastha, "will you please have this brave messenger receive all the required ministrations for his grievous wounds? And when you are done, please come up to the terrace. I shall be there reviewing the situation of the battlefield."

Then he turned to Saran, Jambumali and other ministers and said, "Will you please come up to the roof with me, gentlemen?"

Lanka appeared to be in flames. The rays of the setting sun falling upon the gold plated roofs, towers and steeples, seemed to have set the city on fire. She was a beautiful city, beautiful and gorgeous—the last frontier of non Aryan pride! But now, gradually her flowers were withering away. Her lamps were being put out, one after another, as one by one; her heroic sons were leaving this world of woes. Joy had left her many days ago, but now she had forgotten to weep. She lay sprawling there, wounded in body and mind, like a resigned damsel waiting to be viciously raped.

Ravana went over to the northern side. The battle of the day had taken place beyond the northern gates. The entire seaward side was covered by a city of tents. Amongst the sea of tents, flying the multicoloured flags of Kishkindhya on one sprawling pavilion a saffron standard bearing the image of a rising sun fluttered in the breeze. It was the standard of Koshala. The saffron sun of the Surya clan of Ayodhya was rising above the golden city, while the golden sun of the Rakshasa glory was sinking down beyond the western horizon, painting the environs with the colour of blood. The battlefield ahead was strewn with the dead in their thousands. Jackals, hyenas, stray dogs and other necrophagous animals were having a field day. Vultures wheeled overhead, swooping down to land amongst the dead. Bodies of elephants and horses lay amongst broken chariots and arms, carelessly strewn about. Shadowy figures were foraging about the dead, searching for their near and dear ones. A waft of cold wind blew in from the north carrying with it the offensive odour of carrions and destruction.

Beyond the lines of tents the newly constructed bridge could be seen gleaming in a stretch of white across the cold blue of the sea. Figures could be seen strolling about the bridge with impunity. The sea, that had been the last line of Lanka's defence, had allowed itself to be violated. Ravana, in spite of all his melancholy, could not but marvel at this wonderful feat of engineering. A measured tread broke into his train of thought. Prahastha had come up after arranging for the treatment of the messenger. Without turning Ravana instructed him, "Wake Kumbhakaran up!" His mind was not on the order he issued. How could they have made such a huge bridge in so short a time? He wondered.

✦ ✦ ✦

2

Bridges of Fortune

Rama had stood at the sea-shore, hands akimbo on his waist, a foot planted on a boulder. He was feeling frustrated by the sea. The waves rolled in to break with a resounding din, on the shore. The water churned and heaved, foaming at the top, as it raged towards land, denoting the presence of hidden teeth of jagged cliffs and reefs, enough to rip the bottom out of any passing vessel. Only cutters, piloted by experts in these waters, could dodge in and out of these death traps. But they would not serve his purpose. For an army of the size of the troops under him, he would need a veritable armada, but that was out of question in the given circumstances. He was at a loss as to what was to be done. He turned back and strode over to the camp, where the mammoth Banara army had bivouacked itself.

The beachhead was teeming with humanity. Every available space had been utilised for pitching of tents. Rama went straight in to his own tent and sat down, a dark scowl marring his handsome features. Lakshmana came in but halted as he saw the expression on his brother's face.

"Brother, what's wrong?" He asked.

"I am feeling desperate, brother. I am so close to Janaki, yet she is so far. The sea is raging in between us like an insurmountable barrier. I wish I could dry her up for the army to march across!"

"Pray don't give up hope, brother. I am sure, we can overcome this obstacle as well. Let us call in the Council of War and hear what the others have to say."

One by one they filed into the tent, all the commanders. Rama asked them to sit and went straight to the heart of the problem at hand.

"I have called you in, gentlemen, to discuss how we can cross over to invade Lanka. We can hardly let the puny sea stand between us and victory."

All began putting forth their views, till at length, Jamboban, who had been sitting silently all the while, spoke up.

"I think I have the answer, oh mighty son of Dasharath. We could build a bridge connecting the island to the mainland."

"But that is a colossal task! Who will build it?" Rama asked.

"Nol, here, can get it done. He was a brilliant student of the Deva architect, Vishwakarma. Come on, Nol, speak up!" Jambuban urged.

"I suppose it could be done. The forests nearby have all the necessary timber. This area is rocky. There is no dearth of rocks and boulders. We have the necessary man-power too. I could devise the equipments that we may need. Yes, I think, it can be done," Nol declared. A cheer went up. But this cheer got drowned by a great commotion outside the tent. All commanders rushed outside to see what the uproar was all about.

A cutter had anchored a bit off-shore as the tide was low. From it a skiff had been lowered, and it was coming aground right at that moment. A tall figure stood in it, ostensibly a Rakshasa, dressed in white silk, bordered with silver. He was of a powerful build, like that of a warrior; though he was unarmed, save for a gold-plated mace on his right shoulder and a bejewelled dagger stuck to his waist-band. The heavily moustached person had a full head of luxuriant black hair and his dark-skinned torso was bare. He wore a simple gold chain on his neck as a necklace, and a pair of heavy ear-rings adorned his ear lobes. A gleaming white sacred thread worn over his broad shoulder, running across his chest, declared his Brahmin descent. A golden amulet on his right upper arm denoted a royal lineage. Along with him, seated at the oars of the skiff, were four other Rakshasas, all simply attired. The person leapt down as soon as the skiff was grounded and strode up to the waiting Banaras with measured tread. The cutter that had brought him in, upped anchor turned and sailed off into the blue expanse. Seeing the Banara guardsmen, levelling vicious spears at him, the Rakshasa stopped and declared himself.

"I am Prince Bibhishan, younger brother of the King of Lanka, Ravana. I come in peace. I would like to meet Shri Ramachandra, Prince of Koshala. With me are four of my companions. We come to his aid in the ensuing battle."

Sugriva came forward.

"This is an inauspicious moment for any Rakshasa to come over to our side. What made you leave your brother in the time of crises?" Sugriva asked.

"Ravana has gone berserk. No longer does he listen to a good advice. I had asked him to avoid war by handing mother Janaki over to Shri Rama and to ask for his pardon. This provoked his ire and he exiled me from Lanka."

"You wait here," Sugriva ordered, gesturing to the guardsmen to place the intruders under close guard. Then he strode away to Rama's tent. The other commanders followed.

"What do you suggest?" asked Rama.

"I don't trust him even a wee bit," said Sugriva. "I vote that he should be killed forthwith."

"I too, am of the same opinion," opined Angad.

"I think that he should be thoroughly interrogated," said Sharabh. Jambuban was also against taking him at face value.

"I disagree with you all," Hanuman said after all had finished speaking. "That he comes at an inopportune moment is true. But what harm can he do? I think that he has crossed over due to one reason and one motive. His reason is that he had disagreed with his king, who drove him out, and his motive is to ascend the throne of Lanka after Ravana's demise. Having been a member of Ravana's Council of Ministers, he has inside knowledge of Lanka. During the war, this knowledge could serve as our valuable asset. I therefore say that we should welcome him to our side. We stand to gain all and lose nothing by doing so."

Rama smiled at this debate.

"I think that it is our duty to grant sanctuary to any foe who seeks our protection. I, for one, never relinquish one who seeks my protection, even if it jeopardises my own well-being," Rama declared. "Bring him in to me."

Bibhishan was brought in. At once he prostrated himself at the feet of Rama and asked for his protection. Rama raised him and embraced him like a long-lost friend. Bibhishan gave him all details of the huge Rakshasa standing army and the defence systems of the city of Lanka. Thus he gained the confidence of all detractors and was assimilated.

The bridge was proceeding at a furious pace. The Banaras had all worked with a will. Even Nol, the engineer in charge, was astounded at the speed of work. The hundred *yojana* long and ten yojana wide bridge was completed within five days. All through the days of construction, Banaras, hand-picked by Prince Angad, patrolled the waters day and night, on fast moving cutters, to thwart any attempt at sabotage by Rakshasa commandos. On the third night they had noticed boats leaving Lanka and stealthily proceeding towards the bridge under construction, in the cover on the night. But their attempts were thwarted. Not a single saboteur escaped alive. The waters around the nearly completed bridge ran red with Rakshasa blood. The sharks and barracudas had a feast.

On the sixth day the Banara army crossed over the wonderful bridge. The wide, firm bridge made the crossing easy and in no time the defending troops were overcome and the Lanka beachhead was secured. The Banaras formed a close ring around the walled city, laying a firm siege. Each of the four gates was patrolled by senior commanders while Rama, Lakshmana, Sugriva and Bibhishan stationed themselves on the high ground of the Subel Mountains, near at hand. From their elevated station, they could not only keep an eye on their own troops, but a portion of the inner city was also open to them for inspection. Both sides waited. On three occasions

Ravana sent spies into the enemy camps, but every time, they were apprehended by Bibhishan and his compatriots. The merciful Rama did not allow the spies to be killed but had them released. Again, both sides waited.

Lanka was a densely populated city. Although they had a good reserve of food grains and water, yet after a few days, tension began to mount, as the stores began to deplete. Then the Banaras attacked the walls and breached a part of it. In retaliation, the gates opened and the Rakshasa streamed out for open combat. But, in spite of their valour and the superiority of weapons, the Rakshasas were outnumbered. Both sides sustained a lot of casualties, but the Rakshasas lost a number of commanders. Every day the assault on the walls continued and the Rakshasas had no alternative but to come out again and again in open combat to save the gates and the walls. But the Rakshasas were suffering. Gradually their strength was becoming depleted. Her best warriors were being killed and Ravana was at a loss as to what was to be done next, to save the day for the Rakshasas.

✦ ✦ ✦

3

Meghnad

"Wake Kumbhakaran up," was the order issued by Ravana. He had expected Prahastha.

"Why, father? Your son is still alive."

Ravana whirled around, startled. Not Prahastha, but Meghnad was standing there with a faint trace of smile on his lips.

"But, son, you are my last resort, my ace," said he.

"Father, I can take the invaders on single-handed. Believe me. Then why waste our strength?"

Ravana stared out towards the sea for a long time. After that he sighed and turned.

"All right, my son. I give you leave to go into battle tomorrow."

In the wee hours of morning, the inner sanctum of the Nikumbhila Temple was hazy with smoke of incense. A sweet perfume pervaded the environs. The yajna fire, burning in the central enclosure, leapt up into flames as more ghee was poured into it. Sonorous chanting of prayer hymns lent a touch of piety to the atmosphere. Meghnad was performing the yajna, in honour of the Fire God. Now, the eastern sky was touched with the first blush of dawn and by the time he finished his rituals, the sun will have risen. After that he would arm himself for battle. People said that when he went into battle after completing his yajna, then, with the blessings of the God of Fire, he would be unbeatable.

The sun had risen by the time Meghnad came out of the temple after completing his yajna rituals. A pleasant breeze, fragrant with perfumes from various flowers, wafted around. Birds chirped in the trees around the temple. An air of serenity prevailed, far removed from the din of battle. Meghnad lengthened his strides to follow the path meandering through the grove towards his own palace located beyond its gate.

Meghnad's palace was one of the most elegant of all edifices in Lanka. It was built of marble, bedecked with intricate floral design of semiprecious stones and black jade, interspersed with vines of gold leaves. The gold-plated roof dazzled in the morning sun. A wide flight of marble steps swept up to the foyer. At the foot of the steps, waiting for him with a lighted lamp and flowers on a golden tray, stood his wife, Pramila, the only daughter of Kalnemi, the King of Danavas. Pramila was the light of his life—his one, true love. Asura society was more permissive than many. In keeping with the Asura traditions, there had been many women in his life. But he had loved only one, and that was his only wife, Pramila.

Pramila was a woman of great beauty. But her beauty was not of the dainty type. She was a robust, lively sort and her beauty reflected an elegance that was like that of the

Mahishasuramardini Durga. She was taller and fairer than most Danava girls. But the most striking thing about her was her eyes. They were large and dark, like a doe's, adorned with the most gorgeous eyelashes. Her figure was buxom, with a narrow hour-glass waist. The arms were supple, yet powerful, capable of caressing her lover, doing household chores, but used to drawing a sword, throwing a javelin and bending a bow as well. Her retinue of six, who followed her, were from her own intrepid bodyguards, a hundred strong, of war-like Danavi women, lead by her closest friend and kinswoman, Basanti and Nrimundamalini, each of them perfectly capable of wielding any arms, like any other male commando.

Seeing Meghnad striding in through the main gate, Pramila's eyes lit up. She ran up to him, carefully balancing the gold tray on her hand and taking care to keep the lamp burning. As she reached him, she performed the welcome *aarti*, handed the tray over to Nrimundamalini, put the end of her sari around her neck and stooped low to touch his feet. With a broad smile Meghnad pulled her up and held her close in a tight embrace. Then, hands around each other's waist, the happy couple went up the steps, into their palace.

Pramila led Meghnad straight to his dressing room, which served as the armoury as well. There was another armoury in the temple, in the chamber adjoining the central yajna-room, for, at times Meghnad would get ready for battle right after his yajna. But today, it was different. Today he would be dressed by his dearest wife and armed for victory.

Pramila dressed her husband, lovingly, in flaming orange silk, with gold ornaments to match. For armour, she chose the gold-plated ones and complete with his gold helmet, he looked dazzlingly valiant. The weapons, however, Meghnad chose himself.

After getting ready and taking a frugal breakfast of fruits only, Meghnad came out of his palace entrance. His chariot, drawn by four fiery horses, each as black as the night, was ready, laden with arms. The horses snorted, tossed their heads up and stamped on the ground, eager to sally forth in battle. Dextrously Meghnad climbed into the chariot, looked back at Pramila, smiled, hefted his heavy bow in his left hand and gestured to the charioteer with his right, to move forward. The chariot trundled forth, amidst ululation from the Danavi guards and showers of flower. Pramila, white like a statue in alabaster, joined her palms, touched them to her forehead in a silent prayer to her guardian god. She stood there till the chariot thundered out of the widely opened gates and rounding the curve of the road, disappeared from view.

There was great hustle and bustle in the main square of the city. The army was getting ready to move. The streets were lined with people, all agog with excitement. They had heard that today's battle would be a decisive one. The Crown Prince Meghnad would lead the Rakshasa forces into battle. Meghnad was said to be invincible having defeated even the great warrior Indra in frontal combat, with effortless ease. There was now a crisp purpose in every movement of the soldiers. The Foot Soldiers, in dazzling golden uniform, marched forward, lances over their shoulder and shields over their backs. The chargers of the cavalry trotted forward, the armours on their heads glistening in the sun, their riders, smartly attired and armoured, each carrying a lance from which fluttered the golden flag of Lanka. Elephants came trumpeting from their stables, menacing in their appearance, all of them with swords stuck to the tips of their tusks, swinging clubs or spiked iron balls tied to their trunks. Chariots trundled past, the warriors holding mighty bows in their hands.

A general uproar rent the air as the chariot bearing the bow and arrow standard of Meghnad came into view from far away. Meghnad's figure, flashing gold and fiery orange in the morning sun, looked as heroic as the God of Fire himself. All knew that here lay hope—not only hope of a single victory, but hope of deliverance from the throttling grip of the enemy as well. The drums boomed and bugles trilled. A general shout of "Hail Meghnad, hail Indrajit!" echoed from the farthest hills.

Out there in his pavilion, Rama was arming himself for the ensuing battle, when the Rakshasa cry reached him. Intent on tying his sword to his waist-band, Rama looked up as he straightened. That battle-cry sounded new in his highly attuned senses. It was full of renewed hope. What new development could have occurred? Rama thought as he swung his quivers over his shoulders, having secured his sword to his waist-band. Picking up his awe-inspiring bow in his left hand, he strode out of his pavilion. Lakshmana was there already, as were his generals. Bibhishan too, was armed and ready. At a nod from Rama, Lakshmana put his conch shell to his lips and blew a sonorous note. Bibhishan did likewise, blowing into his own conch shell. The challenging blasts were drowned by the thunderous battle-cry of the Banaras, "Jai Shri Rama!"

The two armies clashed like two bull buffaloes crashing their horns in a frenzy of killing. Today's battle was viciously fought, as arms clashed, voices yelled, elephants trumpeted, blood spurted and the ground underfoot was churned into a quagmire by flowing blood and the wheels of chariots and feet of the fighting men and animals. Meghnad was living up to his reputation, killing at will. His chariot flashed through the warring armies and his right hand drawing and releasing arrows almost without a pause. But the Banara generals excelled themselves led by the vicious strengths of Rama and Lakshmana. The two brothers picked at the Rakshasa commanders as their targets, and began to decimate them systematically. Both were so very skilled in archery, as well as being dextrous with the use of other arms, that their opponents stood no chance at all, as they moved about in the field of battle, like gods of Death personified. The Rakshasas facing them started fleeing towards the city. Meghnad saw that his forces were facing imminent defeat. He signalled to his charioteer. His chariot picked up speed as it thundered along the perimeter of the warring groups to come up to near the city gate. Meghnad vaulted down from his speeding chariot and ran over to the waiting Pushpak.

The Pushpak was fixed up with boards on its outside, painted blue exactly like the clear sky above. On the blue background were drawn white cloudlike formations, to provide an effective camouflage. Behind this screen, the Pushpak remained invisible while Meghnad rained arrows on the adversary forces, giving him the reputation of fighting invisibly from the sky. The engine was already running, as Meghnad jumped aboard, frantically signalling the pilot to move. The pilot revved the engine and the Pushpak lifted off with effortless ease, emitting a thunderous roar. The Rakshasas roared alongwith.

From high above the clouds Meghnad saw Rama and Lakshmana churning through the Rakshasa ranks. The

Rakshasas were now turning tail and fleeing from the tremendous onslaught. Rama turned away from the fleeing foot soldiers and together with Lakshmana took on the charioteers next. Each brother was soon surrounded by more than dozens of chariots. But soon enough the bothers had broken through. It was now the turn of the charioteers to flee. One after another the warriors kept toppling from their chariots, shot through their hearts. Meghnad could but wonder at the tremendous show of power and skill combined. He knew that unless he acted fast, the Rakshasa army was doomed to destruction. He ordered the pilot to hover above where Rama and Lakshmana were.

The brothers were caught unawares at the drone of the Pushpak. Startled, they looked upwards, seeing nothing. But this caused a momentary lapse in their concentration and the Rakshasa charioteers had a chance of slipping away. Rama was the first to recover. He understood at once where this sound was coming from. He fitted an iron tipped arrow on his long bow and aiming at the clouds floating above, let fly. No sooner had the bow twanged, did his pilot let out a shriek. An arrow was sticking through his right shoulder. It was then Meghnad remembered that both Rama and Lakshmana were adept at shooting on hearing the target's sound only with Shabdabhedi Baan. He had to act now, or fail. With infinite care Meghnad chose a slender, though heavy missile, fitted it in the compressed air contraption, gifted to his father by his grandfather and hefted it over his shoulder, yelling at the pilot to hold her steady. He sighted, and fired with deliberate precision. The missile hit the ground in between the two astounded brothers and exploded with a soft 'thud'. It had a vial of a strange nerve gas on its nose which was supposed to shatter on impact. Those in the immediate vicinity would immediately fall unconscious. If they are not shifted from that area, within a short time, their respiration ceased and they died. The foreign merchant who had given him the vials had said that once the respiratory paralysis occurred, there was no salvation for the victims as there was no known antidote. Meghnad was now satisfied that both the brothers were dead and he asked his injured pilot to turn towards the city of Lanka. The Rakshasas yelled "Victory!"

The Banara generals rushed in where Rama and Lakshmana had fallen. They had given the brothers up for dead. From the tents another figure was seen coming running, with a small bag in his hand. It was Sushen, their physician. Sushen was a genius. He was a master of his own art, a great surgeon and also very much adept at toxicology, or the study of poisons. Whenever he saw Rama and Lakshmana fall after the missile had hit the ground in between them emitting a thin vapour, he had understood what had gone wrong. It was probably the same paralysing gas that he had heard about from his colleague in the far eastern country. He knew exactly what was to be done.

Sushen had the insensible Rama and Lakshmana borne as far away from the field of battle as possible. They were laid out in the open and Sushen shooed all the stunned Banara onlookers crowding around, away. The princes needed breathing space. From his capacious bag, he then took out a number of exotic ingredients, added a little Ganges water and honey to it and began to mix the concoction in a mortar and ground it down with a pestle. In the meantime, the breathing of the two unconscious princes had become shallow and irregular. Quickly he called Hanuman and Angad to come over and help in the resuscitation process. They were to blow into their mouths to keep the respiration going, while he prepared the medicine to his satisfaction.

Meghnad was accorded a hero's welcome when he returned to the city. The king was waiting at the top of the steps in the Royal Palace. He embraced his son closely and ushered him in to his private chamber. The whole city was shaking with cries of 'Hail'! People sang and danced out in the streets. Alcoholic beverage flowed like water. Every house was decorated with lighted lamps. The martial bands played, together with the sometimes discordant, accompaniment of civilian music. People cried, "Rama and Lakshmana are dead! We have won the war!"

Out in the darkness of the Ashoka grove still bearing the signs of devastations at the hands of a single marauding intruder, a lone woman wept in silence. No one spared her a thought. Her keepers fell asleep one after another in a drunken stupor. But she sat there, devastated and alone, her back to her only support, the trunk of an ancient tree, waiting for a definite news from the palace. But none came. Gradually all din of celebrations abated and the city started sliding into the clutches of all consuming slumber.

After paying his respect to his parents, Meghnad ran out to where his chariot stood. He gave the charioteer leave and vaulted into the driving seat. The four black horses responded to the loving touch of their master's rein and broke into a thunderous gallop. Pramila left her palace and came running down the steps as the prince reined in. With one strong hand,

Meghnad swooped her up and with the other he manipulated the reins to turn the chariot about. Then they sped off to their country resort. The hundred Danavi guards leapt up on their own horses and galloped after the chariot. The chariot with its retinue thundered out of the unguarded western gate and disappeared into the darkness.

There was a great commotion in the Rama camp. The unconscious brothers had begun stirring. Soon normal respiration returned and with it returned their colour. Within a short while, they had regained full consciousness. The Banara soldiers leapt up shouting. Cries of "Jai Shri Rama" and "Jai Sushen" rang out again and again.

Lankans was still rejoicing, though understandably, in sleepy languor, when they heard the roars of the Banara troops. A stunned silence fell over the city. Ravana jumped up in agitation and called for the chief of his spies.

"Yes, Your Majesty," the spy reported, "Both of them have been brought back to life. They are now eating a huge dinner. The people are saying that the great bird, Garuda had come in and have scared the venomous bonds away. This is sheer magic!"

"Black magic!" growled Ravana. Then he turned and beat the great gong hanging near the corner. The spy crept backwards and disappeared. When the sentry entered, Ravana gruffly ordered him to get the Prime Minister, Prahastha.

"Yes, Dashanan, I have heard it all. What do you aim to do now? Recall Meghnad?" Prahastha asked.

"Where is my son now?" Ravana asked.

"From what I have heard, the Crown Prince is promenading with his wife in the country resort."

"No, no. He needs to relax for a while for what he did today."

"Then, what is your plan?"

"I am thinking of leading the troops myself tomorrow morning," declared Ravana.

"That is preposterous, and you know it," Prahastha replied, waving his hand as if driving an errant mosquito away. "You are our last hope and we can never afford to lose you. Think of someone else."

"But no one else remains, except you, Jambumali and Kumbhakaran. Kumbhakaran is sleeping away his soused sleep and I cannot allow you or Jambumali to go out into battle. Both of you are aged now and would be no match for the Raghava brothers."

"Then there is no way out. We are trapped now," Prahastha sounded really worried. Ravana did not speak for a long time. He paced about in the room like a caged tiger, hands clasped over his back, his careworn head bowed. Then he stopped in his stride.

"There's nothing to be done. Wake Kumbhakaran up."

But it was easier said than done. Scores of Rakshasa guards pushed at him, yelled, beat drums and bugles right into his ears, but he could not be woken up from his drug induced stupor. At last, it was nearly at dawn when he could not withstand the onslaught any longer and came awake with a grunt and a roar, seriously displeased at his sleep having been disrupted. Prahastha stood nearby to speak to him as he came back to his senses.

"The king wants to speak to you," informed Prahastha.

"What about?" gruffly asked the irate Kumbhakaran.

"We are facing serious loss in the battlefield. All the commanders have been killed one after another. Yesterday, Prince Meghnad had killed Rama and Lakshmana in battle. But by some black magic their life has been restored and they will take to the field later today, rejuvenated. The king requires you to take charge of the Rakshasa troops."

Kumbhakaran stood, stretched and yawned.

"Come, uncle," said he," Lead the way."

Meghnad was blissfully unaware of all this. The whole night the couple had enjoyed songs and dances and after retiring, they had indulged in a bout of exquisite, prolonged foreplay and had just fallen asleep after making some deeply satisfying love, as the sun peeped out of the eastern seas. The battle-cries of the Banaras could not penetrate into the amorous environment of their haven of bliss.

✦ ✦ ✦

4

The Fall of the Last Pillars

The golden goblet clanged as it fell on the heap of other empty goblets and rolled away, uncared for. Kumbhakaran had flung it away after quaffing it empty at one go. With his right hand he tore a piece from the leg of the peacock, roasted whole, and munched thoughtfully. The food and drinks had fortified him, but they had failed to cheer him up. He stood up and moved over to the window.

The sky was overcast like his dark mood. He did not like it at all. The empire that he had helped build up with the sweat of his brows, was now tottering on the brink of disaster. When he had first heard about the abduction of Sita, he had been filled with a foreboding that perhaps events had run their full circle. Was this last war really needed? But that was the decision of his mentor, and who was he to question him? The wails of bereaved widows and mothers rent the air of Lanka, replacing the music that sounded in this city day in and day out. Lanka was finished, and he knew it. Today he was going out for the last time in his illustrious military career. Immersed in thought, he had not heard the door open.

"Father," someone called. Kumbhakaran looked up with a start, his reverie broken. Nikumbha was standing there at the door. He was fully armed. Kumbhakaran's heart swelled with filial pride at the sight of his valiant son.

"So, my son, you are ready?"

"Yes father. Today I am so happy."

"Why my son? When everybody around us are weeping their hearts out, what makes you happy?"

"Today, for the first time in my life that I have got the opportunity of fighting alongside my mighty father! That alone makes me happy."

"Your father, Nikumbha, is now a mere shadow of his former self. I feel it in my bones that I am going into my last battle. I shall not return."

"Not while I am alive, father."

"That is what I am more worried about, my son!"

No reserve forces were held back to fight another day. At the challenging call from the conch shells of Lakshmana and Bibhishan, the gates opened as if on cue and the last remaining Rakshasa warriors marched out for a decisive battle. This time their columns were led by the elephant brigade, followed by the chariots. The cavalry and foot soldiers streamed out after them. Kumbhakaran was sitting atop the giant lead elephant, Bhayangkar, with Nikumbha following close behind. True to his name, the elephant Bhayangkar was really terrifying to look at. Towering high above the other animals in the pachyderm brigade, he was bedecked all in iron armours. His legs were encased in iron covers from which jutted vicious looking spikes.

In his trunk he swung a huge spiked ball of iron attached to a heavy chain. His beady, red-rimmed eyes darted about here and there in search of his enemy, as his huge ears flapped in eager anticipation. The charioteers were led by Ravana's son Atikaya and the last of the commanders, Narantak, Devantak and Trishira. The cavalry was led by Mahodar and Mahaparsha.

"My lord," said Bibhishan to Rama, "Ravana has thrown in the last of his generals into the fray. If we win the field today, then, except for Meghnad, no other warrior remains who will take command of his forces, other than himself. It is time the lion is goaded out of his lair. We have to win today and then devise a method of getting rid of the notorious Meghnad."

Rama, Bibhishan and Sugriva were standing on top of the Subel hill, keeping a close watch on the proceedings.

"What are your orders today, my lord?" asked Sugriva.

"Tell Lakshmana to go for the charioteers, along with Angad. You, my friend, lead the attack against the elephants. Take the mighty Hanuman, Nol, Neel, Dwivid, Mainda and Sharabh with you. Go for the warriors. Try to bring them to ground. After that, send enough men to make the elephants run for the city, trampling their foot soldiers on the way."

Makaraksha stood in front of him once again; palms joined together, blood flowing from his scalp wound to mingle with his tears. He had several fresh wounds on his body. Some of his old wound appeared to have reopened. Ravana sat on his throne in a stunned silence. Prahastha stood beside him, his hand resting on the shoulder of his king and nephew.

"So, messenger, Kumbhakaran too is dead? And Atikaya and Nikumbha and all the other commanders?" Ravana said after a long period of silence.

"Yes, sire." The messenger was barely audible.

"It is alright, messenger. You have done your job. Now you go over to the surgeon's and get yourself treated," Prahastha instructed him. Makaraksha paid obeisance and left.

Silence prevailed once again.

Suddenly the door of the chamber crashed open. Queen Dhanyamalini rushed in, her hair dishevelled, her dress in disarray, her eyes red and flashing fire, dry as the desert sand. Her attendants followed her, all weeping uncontrollably, disconsolate at their mistress' distress.

"What do I hear, my king? My son, the valiant Atikaya, is dead! How did it happen, my husband? How could you allow it to happen?"

"Yes my queen, what you heard is true. Atikaya is dead. But his death was not futile, my dear. He had fought like a lion, accounting for countless enemy soldiers, before falling in frontal combat," gently replied Ravana.

"He was the only treasure I had, my lord," said the queen with a dry sob. "He was the only solace I had. I had given him to you for safekeeping. Why have you lost him? Tell me, my king, what have I to live for now?" A stunned silence followed, broken by the queen's sobs. Ravana stood up and came over to her, placing his heavy arms on her shoulders.

"Look at me, my queen," he said quietly. "Here you lament the death of one son. But, look at me, my lady, my heart is being ripped asunder day in and day out at the loss of a hundred sons! What of me? What have I to live for?"

Prahastha excused himself and went away. He went straight up to the aviary that housed the messenger pigeons. He selected the fastest pigeon, scribbled a note hurriedly, tied it to its foot and released it. The pigeon stretched its wings and took to flight. Enough of daylight remained to show it the way.

✦ ✦ ✦

5

The Death of Hope

Meghnad and Pramila were sitting on a marble seat by the side of the lake that was the main attraction of this country resort. Swans were swimming about in their graceful elegance. Lotuses bloomed near the shore. Three cormorants took to flight across the azure sky towards an unknown destination. A fragrant breeze, laden with the perfumes of flowers, blew. Birds chirped as they made their ways to the rookeries in the rows of trees all around, preparing to settle themselves in for the night. A sense of serenity prevailed.

The sound of a pair of running feet broke into their reverie. A Danavi guard was running in holding a carrier pigeon in her hand. Meghnad leapt up, strode over to the guardswoman and gently prised the pigeon away from her grip. There was a small message tied to the pigeon's foot. He opened the message, handing the pigeon over to the guard, and read intently. An anxious Pramila came over and stood beside her husband.

Meghnad's handsome features had paled. He turned to Pramila.

"Our vacation comes to an end, dear lady. Duty calls."

"Why, husband, what is wrong?"

"It appears that due to some divine intervention, Rama and Lakshmana, both of whom I had seen falling in battle, have been restored to life. Not only that, today they had taken to field and have killed uncle Kumbhakaran, untimely aroused due to the emergent conditions, along with my brother Atikaya, cousin, Nikumbha and have wiped out the last of our commanders. Now no one remains who can take charge of the Rakshasa forces. Unless I return, father will take to field and this I cannot allow."

"What do you intend to do, dear?" asked Pramila.

"I shall go back to Lanka right now."

Meghnad called for his chariot. It was brought up immediately. He leapt up into the chariot and reached out for Pramila.

"Take care, my love. Stay here till I return. Do not worry."

"But, dear, won't the gates be closed with the Banaras patrolling about?"

"Who has the power to stop Meghnad rushing to respond to the call of his motherland, dear?" Meghnad replied with a smile. "Don't you worry."

The chariot thundered away. Pramila stood rooted to the same spot—her world in turmoil. He told her not to worry. But she worried, oh God, how she worried!

The sentries atop the western gate spied the chariot driving in like a whirlwind from afar. Stealthily they removed the retaining bolt from the gate and waited with bated breath, tensely waiting to open it wide at the last moment. The chariot thundered in. The Banara troopers were caught off-guard at its sudden appearance. It swept past them before they could react and entered the city through the momentarily opened gate.

Ravana was astonished at the sight of Meghnad. He ran to his son and buried his tired face in the younger man's shoulders. In a moment of desperation the son assumed the father's role and patted his back in reassurance.

"Father, I am here now. So stop worrying. Tomorrow I shall lead the forces into battle. I know not due to what divine trick Rama and Lakshmana have been restored to life, but they will be dead tomorrow. This is my promise."

"That's fine, my son, but I would suggest that first of all you do your ritual Yajna at the temple at Nikumbhila. Take the blessings of the God of Fire and be invincible. You are my last hope."

It was dead at night. All were asleep at Rama's camp. Only the soft tread of the patrolling sentries could be heard. The burning torches planted in the ground served to throw more shadows than light. An owl hooted in the distance.

Outside the pavilion flying the colours of Koshala, two figures could barely be discerned in the shadows, engrossed in the deepest of conversation. One of them nodded. The other melted in the darkness. The first shadowy figure moved over to the entrance flap of the pavilion.

"Are you awake, my lord?" asked he.

"Bibhishan," Rama's voice asked from inside of the tent.

"Yes, sire, it's me," Bibhishan replied.

"Enter."

Bibhishan entered the pavilion. There was a small lamp burning at one side of the sprawling tent. The tent itself was bereft of furniture of any description. Rama was sitting up on his bed, if that could be called a bed at all! It was merely a clean sheet laid over the ground with a bundle of clothes serving as the pillow. There was another similar bed on the other side. It was now occupied and a slight snoring from there proving that Lakshmana was indeed fast asleep.

"My lord, I apologise for waking you up at this unearthly hour, but I have my reasons." Rama nodded silently and waited.

"Meghnad has returned to the capital. He will be leading the Rakshasas tomorrow. Moreover, in the wee hours of morning, he will go to the temple at Nikumbhila and offer his puja at the altar of the Fire God. He will be there till sunrise. After that he will arm for war."

"Meghnad is the last barrier to be crossed. He is adept in techniques we are not familiar with. We cannot hope to win this war, unless Meghnad is taken care of," Rama observed.

"I know of a secret passage into Lanka that leads right up to the inner sanctum of the Nikumbhila temple. The passage is really tough going, though, and will permit only one person through at a time. I could take Lakshmana with me and show him the way. During pujas, Meghnad will be unarmed. That is the best time to kill him. He would not be able to fight back."

"But Bibhishan, that is preposterous. It will go against all laws of chivalry and will be an act of downright cowardice! How can I condone such a mean trick? No, my dear man, I am a Kshatriya. We never wage war on unarmed adversary. Winning the war is important, but not at any cost. I cannot allow the heroic Meghnad to be killed by deceit."

"My lord," said Bibhishan gravely. "Meghnad is the only person who stands between us and victory. If he is no more, then my brother would not be able to withstand your attack at all. There is no other way by which we can remove Meghnad. And sire, one who resorts to meanness himself by hiding behind the clouds and firing lethal missiles upon the unsuspecting enemy below, is he worthy of your magnanimity? Come, my lord, let me awaken Lakshmana and listen to what he has to say."

Lakshmana awoke with a start and grabbed his sword in reflex. When he saw that it was Bibhishan, he relaxed. Then, hearing the point of discussion, he came over to Rama's bed and sat down on the ground.

Rama relented after a long debate and that too with all reluctance. Once he got the nod from his brother, Lakshmana did not waste much time and started to get ready. But a great commotion outside, made him stop.

Pramila was worried, exceedingly so. She was now blaming herself at allowing him to go alone. For some time she walked by the lake. But the serene environment failed to soothe her. Then she went inside and did her hair. She took up her needlework and threw it away in chagrin. This solitude, coupled with anxiety, was killing her. At last she could bear it no more and jumped up. She called out for her kinswoman, Basanti.

"Basanti, I am going to Lanka," she declared.

"What!" exclaimed Basanti. "Are you out of your mind? Have you forgotten that the army of Rama is surrounding the fair city like an impassable sea? Do you think that they will allow you safe passage?"

"But my husband has gone over. Then why can't I?" asked Pramila.

"He was only one person, passing like a whirlwind. How can a few monkey-men block his path?"

"Basanti, sitting alone here, doing nothing but worry, it will be the death of me. My husband has gone there, and it is my duty to be by the side of my husband, come what may."

"I do not think that this move is advisable, especially in the circumstances that the western gate is probably being manned by heavily armed enemy troops."

"Basanti, can anyone obstruct the seaward flow of a raging river? I am a trained soldier, so are you all. I shall enter the city of Lanka by force. The enemy can come in my way at his own peril!"

With this Pramila left her seat and entered the armoury to arm herself. By the time she emerged, armed to her teeth, her fiery mare, Baraba, was ready and waiting for her; and so were her hundred armed Danavi guards, led by the war-like Nrimundamalini. Pramila vaulted on to the back of her mare and with her small picket of resolute soldiers, thundered on towards Lanka, at full gallop.

Hanuman challenged the ladies' army at the gate of Lanka. Pramila and her band drew rein and Nrimundamalini stepped forward.

"Who may you be to stop the daughter-in-law of the King of Lanka from entering the city to meet her husband?"

"This is Hanuman, the son of Anjana and Keshari, born through the auspices of Pavan, the god of winds. It is my privilege to serve my Lord Rama."

"Then take me to your lord. I do not want to waste time arguing with underlings such as you."

Hanuman was amazed at the blatant show of raw courage. He bowed to Pramila and gestured that they should follow him to the camp of Shri Rama. The Danavi platoon followed him in disciplined military formation, chins jutting out and heads held high. The Banara sentries marvelled at the spectacle and started talking excitedly amongst themselves. This was the commotion that Rama and Lakshmana had heard.

On entering the pavilion, Nrimundamalini paid homage to the feet of Ramachandra. With a mild bit of astonishment, she noticed Lakshmana putting on battle dress at this time of the night. But this did not concern her, so she turned towards Rama and bowed waiting for permission to speak. Rama nodded.

"Hail to the valiant son of mighty Dasharath and prince of Ayodhya. I come with a message from my mistress, Lady Pramila, wife of Crown Prince Meghnad. She pays her homage at your feet and requests safe passage into Lanka, where she goes to meet her husband. If you deny her entry, then she demands battle. She challenges any one of your mighty contingent, any person of your choice, to a duel, with any arms that you may choose. The choice, my lord, is yours."

Rama sat there, looking at the envoy, bemused. Then he stood up and strode out of the tent, motioning Nrimundamalini to follow him. Once outside, he stood there with hands behind his back, looking at the platoon of guardswomen and Pramila. He was struck with the courage and show of might of this handful of women. Rows of standards fluttered in the breeze. They were standards of the Rakshasa gold with the imprint of a vicious trident—Pramila's own colours! The trident of Pramila was going to be united with the bow and arrow of Meghnad. Pramila, sitting relaxed on her steed, cut a truly war-like figure. She was dressed is a blood-red sari, interwoven with gold thread. Her gold-plated breast plate and helmet flashed in the light of the myriads of torches held aloft by the Banaras. The black horse-tail plume attached to the crest of her helmet, bobbed with every movement of her head. Over her back were slung her bow and a quiver full of iron-tipped arrows. A sword, in its golden scabbard inlaid with precious stones, hung from her waist. In her right hand she held a vicious trident, while in her left she held a gold-plated shield that had been forged by none other than Maya, the king of Danavas. It seemed as if she was the Goddess Durga herself, ready to take on the might of Mahishasura. Strangely enough, she did not hold on to the bridle of her horse. Her poise was extra-ordinary and her command over her steed was exemplary. She directed her horse with crisp voice-commands. Closely surrounding her on all sides were her hundred guards-women, dressed in black and gold. All of these women were armed to their teeth. The sight was enough to send the stoutest heart quaking.

Seeing Rama, Pramila and all her guards alighted from their mounts and joined their palms, bowing low. Rama nodded to them.

"I, my lady," Rama addressed Pramila directly; "I am born of a Kshatriya lineage. We can recognise valour when we see it and respect it too. I have no war with you. I not only permit you entry into this fair city, but to ensure your safe passage, I shall send you on your way with an escort of my men." He nodded at Hanuman and Angad to do the needful and turned back into the pavilion. The Danavis vaulted on the backs of their mounts and spontaneously gave such a cry that made Rama break his stride and turn back in amazement. They had cried "Jai Shri Rama!"

In the confusion of Pramila and her retinue entering Lanka, no one noticed the fully armed Lakshmana and Bibhishan, sporting his heavy mace, slip out of the side of the pavilion.

The two of them hurried towards the sea shore under the light of the stars. There, with unerring precision, Bibhishan located a rounded boulder and pushed it aside with his immense strength, to reveal a narrow flight of steps leading into the bowels of the earth. Bibhishan stopped to light a taper he was carrying and stepped down along the staircase. Lakshmana followed. Tentatively, step by step they went down, apparently interminably, till at last they hit a sandy bottom. A narrow path ran on, gradually sloping upwards. They walked on through this narrow passage, until they reached another flight of steps. Bibhishan with hand signs told Lakshmana that they were almost there and climbed up these stairs. At the top, this stair-well terminated into a round opening which was covered by a round stone. Bibhishan gently pushed at this stone and grunted in satisfaction when it moved easily. Then they waited.

Meghnad was elated on seeing Pramila, though he thoroughly chided her for undertaking such risks at coming into Lanka in these troubled times. The whole night they lay awake in each other's arms, talking and talking. At last, when the night was almost at its end, Meghnad left his bed. He roused the dozing Pramila.

"Come, my dear, let us wash up and go to mother's house for her blessings, before I leave for Nikumbhila."

In spite of the early hours, everyone was up and about in Queen Mandodari's palace. Servants came running in to receive the princely couple as their chariot rolled up the driveway. Meghnad knew all of them well and so did Pramila. Meghnad threw the reins to one of the servants.

"Hold these for me for a while, will you good Bilola? I won't be too late."

An elderly woman, Trijata, came running, shouting, "Welcome prince, welcome princess!" Meghnad smiled. Pramila too, was all smiles as she joined her palms in greeting Mandodari's chief of household.

"Ah, mother Trijata!" exclaimed the prince. "You are up already!"

"Oh yes, son," replied Trijata. "I seldom sleep at night. This joint pain of mine keeps me awake. And the quack of your household physician tells me that nothing is wrong with me. Someday I shall kill the demented, old sawbones!"

Meghnad laughed heartily at this.

"I'll wait for the day, mother. Now tell me, is the Queen awake?"

"What do you say son! Of course she is awake. She has already taken her bath and is getting everything ready for her pujas to Lord Shiva, for your well being!"

"Please inform her that we have come, will you?"

"Of course I shall, though I think she has already got the news. Ah, there she comes!"

Mandodari, chastely dressed in a raw silk sari with red border, was looking very fresh, despite the early hours. Coming up with a huge smile, she performed a welcome aarti for her son and put a red tilak on his forehead to the auspicious sound of a small conch-shell, being blown by one of her attendants. Meghnad and Pramila touched her feet. She touched each of them under their chins and kissed the tops of their heads.

"Mother, I shall not tarry, or I'll be late," said Meghnad. "I am on my way to Nikumbhila. I intend to go to battle today, mother and have come to seek your blessings."

Holding back her tears, Mandodari smiled at him. It seemed as if the sun was shining through banks of rain-clouds.

"Of course you have my blessings, son. Go on. Come back in victory." Meghnad turned to go. "But son, please let Pramila stay here with me till you return. You'll stay, won't you my daughter?"

"Oh yes, mother. I shall stay with you as long as you wish," said Pramila with a smile, although her heart was aching to be with Meghnad. Oh Pramila! What had you done! Had you stayed on with your husband during his yajna then history would have been written otherwise!

Meghnad drew up at the gate of Nikumbhila and alighted from his chariot. Then he walked bare-feet along the path through the grove, towards the temple. There, after taking a dip in the nearby lake, he dressed in red silk, for his yajna.

A fire blazed in the small pyre in the centre of the room. Having lit the incense sticks, Meghnad poured offerings of ghee into the fire, making the flames leap up in glee. A perfume from burning incense filled the room. The sonorous note of "Om" resounded all through the temple. Meghnad made more ghee offerings and began his invocation for the Fire God and his wife, Swaha. He was so deeply engrossed in his puja, that he did not notice the furtive movement of the stone slab placed in a corner of the room, as it slid gently back. Bibhishan and Lakshmana pulled themselves out of the hole and slipped over to merge with the shadows unnoticed.

When the yajna had reached its zenith, at a cue from Bibhishan, Lakshmana showed himself to Meghnad. Through the haze of smoke Lakshmana's handsome figure had an almost divine appearance. Meghnad mistakenly thought that the God of Fire had come to his devotee. He prostrated himself at Lakshmana's feet.

"Rise, prince, for I am not your guardian god, but am your harbinger of death," said Lakshmana. Meghnad peered through the pall of smoke.

"Is it you, Lakshmana? Come to kill me, I suppose. But how could you enter? The door is barred from the inside!"

"That is of no concern to you, Rakshasa. Prepare yourself for death." Lakshmana grabbed at the grip of his sword. Meghnad smiled.

"Do you think that Meghnad is afraid to die? If you think so, then you are mistaken, Lakshmana. But let me tell you one thing. Now, you may be my adversary, yet you are a guest in this household. The traditions dictate that first of all you should take some rest, then have your repast. Enjoy them, prince, while I get ready for battle. I am never averse towards a duel fought on even terms. You are a valiant man, Lakshmana. You too, must be welcoming this duel? Please give me a moment; I shall get ready as soon as possible."

"Nothing doing," Lakshmana growled. "You are fated to die in my hands! Now!"

"What!" Meghnad was incredulous! "You mean to say that you shall strike down an unarmed foe? Am I hearing it right? You are going to break the codes of Kshatriya chivalry!"

"The word 'chivalry' is unbecoming of you. What becomes of your chivalry when you rain down arrows and missiles from your hideout behind the clouds, where the enemy cannot reach you? Where was your chivalry when you stood still while that villainous father of yours broke into another man's residence like a common thief to steal his dearest wife?

The term 'chivalry' is unbecoming of you, son of a felon! Now die!"

Lakshmana made to unsheathe his sword. But he had not bargained for the reflex of the Rakshasa warrior. Meghnad grabbed a heavy copper utensil and threw it underhand at Lakshmana. The vessel struck Lakshmana on his forehead. His knees buckled and he crumpled down with a momentary blackout, blood streaming from a cut on the forehead. Meghnad took this opportunity to leap for the side door that led to the armoury adjoining the inner sanctum. But a mace-wielding figure materialised through the haze, to block his path.

"At last," said Meghnad, "At long last I understand how Lakshmana could enter the Nikumbhila temple. So it was you, uncle, who led him through the secret passage? You had deserted your own, that I know. But I had never thought that you would stoop so low!"

"I serve Lord Rama," Bibhishan said.

"You serve him? You, Prince Bibhishan, brother of the Rakshasa emperor, serving a common Kshatriya forest dwelling pauper! What a shame, uncle, what a shame! But we can talk about it all later. Now, uncle, please let me pass. I shall go to the armoury and come back armed to give Lakshmana a fair fight. Please uncle, let me go through!"

"That I cannot do."

"So you too are afraid of Meghnad's feat of arms are you?"

A soft groan was audible from the other end of the room. Lakshmana was coming back to his senses. Like a lion leaping on to his prey, Meghnad leapt upon Lakshmana with a roar. The two of them grappled together, their strengths almost evenly matched. Gradually however, Meghnad began to prevail upon his opponent. He began to push Lakshmana towards the yajna fire. With an intense effort Lakshmana freed his right hand. He whipped out a vicious looking dagger from his belt and plunged it straight into the Rakshasa's chest, right up to the hilt. It was instant death for the Rakshasa hero. Lakshmana pushed the dead Meghnad away and pulled his dagger out. Blood flowed from the lethal chest wound unabated. Bibhishan stood there, agape and transfixed.

"Take a grip on yourself, oh heroic Rakshasa," Lakshmana hissed out the words. "Now is not the time to stand and stare. We have to leave fast. If we are caught out here, then we are done for. Come, dear friend. Don't waste time!"

With this Lakshmana grabbed the wrist of the older man and pulled him towards the entrance of the secret passageway. In the frenzy of combat he had not noticed that his signet ring had been ripped off from his finger and was now enclosed in the fist of the deceased Rakshasa crown prince.

Ravana was getting restless. It was not like Meghnad to be ever late for anything. Yet today he was late. Ravana could not wait further. He called a sentry and sent him on to Nikumbhila to find out what was taking the prince so long.

The sentry had come back from the temple, alone. He stood there in front of his king, head bowed in grief, quaking from head to foot. Ravana sat in a stunned silence. He could not believe his ears. His eyes were dry and red. All his tears had been exhausted. Prahastha came in silently to stand beside his king. He had visited the inner sanctum of the temple himself and had seen everything with his own eyes. Silently he motioned the sentry to leave. Ravana turned towards him.

"You know uncle?"

"Yes, Dashanan, I do."

"Meghnad has been killed! Stabbed to death inside the temple! Within the precincts of the palace! Unbelievable!"

"But unfortunately true."

"But who could have done this heinous act!"

"I think I have the answer."

Prahastha opened his palm. A signet ring nestled there. Ravana reached out tentatively and took the ring in his hand. It was a heavy, but simple ring marked with the crest of the house of Koshala, over which was inscribed the letter 'La' in Sanskrit script.

"Lakshmana!" Ravana was hoarse in his whisper. It sounded as ominous as the hiss of a king cobra. "Prime Minister, prepare the men for battle. Today I go myself, standing in for my deceased son. Let the army march!" Prahastha left as silently as he had entered. Ravana sat there in silence, alone, with his heart-breaking grief for company. He sat there for a long, long time. How long, he had no idea.

The door to the chamber opened silently once again. Mandodari entered. She was still dressed for puja, the puja she had been offering for the well-being of her only son. She was devastated, but the sight of her husband devastated her further. Seeing him reminded her of a proud coconut tree struck by a thunderbolt.

"My king," she gently called. Ravana looked up, his eyes unfocussed. Then he registered who it was.

"Mandodari," he said. "You too have come to blame me for your son's death?"

"No, my lord. I know that your loss is as great as mine. I was worried about you. That's why I came running."

"I hate myself, queen. All these deaths...all could have been avoided!" Mandodari kept silent. "Let us go away, Mandodari. Far away from it all. Just you and I. The world is so harsh a place, Mandodari..."

Prahastha entered.

"The army waits, Your Majesty!" Ravana sighed and straightened.

"I'll be back, queen. Some unfinished job remains..."

✦ ✦ ✦

6

The Flames Burnt Dark

Prahastha sat in his balcony, eyes fixed upon the sea shore. Of the rows and rows of pyres, the two largest ones still burnt merrily, throwing up leaping tongues of flame in an endeavour to lick the sky. In those pyres, the hopes of Rakshasas were being burnt to ashes. People were scurrying about the pyres, busy, but doing little. A short while ago the Lankans had lined the streets cheering the new leadership, "Jai Shri Rama" and "Jai Maharaj Bibhishan". One had to come in terms with facts. Meghnad was no more. Neither was king Ravana. An era had ended. Pramila, the flower, withered away just as it had blossomed, had been brave enough to accompany her husband on his onward journey. She had mounted the pyre of her husband in silence and had been silent even when the flames had shot up, engulfing her.

That day, Ravana had been irresistible. Mad with the grief for his son, he had effortlessly churned through the enemy forces. All their generals, even Lord Rama, had not been able to contain him. At long last they were seeing the Ravana of old. Ravana had made a beeline, straight for Lakshmana. The battle had been bitter. Lakshmana was indeed a great warrior. He had not yielded a little bit under the savage onslaught. Finally Ravana could get the better of him. The lethal arrow had streaked like a tongue of fire and passed through Lakshmana's trunk. Lakshmana had fallen down, dead. Mission accomplished, and his son's death avenged, Ravana returned to the city.

But miracles do happen. The apparently dead Lakshmana had been brought back to life by some exotic medicinal herbs prescribed by their genius of a surgeon and brought in by the indomitable Hanuman, from the mainland. This news had shattered all resolves of the Rakshasa king. He was so devastated that he did not have any heart in the war anymore. At night he had visited Sita to ask for her pardon.

"To what avail?" Sita had asked as she had placed a blade of grass in between herself and Ravana, symbolising the barrier that existed between the hostage and the king. "You have destroyed my life almost as effectively, as you have destroyed Lanka. Now you have the audacity of asking for pardon?"

Ravana had no answer to this. He had stood there in silence with his head bowed—a broken man.

"Sita, I have wronged you," he had said at last, after a long pause of silence. "Come morning, I march to my death. I shall not be back to see you again. Very soon you shall be united with your victorious husband. Just tell him, on my behalf, that Ravana had never shown any disrespect towards you. Your husband is a valiant man. I aim to court death in his hands. None deserves to defeat Ravana more than he does." Then he had turned towards Sarama, the wife of Bibhishan, who had been kneeling there at Sita's feet.

"Sister, tell Bibhishan when he triumphantly enters Lanka, that I leave him a kingdom without any foe. All my men are dead. There will be none to resist his kingship. Tell him that I know that he would be a good ruler of the Rakshasas who remain. Tell him that in spite of all that had befallen, Ravana still loves his youngest brother with all his heart."

With this, Ravana had turned abruptly and had left the Ashoka grove. An onlooker would have been astounded to see something that no one had ever seen before. Tears were streaming down over the cheeks of the proud Emperor, yet his head was held high.

All through the night Ravana had sat with his queen, in the temple, holding her hands. In the morning he had gone into battle with a slight smile on his lips. He had gone straight up to Rama and had engaged him. The battle that ensued was not at all like any other that the warriors of either side had ever witnessed. The best of the Rakshasas was locked in arms with the best of the Kshatriyas. None would yield an inch of ground. The world appeared to stand still to watch the tremendous feat of arms between two greats. Time after time Ravana cut through Rama's defences, to the extent of cutting down his bow on three occasions. But Rama was indomitable that day. Every time his bow broke down, he picked up a new bow to launch a fresh onslaught on the Rakshasa King. But soon it was apparent that Ravana was courting death. He had come into battle without his armour! He was laughing and had dropped his guard when Rama had drawn the lethal arrow. He was still laughing when the arrow had entered his chest.

An era has come to an end, thought Prahastha. Bibhishan had offered him an important post in his cabinet, but he had politely declined. Lanka had now become a vassal state of Koshala. The ideas about Rakshasa dominance, self determination for non Aryans, all had become empty dreams. Prahastha took a dagger out and tested the razor-sharp blade. He looked upwards towards the summit of the Trikuta hills. The flame of Rakshasa pride was still burning bright. Now it seemed a joke.

With his right hand Prahastha placed the blade of his dagger on the left wrist. His pulse throbbed underneath the blade. Fastidious by nature, he had kept a basin under his left wrist. When he went, he wanted to go clean. Calmly he sliced through his pulsating artery. Blood squirted out. Then he sat back and relaxed. Ah Ravana! The dreams you had had! The visions that we shared! It felt so good that Ravana had left the world with his head held high, holding aloft the golden flag of independent Lanka.

The sky had become overcast. Soon the rains will begin to wash out all traces of the previous regime. The world darkened before his eyes. He looked upwards. The pride of Rakshasa regime was still burning bright. But gradually the light was becoming dim. The sun of Asura glory had set. The day of the Aryasura had come to an end. At last all became dark. Even the leaping flames on the Trikuta summit burnt dark.

✦ ✦ ✦